GUNPOWDER TEA

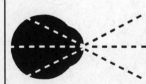
This Large Print Book carries the
Seal of Approval of N.A.V.H.

THE BRIDES OF LAST CHANCE RANCH

GUNPOWDER TEA

MARGARET BROWNLEY

THORNDIKE PRESS

A part of Gale, Cengage Learning

GALE
CENGAGE Learning·

Farmington Hills, Mich • San Francisco • New York • Waterville, Maine
Meriden, Conn • Mason, Ohio • Chicago

GALE
CENGAGE Learning®

LIBRARY OF CONGRESS CATALOGING-IN-PUBLICATION DATA

Brownley, Margaret.
  Gunpowder tea / by Margaret Brownley. — Large print edition.
     pages ; cm. — (A brides of Last Chance Ranch series ; #3) (Thorndike Press large print Christian historical fiction)
  ISBN 978-1-4104-6562-7 (hardcover) — ISBN 1-4104-6562-4 (hardcover)
  1. Large type books. I. Title.
PS3602.R745G86 2014
813'.6—dc23   2013044057

Published in 2014 by arrangement with Thomas Nelson, Inc.

Printed in Mexico
1 2 3 4 5 6 7 18 17 16 15 14

To GTF
Who makes all things possible

**Heiress
Wanted**

Looking for hardworking, professional woman of good character and pleasant disposition willing to learn the ranching business in Arizona Territory. Must be single and prepared to remain so now and forevermore.

CHAPTER 1

Pinkerton National Detective Agency: We never sleep.

New Orleans, 1897
Miranda Hunt drew a linen handkerchief from the sleeve of her black mourning frock and dabbed the corner of her eye. Only the most discerning person would spot the foot tapping impatiently beneath the hem of her skirt. Or guess that her respectfully lowered head hid a watchful gaze.

As far as anyone knew, she was exactly who she purported to be: Mrs. James Kincaid the Third, friend of the deceased.

"Such a modest man," one of the mourners, a middle-aged woman, lamented, looking straight at Miranda. "Wouldn't you agree, Mrs. Kincaid?"

"Most definitely," Miranda replied. From what she knew of Mr. Stanton, he had much to be modest about.

Everything in the stately mansion from the polished marble floors to the gold filigree ceilings was due to Mr. Stanton's marriage to the heiress of a flypaper empire. The rich knew how to live, and judging by the carved oak coffin edged in gold and lined in silk, they also knew how to die.

An elderly gray-haired man approached her chair and put up his monocle. "Would you care to pay your last respects, Mrs. Kincaid?" He was stoop-shouldered and spoke with a lisp.

Miranda stood with a solemn nod and crossed the elegantly furnished parlor to an alcove near the grand piano. Tall palms stood like sentries guarding the open coffin. The deceased was perfectly laid out in a fine tailored suit, his white mustache and hair neatly trimmed. Had it not been for the silver coins concealing his eyes, one might think him merely asleep.

The last few petals of Miranda's rose fluttered to the floor but she dutifully laid the wilted stem by the dead man's side. She allowed a ladylike sob to escape and drew a handkerchief to her cheek — all for the benefit of the monocle-eyed man.

Like all operatives of the Pinkerton National Detective Agency, Miranda was an expert in disguises. Blending in was the key to nabbing an unsuspecting criminal and that took a certain amount of concentration, attention to detail, and, of course, acting ability.

Today, it took considerably more. It took a steadfast stomach to eat the Russian fish eggs and liver paste that the rich called food.

Returning to her seat, she strained to hear three young women whisper among themselves. A private detective had to listen to an amazing amount of gossip, which went against Miranda's Christian upbringing. But between the "he dids" and "you won't believes" was where an operative often gleaned the most useful information. Certainly God made allowances for those fighting for law and order. At least Miranda hoped He did.

The hands on the longcase clock swept away another hour and Miranda's spirits sank, but her vigilance remained. So far this week she had attended two weddings, three funerals, and a baptism without a sign of the man known as the Society Thief.

Though he excelled at what he did, he was considerably more than just a criminal; he was her stepping-stone to bigger and better assignments.

He had been a bane to the city's upper class for more than a year. No jewel was safe from his sleight of hand; no wealthy man's corpse immune to his pilfering fingers. Catching him red-handed would prove to the Pinkerton brothers once and for all that she was ready for more than the jobs no other operative wanted. At the age of twenty-four, she was ready for a real challenge.

She had just about decided that this funeral was a waste of time when she spotted the straw boater. It was always the details that tripped up a person and today it was the hat. Senses alert, she studied the latecomer. The fact that he'd failed to give his head-covering to one of the servants like the other male guests made him suspect. There was always the possibility that he planned on using his hat to conceal a dastardly deed. Or perhaps he simply kept it so as to make a quick escape.

Slender of build, he had short black hair and a pointed beard. He was immaculately dressed in a black sack coat over gray trousers and vest. A short turnover collar showed above a floppy bow tie.

The other male guests wore silk suits and linen shirts, appropriate attire for a warm spring-like day, but this man wore wool — the fabric of choice for pickpockets. Wool didn't rustle like other fabrics, allowing the

10

wearer to move without detection.

The man's gaze met hers and she gave her fan a coquettish flick and smiled. Confident enough to think she was flirting, he smiled back. The scene was set.

A rush of excitement raced through her as it always did whenever she was about to nab a suspect. *You should see me now, Papa. Maybe then you wouldn't have been so against me becoming a detective.* She moved across the room, but the deceased's widow reached his side first.

"I'm Mrs. Stanton," she said. "And you are . . . ?"

"Harry Benson. Your husband and I were business acquaintances. I apologize for being late."

A rehearsed response if Miranda ever heard one. He lowered his head and said something more, but his voice failed to reach her straining ear.

The widow blushed. "Thank you, Mr. Benson. That's very kind of you to say." She gestured toward the enormous table of delicacies. "Do help yourself."

With a swish of her black taffeta skirts, Mrs. Stanton walked away. A snap of her fingers sent servants scampering to the kitchen for more plates of pâté and caviar. Had the woman realized that Mr. Benson

11

had taken her quite literally and helped himself to her diamond brooch, she might have been less inclined to worry about his appetite.

Miranda quickly moved toward her prey. "Mr. Benson," she said by way of greeting. "I'm Mrs. Kincaid. Perhaps you know my husband?"

"I'm afraid not." Raking her over, his gaze settled for a split second on her diamond necklace before belatedly meeting her eyes. The necklace had been borrowed from a local jeweler and the Pinkerton agency would have to pay quite handsomely should it disappear. Miranda meant to see that it didn't.

"Would you care for some refreshments, Mrs. Kincaid?" he asked.

"Yes, thank you."

"Allow me." The nature of the crime required a pickpocket to make physical contact with his target, so it was no surprise when Mr. Benson, or whatever his name was, offered his bent elbow.

Since a detective needed to get as close as possible to a perpetrator, she slid her arm through the crook of his.

They strolled like two old friends to the refreshment table. A pickpocket's second order of business was to distract his intended victim. Mr. Benson did this by "ac-

12

cidentally" spilling cider on her dress.

"Oh, forgive me." He drew out his handkerchief and quickly dabbed at her skirt. Like any good victim, Miranda allowed him to do so.

"How clumsy of me," he murmured. "I do apologize."

In the blink of an eye, he had expertly relieved her of her jewels — a true professional if she ever saw one. Any pickpocket worth his salt took pride in his work and would never be so inelegant as to cut a lady's dress or a gentleman's apparel. While he pocketed the necklace with one hand, Miranda just as efficiently matched his professional pride by slipping a handcuff on his other.

His mouth dropped open but it was the gun that turned him pale as the corpse.

"It w-was an accident," he stammered. He cast a nervous glance around the room but no one paid them any heed. "I'll be happy to make compensation for the d-dress."

"This old thing?" She smiled. "You needn't worry about it, but you might be a tad bit concerned about your pockets."

One eye twitched and sweat dotted his forehead. "Who . . . who are you?"

"A thief's worst nightmare," she replied, raising a palm to reveal her Pinkerton badge. "It might interest you to know that the police are waiting for my call."

Before Miranda could clamp the second cuff around his wrist, a female servant dropped a tray and screamed, "She's got a gun!"

A collective gasp rose from the mourners but before anyone had a chance to move, the pickpocket grabbed for Miranda's weapon.

"Stop," she hissed.

They struggled and the derringer arched back and forth between them, the loose handcuff swinging from his arm. The gun went off with a deafening bang. Overhead, the crystal chandelier shattered and glass sprayed down like silver rain.

Guests scrambled beneath the buffet table. Others dived behind sofas and chairs. One robust woman fainted dead away.

The weapon went off a second time.

The pickpocket was good at his craft but was no match for Miranda. With a well-placed knee and a perfectly aimed blow, she gained control of the gun. Doubled over in pain, the thief could do nothing to prevent her from snapping the second steel bracelet around his wrist.

Her derringer in one hand, she pulled an array of watches, bracelets, and necklaces from his pocket with the other and dumped them on the buffet table. The palm nippers used to snip jewelry free from an unsuspecting neck or ear, she kept. One never knew when such a tool might come in handy.

"Calm down, everyone." Miranda held her badge over her head for everyone to see. It was now just a matter of calling the police. "Everything's under control."

"Not everything," the widow cried. She had thrown herself across the coffin and her feet flopped about like newly caught fish. "You shot my husband!"

Miranda's stomach churned as she hurried down Fifth Street to the three-story building housing the Chicago headquarters of the Pinkerton Detective Agency. One hand tucked in her muff and the other holding on to her hat, she kept her head down. The icy wind blowing off Lake Michigan sliced through her gray woolen skirt and chilled her to the bone.

Summoned to the office posthaste, she dreaded her meeting with Mr. William Pinkerton. She was definitely in trouble. A large black-and-white eye on the face of the building seemed to confirm it. Today the firm's logo appeared to glare down at her.

She battled the heavy door leading to the

15

lobby. It was still early, which meant that none of the other operatives or secretaries had arrived yet. She alone had to face the principal.

Inside the building, she straightened her hat, wiggling the hat pin in place. She then held her chin high, ready to explain and, if necessary, defend her actions. Thus braced, she took the elevator to the top floor and marched right past the detective room and into the principal's wood-paneled office.

William Pinkerton greeted her with a curt nod and waited for her to be seated. He then paced back and forth in front of her, hands clasped behind his back.

He shook his head, his heavy jowls jiggling and his walrus mustache drooping. "You shouldn't have shot the dead man."

"Yes, that was most . . . unfortunate. But as I explained to the widow, except for the hole in his head and dislodgement of coins at his eyes, her husband's . . . uh . . . condition remained unchanged."

Pinkerton regarded her from beneath slanted brows. "The last thing the agency needs is more bad press and now Mrs. Stanton threatens to bring about a lawsuit."

She grimaced. "I . . . I don't know what to say. The man was dead when I got there and dead when I left."

"You should never have tried to restrain the thief yourself. Your instructions were to identify him and then call the police. That was all."

"If I had called the police first, we would have lost him. I caught the Society Thief and that's more than Stands or Masters did." The two operatives had worked on the case for six months without success.

Pinkerton stopped pacing. "Many believe that a woman has no business fighting crime."

"Including your brother," she said. She'd heard the two arguing over that very subject not long ago.

He nodded. "Including Robert. But unlike my brother, I believe women have an advantage over men when working undercover." Pinkerton sat on the edge of his desk and rubbed the back of his neck. "I promised Charles to watch out for you, but I can't do that if you continue to take unnecessary risks."

A dark cloud entered the room at the mention of her father. If it hadn't been for a careless Wells Fargo detective, her father might still be alive. "Papa was one of your best operatives. He taught me everything I know about detective work."

"That doesn't make me feel any better,"

Pinkerton said. "Your father took his share of unreasonable chances."

Miranda tightened her fingers around her fur muff. She still hadn't gotten over her father's death three years earlier. Her only consolation was carrying on the work he loved so much.

"My father might have taken unreasonable chances, as you call them, but he captured more criminals than all your other operatives put together." She leaned forward. "I want to be treated like every other agent. If I were a man, we wouldn't be having this conversation."

Pinkerton blew out his breath. "You're your father's daughter through and through." He folded his arms across his chest.

Miranda chewed on her lip. "You aren't thinking of letting me go, are you?" She feared that more than anything in the world. To be relieved of her duties would be an affront to the memory of her father. It would also break her heart to give up the work she loved.

"On the contrary. The governor of Arizona Territory has asked for our help. He wants to hire us to track down a man who has terrorized the county for more than a year. I'm sure you've heard of the Phantom."

Her mouth dropped open. "You want *me* to track down the Phantom?"

"Normally this would be handled by the Denver office, but they lack relevant personnel," he said. "If you're successful, it would put a shine on our tarnished reputation."

She frowned. *Relevant personnel* seemed like an odd term to use and she had no idea what it meant. "But the law —" Pinkerton agents were accused of employing bullying tactics during the union riots and using undue force. That led to Congress passing a law preventing the government from hiring private detective firms. The law had cut into the agency's work, but so had the increase in competition.

"The Anti-Pinkerton law prevents the U.S. government from hiring us. It says nothing about territories." He stood and walked over to a map pinned to the wall. Arizona Territory was riddled with black Xs.

He jabbed the map with his finger. "All the robberies committed in the last year are marked."

Miranda joined him. Doing a quick count, she stopped at twelve. Even the James gang in their glory days hadn't been that active.

"As you can see, the robberies are centered in the southeast portion of the territory — in Cochise County, to be exact. They tend to be centered around . . . here." He pointed to a blank space between Tombstone and a little town called Cactus Patch.

She squinted at the tiny dot that marked the town. "Doesn't look like there's much there but desert."

"That's why the governor asked for help. The long-range manhunt is taxing local authorities." His finger made a circle on the map. "This is a cattle ranch called the Last Chance. As you can see, it's the most centrally located to the robberies. Unless I miss my guess, that's where we'll find the leader of the gang. And even if he's not hiding out at the ranch, he's got to be somewhere nearby." He plucked a newspaper clipping from his desk.

"It gets even more interesting," he continued. "The ranch is owned by an old lady named Eleanor Walker. I believe she's a bit soft in the head." He read the piece aloud. "Heiress Wanted." He chuckled and stroked his mustache. "Now I ask you. Does it sound normal for someone to advertise for an heiress?"

"It does sound odd," she agreed.

"Yes, but also fortunate." He read the rest. Not only was the "heiress" expected to learn the cattle business, but she also had to promise to forgo marriage. "So how do you feel about cattle ranching?"

He didn't have to ask how she felt about forgoing marriage. No man would be so foolish as to marry a Pinkerton operative. "I think ranching is a dirty business but someone's got to do it."

"Yes, and as it turns out, that someone is you."

She gaped at him. "You want me to answer that advertisement?"

"Yes," he said, though he didn't look happy about it. "Miss Walker might be fey, but I'm sure she would notice if a male operative showed up wanting to be her heiress."

Aha! *Relevant personnel* meant female. For once her gender worked for and not against her. She forced herself to breathe. It was the assignment of a lifetime. It was what she wanted, had prayed for, and worked so hard to achieve. Still, there was a big difference between tracking down criminals in a city like Chicago, Boston, or New Orleans and hunting for them in the Wild West. Every horror story she'd ever heard from other operatives came back to taunt her.

"But . . . but I know nothing about cattle or even ranching."

"The advertisement clearly states that the

21

ranch owner is looking for someone willing to learn. While you're learning, you will track down Mr. Phantom, whoever he might be." He gave her a stern look. "That's all you will do. Track him down. Once you identify him, you will then notify local law enforcement. You are not to go after him yourself. Is that understood?"

"Perfectly."

He reached across his desk for a thick portfolio. "Here is a complete dossier on Miss Walker and the ranch and what little we know about the gang leader. You'll also find your train tickets and expense money in here." He put the thick binder in her hands. "The ranch owner has been notified and is expecting a Miss Annie Beckman, which, of course, is you. As usual, you will send daily reports on your progress to the name and post office box listed in your dossier, in cipher. Any questions?"

Surprised to find herself shaking, Miranda forced herself to breathe. Finally, finally she had gotten her wish. Too stunned to think, let alone ask questions, she stared at the manila folder in her hands.

"None at the moment."

"Then I'll let you get to work. Your train leaves first thing in the morning."

That didn't give her much time to study

the material and plan a new identity. "Thank you. I'll do my best." *If only Papa could see me now!*

"I expect nothing less, but I mean it — you're to take no unnecessary chances."

"I understand, sir." She headed for the door but he called after her.

"One more thing, Miss Beckman," he said, addressing her by her new name. "Don't shoot any more dead men."

CHAPTER 2

A gullible fool can locate a swindler faster than the smartest private eye in the world.

Arizona Territory

The *Southern Pacific* ripped through the desert with unnerving speed. The smell of burning wood and red-hot steel pervaded the car with a sense of urgency. The train was late and the engine driver seemed determined to make up for lost time.

Miranda stared out the window while going over her new identity. From this moment on, she couldn't just think of herself as Annie Beckman. She had to *be* Annie Beckman. With her golden-brown skin, dark hair, and high cheekbones, she could hardly hide the Indian blood inherited from her Kickapoo mother but most everything else was fabricated . . . except for perhaps her age and propensity for sweets.

Watching the scenery fly by, Miranda

mentally let her true identity slip away with it. By the time she pulled her gaze away from the mindless blur beyond the smoky windows, the transformation was complete. She *was* Annie Beckman.

Annie dug in her drawstring purse for her gold pocket watch. It was only twenty minutes later than when she last looked. It seemed like an hour.

Thankfully, the man on the seat next to her was deep in slumber but he was no less obnoxious in sleep than awake. His mouth hung open, allowing the most despicable hog-like sounds to escape. At least now he wasn't puffing away on his vile cigar. His neatly patched trousers and pressed boiled shirt told her he was married, which made his unseemly passes all the more disgusting.

She sighed and dropped the watch back into the satiny depths of her purse. A short, skinny man walked down the aisle, unaware that he had dropped an envelope. She lifted her hand to call to him, but not wanting to wake the man by her side or the one across the aisle, she changed her mind. She stood and grabbed the back of the seat in front of her in an effort to gain her balance.

She reached the owner of the envelope just as he took his seat. "Sir, you dropped this." He gave her a cursory glance before grabbing it out of her hands and slipping it into his vest. He didn't even bother thanking her.

Most would blame his curtness on bad manners, but her Pinkerton training came into play and now, as always, she dismissed the obvious. Unless she missed her guess, whatever was in that letter was important and he was irritated at having so carelessly dropped it.

She made her way back to her seat, aware that the stranger across the aisle was now awake and staring at her. His blue-eyed gaze seemed to penetrate her very thoughts. Neither his rugged whiskers nor ragged cut of sandy hair took away from his good looks.

Normally Annie could glance at a person and know immediately his or her marital status, profession, and financial circumstances. She guessed that the pale-faced woman in back was a mail-order bride on the way to an unknown future; that the pock-faced man seated directly behind her with the toothbrush sticking out of his waistcoat pocket was a traveling salesman; and that the middle-aged man next to him a land developer.

But the blue-eyed stranger was an enigma. He sat tall, shoulders straight, fingers tapping impatiently on his lap. He was dressed like a cowpuncher in dark trousers, striped shirt, and vest, his boots scuffed and his red kerchief wrinkled. Such casual attire didn't seem to belong on his rigidly alert frame. Only the gun at his side seemed at home.

He appeared to be waiting for something. Or perhaps he was simply anxious for the trip to end. If so, that made two of them.

She pretended to ignore him. It wasn't the first time she'd caught him staring. For one brief moment, she considered the possibility that he'd guessed her occupation but immediately discounted the thought. Both her powers of observation and her careful attention to every last detail were beyond reproach. That was why she always got her man or, in some cases, her woman. Though this was the most challenging assignment she'd ever embarked upon, she was completely confident that she would succeed.

She took her seat and tried to ignore the porcine sounds emitting from the sleeping man next to her. The *clickety-clack* of the train had a lulling effect and her lids soon drifted downward. There was nothing much she could do before reaching Cactus Patch so she might as well catch a little shut-eye. The nature of her job sometimes required her to grab sleep at odd times.

She had just about drifted off when something startled her into full wakefulness. Two male passengers were on their feet rushing up the aisle. Confusion — a curse — and a collective gasp.

A man stood in front of the swaying car holding a gun. "Don't anyone move!"

Annie drew in her breath. She was almost positive he was the man with the envelope. The traveler next to her opened his eyes and blinked. For once his open mouth produced no sound.

"I said don't move," the gunman bellowed, brandishing his weapon toward a male passenger in the front seat. With his hat low and kerchief high, it was impossible to see much of the outlaw's face — just enough to know he meant business. He was joined by two others, all three faces hidden behind red kerchiefs.

Annie resisted the urge to reach for the weapon secured beneath her skirt. Could this be the Phantom gang she'd heard so much about? Possibly. Still, she couldn't afford to blow her cover until she had tracked down the leader. Until that time, her job was to observe and act like just another hapless traveler.

"Empty your pocketbooks," the gunman ordered. He spoke in a lazy drawl that contrasted oddly with his quick movements and darting gaze.

An older woman seated two rows back from the bandits shook her head like she was scolding a wayward child. "Heavens to Betsy. Can't a body go anywhere without being robbed?"

Annie had noticed the woman earlier. It was impossible to miss the face paint and the bright purple skirt and shirtwaist. The attire would be shocking for someone much younger, but on a woman old enough to be her grandmother, it was downright scandalous. Clearly she was a woman with no reputation to protect. The way she argued with the gunman suggested she wasn't all that concerned about her physical safety either.

"I demand that you stop this nonsense right this minute, young man. If you don't, I'll —"

The gunman whirled around to face her straight on, the muzzle of his pistol practically in her startled rouged face. "If you don't shut up, they'll be one less passenger on this train."

"Well, I never . . ." The woman gave a disgusted nod and glanced around as if to see how many troops she could rally. Seeing none, she fell silent.

Having made his point, the masked bandit signaled his partners with a toss of the head.

The other two outlaws set to work gathering loot from the passengers and dumping the jewelry and cash into burlap sacks.

Annie clutched her purse tightly. There was nothing inside to identify her, of course. No Pinkerton operative would be so careless. The only personal item she carried was her father's gold watch. Ever so slowly she slipped her hand into her purse and curled her fingers around the timepiece. With a quick glance at the armed bandit, she slid it into the folds of her skirt.

Gradually, one of the outlaws worked his way to her side. "Your purse, ma'am," he said as politely as if asking her to dance.

The lower half of his face hidden by the triangular fold of his kerchief, only his blue eyes gave him away. She frowned. She hadn't pegged him as an outlaw, nor had she noticed his seat empty. Either she was losing her touch or he was extremely clever. Neither explanation offered much comfort.

Swaying slightly with the movement of the train, he took her purse and riffled through it, his hands almost too big for the task.

He gave her a questioning look. "Your watch, ma'am."

She imitated the shocked, frightened look of the other passengers. "Please."

He thrust out his hand. "Your watch." He

sounded almost apologetic but no less persistent.

The watch would command but a quarter of its worth. If this was indeed the Phantom gang, they were nothing more than a bunch of petty robbers, one notch higher than pickpockets.

She sucked in her breath and reached beneath the fabric folds of her skirt. He took the watch, but instead of adding it to his bag, he slid it into his vest. She frowned. A thief among thieves.

He seemed amused by her reaction. Or perhaps she only imagined the slight incline of his head and wry twist of his mouth. The outlaw returned her purse and, without bothering to relieve her seatmate of his belongings, moved away.

While one masked man kept guard in front, the other two worked with quick, efficient movements up and down the aisle, stopping only long enough to collect watches, rings, pendants, and money from the other travelers.

The entire operation was over almost as quickly as it had begun.

As if on cue, the train slid into the Cactus Patch station and rolled to a stop, announcing its arrival with a piercing whistle. The outlaws pushed past the dark-skinned porter and left the train with their ill-gotten booty before anyone else had a chance to move. A collective sigh rose from the passengers, followed by muttered curses.

"Land sakes!" exclaimed the matronly woman with the painted face. "There ought to be a law against such scoundrels."

"Ma'am, there is a law," bellowed an indignant Englishman, caning his way to the exit.

"Harrumph!" The woman picked up her satchel and followed him down the steps to the open-air platform, complaining all the while.

Every passenger left the car, even those who planned to continue on to Flagstaff.

Annie rose to let her seatmate pass but was the last to leave the train. After checking to make certain her weapon was secured to her leg, she straightened her plain but practical felt hat and brushed the cinders off her blue traveling suit. Dark hair secured into a tidy bun, she looked like a woman on the way to a job interview, which was exactly the plan.

She quickly rehearsed her story. Her father never started a new assignment without prayer and neither did she. *God, give me wisdom and courage as I track down that no-good scoundrel of a Phantom. And,*

oh yes — tell Papa I'll get his watch back.
Amen.

Thus braced, she left her seat, though she wasn't anxious to join the noisy crowd on the platform. Stepping outside was like walking into a hot oven. It had been a brisk forty degrees when she left Chicago five days prior. Cactus Patch had to be at least fifty degrees warmer.

Blinded by the sun, Annie tried to make sense of the chaos that greeted her. Everyone was talking at once.

A male voice thundered, "Quiet! All of you." The travelers fell silent and turned toward the marshal standing on a soapbox. As if to introduce the speaker, hissing steam belched across the platform, forcing travel-weary passengers to scramble out of the way.

Obviously relishing the moment, the marshal waited until he had everyone's attention before speaking. The mustache drooping down to his jaw gave him a comical look.

"I'm Deputy Marshal Morris," he said. He blew on his knuckles and gave the shiny badge on his leather vest a quick rub. "All three of the outlaws have been arrested and will be prosecuted to the full extent of the law."

The news was greeted by applause and

murmurs of approval, the woman in purple the most vocal. "It's about time the marshal earned his keep."

It was then that Annie noticed the three men in handcuffs lined up in front of the baggage room and telegraph office. She couldn't believe how quickly the bandits had been apprehended. Lawmen in Arizona Territory were evidently more efficient than in other parts of the country.

"I say hang them," someone yelled.

"When do we get our belongings back?" another demanded.

The older woman shook her fist, her rouged face fraught with outrage. "They took my wedding ring. It's a crying shame that a body can't take a trip without being molested."

The marshal looked in her direction. "You'll get it back, Bessie."

"See that I do."

The woman named Bessie leaned toward Annie. "Are you all right, dear? You look so tense."

Alert was more like it but Annie afforded the woman a withering smile. "I'm fine, thank you." She fanned her face. "It's just so hot and I've never been robbed before."

The woman commiserated with a pat on the arm and a sniff of her well-powdered

34

nose. "Don't worry. You'll get used to it."

The other passengers began moving away. Some left the platform and headed for horses and rigs parked nearby. Others returned to the train but the woman named Bessie remained by Annie's side. Curiosity seeped through the paint on her face like sun peering through clouds.

"Are you heading for Flagstaff?" Bessie asked.

"No. I'm heading for the Last Chance —"

"Mercy me!" Bessie's hand flew to her chest. "Not another one!"

Annie drew back. "Another . . . what?"

"Heiress, of course. That makes how many now? Ten, twelve . . . I've lost track."

Annie blinked. "Are you saying other women have applied for the . . . job?"

"Yes, but none stayed for very long." Bessie puckered her red lips and lowered bright blue eyelids. "Never in all my born days did I hear of advertising for an heiress. Not till Miss Walker got it into her fool head to ignore good taste and proper manners."

The woman with her garish paint and purple dress was a fine one to talk about good taste and proper manners, but of course Annie kept such thoughts to herself.

Bessie looked her up and down like a dressmaker taking measurement.

"Do you have any idea what you're letting yourself in for?" she demanded more than asked. "A little bit of a thing like you . . . having to deal with the likes of Miss Walker."

Standing five foot eight in bare feet, Annie could hardly be called *little,* but she tried to act appropriately worried. "Is Miss Walker really that difficult?" There wasn't much Bessie could tell her that Annie didn't already know. The dossier William Pinkerton supplied gave an in-depth portrait of both the ranch and ranch owner and Annie had practically memorized it.

Before Bessie could reply, a passerby wearing a derby and spectacles called over his shoulder, "If I had a choice between facing Miss Walker or a charging bull, I would take the bull." He kept walking.

"Don't pay any attention to Mr. Green. Miss Walker won't gore you. I'll say that much for her. By the way, most everyone calls me *Aunt* Bessie. What do I call you?"

"My name is Annie Beckman." Her new name fell flawlessly from her lips, thanks to hours of rehearsal.

"Annie it is. My sister's over there with a wagon and you can ride to town with us. From there you can rent a rig to take you to the ranch."

"That's very kind of you." The town appeared to be about a mile away and she didn't relish walking that distance in the sizzling desert heat. But getting to know the chatty woman was the real reason for accepting a ride. "I just need to get my carpetbag."

She turned and headed toward the baggage room where the porter had tossed trunks and baggage into an unorganized heap.

She neared the outlaws. Handcuffed and tied to a single rope attached to the back of the marshal's horse, the thieves could cause no harm. Still, the blue-eyed bandit staring straight at her gave her pause. If she didn't know better, she would swear he could read her thoughts.

At least a head taller than his two accomplices, he showed no remorse at his capture — unlike his partners, who looked dead serious and glared at Annie as if their current predicament were entirely her fault.

The marshal greeted her. "Ma'am?"

She pointed to the tall outlaw. "He stole my watch."

"And your name is . . . ?"

"Annie Beckman."

The marshal turned to the tall, staring bandit. "Is that true?" asked the marshal. "Did you take this lady's watch?"

"I do believe the woman is lying," he said, his voice as smooth as warm syrup.

It seemed from the gleam in his eyes that he wasn't talking about the watch and Annie shot him a visual dagger. He couldn't possibly know her identity but his accusation was nonetheless unnerving. Something about the man didn't sit right but she couldn't put her finger on what it was.

"I'm sure the marshal knows better than to take the word of a thief," she said.

A hint of humor suffused the outlaw's face and Annie had the strangest feeling she was cornered, much like a mouse trapped by a cat.

"If he's wise, he'll be equally cautious about believing everything the lady says," the thief replied in a lazy drawl that hardly seemed to suit him.

The marshal made an impatient gesture. "All right, that's enough." He turned to Annie. "If you're leaving for Flagstaff, give your address to my deputy and your belongings will be mailed to you."

"That won't be necessary," Annie said. "I'm heading for the Last Chance Ranch." This got no response from the marshal but she sensed a subtle reaction from the outlaw. What was it about this man that had her on tenterhooks?

"Come into the office in a day or two and I'll make sure that your property is returned," the marshal said.

"Thank you, I'll do that." Whenever a Pinkerton started a new assignment, the first order of business was to notify local law enforcement. The outlaw had no way of knowing it, but he actually did her a favor by stealing her watch. That gave her a legitimate reason to visit the marshal's office and would draw no suspicion.

She glanced at the outlaw whose gaze never left her face. "Is this the Phantom gang I've been reading so much about?" she asked.

"It's them, all right," the marshal said with more than a little pride. "Some of 'em. Unfortunately, the leader is slippery as a greased hog. Even his men don't know who he is. But I'll catch him. You can be certain of that."

Not if I catch him first. Out loud she said, "Good luck, Marshal."

Reins of his horse in one hand, the marshal grabbed the cantle and swung onto his saddle. With a click of his tongue the gelding moved forward and the prisoners shuffled behind.

"Yoo-hoo!" Bessie called. "Over here."

Pulling her gaze away from the departing

39

outlaws, Annie hurried to the baggage room, her mind still on the train robbery and the puzzling — but no less handsome — thief.

CHAPTER 3

A private eye's best friend is a woman with a secret too good to keep.

David Branch, aka Jim Taylor, aka John Crankshire, aka Tom Kindred, leaned against the dull steel bars. The jail cell measured a stingy eight by six feet and barely accommodated one man, let alone three. It had adobe walls, a dirt floor, and a low ceiling hardly high enough to contain his six-foot stature. Mexico had better hoosegows than this and that was saying something.

His real name was Jeremy Taggert but that name seemed as surreal as the hundreds of aliases he'd used through the years.

The man known as Grady sat on the single lumpy cot. His face disfigured by smallpox, he had the physique of a bird and disposition of a rattler. He made up for his short stature by acting unbearably superior, a flaw that Taggert intended to use to full advantage.

"Somebody squealed." The man named Squint stared at Taggert with buttonhole eyes. "That's the only 'xplanation."

"Maybe." One shoulder against the wall, Taggert hung his thumbs from his waistband. "Or maybe the marshal decided to greet the train as a precaution."

Squint's face puckered like a prune. "Makes sense, I guess. We have been kinda active."

Grady gestured with his arm. "You two don't know whatcha talkin' about."

Squint glarcd at him. "I suppose you do?"

"Yeah, I do. I've been around a lot longer than either one of you. I know how the Phantom operates."

Taggert remained silent and waited, careful not to reveal undue interest. He still didn't have a clue as to who the Phantom was and only a hint of where he might be hiding. Far as Taggert could tell, Grady was the only one who had actually met the man.

"Suppose you tell us how he operates," Squint said. "Or you just mouthin' off to hear yourself yak?"

Taggert decided to add a little more fuel to the fire. "He just likes everyone to think he knows more than he does."

42

It worked, or at least Grady's face grew red and the veins in his neck stuck out like thick blue cords. He glanced around as if checking for eavesdroppers. "Him and me . . . we made a deal."

Taggert narrowed his eyes. "Go on."

"I was to round up a couple of guys and keep the authorities hopping from place to place by robbing trains and stages. It worked out well till Barnaby got himself shot." Barnaby was the gang member Taggert replaced.

"That's why you recruited me," Taggert said. Several weeks of hanging around saloons and hinting that he was on friendly terms with some well-known outlaws got Grady's attention.

"Like I told you, we can keep the jewelry but the Phantom gets the cash."

Taggert shook his head. "I still don't understand why we can't just keep it all. What do we need the Phantom for?"

Grady's eyes rounded with greed. "He told me there was somethin' bigger down the road. Something real big. And if I did what I was told, I'd be rich. We'd all be rich."

"How do I know you're telling the truth?" Taggert's gaze traveled between the two men. "I only have your word that we're working for the Phantom. You can't even describe him."

Grady glared at Taggert. "I told you, I only met him the one time. It was dark and the Phantom kept his head down."

Squint cursed beneath his breath. "Now what?"

Grady lowered his voice. "I'll tell you what I think. I think the boss leaked the train robbery to the marshal."

Squint frowned. "Why would he do such a thing?"

Grady's eyes glittered. "So the marshal would be occupied while the boss robbed the bank."

Squint looked flabbergasted, or at least his eyes opened the widest Taggert had ever seen. "Are you sayin' we ain't nothin' but a bunch of *de*-coys?" Squint kicked the wall, his boot leaving a scuff mark. "Now ain't that grand? He's got the money and we're in jail."

"The boss will get us out," Grady said, though he didn't sound all that certain.

"If he doesn't leave town first," Taggert said, throwing another verbal log into the already heated discussion.

"Oh, he ain't gonna do that," Grady said. "He's got hisself a good safe hideout."

"In Cactus Patch?" Squint asked. He

44

made a face. "It's foolhardy to rob a bank in the town you call home."

Grady gave a mirthless laugh. "The Phantom don't know it, but after I dropped off the loot one night, I hid and waited for him to retrieve it." He lowered his voice to a whisper. "And he headed straight for a ranch."

Taggert folded his arms. "Sure he did." According to everything he'd heard, the Phantom didn't leave enough tracks to trip an ant.

"It's true," Grady insisted.

Squint gave him a look of disdain. "You don't know nothin' 'bout nothin'."

"You got that right," Taggert muttered. "Grady just likes us to think he knows."

It was a challenge Grady couldn't pass up. He leaned forward. "I'm tellin' you, the boss hides out at the Last Chance Ranch. That's his headquarters."

Squint regarded Grady with disbelief but Taggert showed no emotion. "The Last Chance, eh?" That pretty much confirmed what Taggert already suspected but he was careful to hide his excitement behind a disinterested yawn. It was the second time Taggert heard the ranch mentioned that day and a vision of a dark-haired beauty came to mind. He had never seen eyes like hers, a

45

mixture of caramel brown and dark green that reminded him of dense forests and deep waters.

He recalled Miss Beckman handing something that looked like an envelope to Grady and that made her suspect. Perhaps the Phantom was finally feeling the heat. If so, he may have found another way to communicate with his men. That would certainly explain the envelope and the lady's interest in the ranch.

Taggert didn't dare confront Grady with this theory as it would only arouse suspicion.

So what had she given him? Directions as to where to leave the loot collected from the train passengers? Instructions for the next heist? And what had he done with the envelope? His pockets had been empty when the sheriff checked.

Just as important, what was Miss Beckman's business at the Last Chance?

The woman had secrets, no doubt, and uncovering secrets was what Jeremy Taggert, aka David Branch, did best.

Bessie's sister, Lula-Belle, drove the wagon through town slow as water traveling uphill. Sitting between the two older women, Annie had to keep swiping the feathers from

Lula-Belle's hat away from her face.

Lula-Belle's dour expression matched the drab gray color of her dress. The two women were such complete opposites in dress and disposition it was hard to believe they were sisters.

Earlier, Annie persuaded Lula-Belle to stop at the post office, where she arranged for a mailbox, another crucial task at the start of a new assignment.

She was now anxious for her journey to end. The sooner she arrived at the ranch and settled in, the sooner she could get to work. If only it wasn't so hot. Perspiration ran down the side of her face and she dabbed it away with a handkerchief.

Cactus Patch was a town of sun, sand, and shimmering air. Adobe buildings with false-faced fronts lined the street on both sides. They passed several saloons, a general mercantile store, and a hotel. Opposite the hotel was a doctor's office and, at the end of the street, a windmill and stables. Tall green posts rose above the rooftops, draped with a network of wires.

"Those posts belong to the Arizona Telephone and Telegraph Company," Aunt Bessie explained with a prideful look. "Cactus Patch now has the telephone and I'm in charge of central."

"Really?" Annie knew that nearby Tombstone had telephones but hadn't expected Cactus Patch to have them too. Perhaps the little desert town wasn't as behind the times as she'd imagined. That would certainly make her job easier.

"Just got back from St. Louis for special training," Aunt Bessie continued.

Lula-Belle made a disgusted sound from the driver's seat. The feathers on her hat drooped in such a way as to match the disapproving curve of her mouth. "A woman's place is in the kitchen, not minding everyone's business."

Aunt Bessie lifted her nose. "For your information, the telephone company prefers women operators to men or boys." She turned to Annie to explain. "Women are much more dependable. You'll never catch us drinking beer or using profanity. And we're always on hand."

"That's true," Annie said. "We used to have telephone boys in Chicago but they left their posts to play in the snow and were replaced by girls."

"Are you from Chicago?" Aunt Bessie asked.

"Yes," Annie said, though she was actually from Peoria. It was essential to stay close to the truth without giving too much away. In

48

any case, it wasn't always easy to hide the nasally vowels and dropped letters of her native Illinois dialect.

Bessie's sister opened her mouth to say something but was distracted by a man waving for them to stop. News had traveled fast and already a crowd lined the street and clamored for details of the town's latest robbery.

Lula-Belle glowered as she tried to steer around the mob but Bessie appeared to be in her glory and broke into a buttery smile. The sudden attention didn't make her look younger than her sixty-some years but certainly more spry.

She answered questions left and right. "Yes, there were three of them," she yelled.

"Never saw any of them before in my life," she shouted at a woman in a poke bonnet.

"Yes, of course I feared for my life."

"Her name is Annie Beckman and she's Miss Walker's latest heiress."

Annie smiled and waved. People back home were much more circumspect. At least they didn't shout one's business out in public. Aunt Bessie showed no qualms in telling one and all everything she knew and a few things she didn't. She was, in essence, an operative's best friend.

A tall, skinny man with a thin mustache

ran up to the wagon.

" 'Xcuse me, ma'am. Name's Stretch. I'm headin' for the Last Chance now. If you'd like a ride, I'd be happy to take you there."

It was an offer too good to pass up. "Thank you," Annie said. "I'd be most grateful."

"Now isn't that nice?" Bessie's head bobbed up and down with approval. She slanted a blue-lidded gaze at the ranch hand. "See that Miss Walker doesn't give her a hard time."

Stretch lifted his hat and raked a hand over his black curly hair. "The boss lady will give her a hard time, all right. Ain't nothin' I can do 'bout that."

Moments later Annie was seated in a buckboard behind a black gelding next to the man named Stretch. She glanced in the back of the wagon. It was filled with what looked like newly purchased supplies, including cans of kerosene, boxes of leather soap, and a roll of barbed wire.

"Help yourself to some water," Stretch said, indicating the canteen on the seat between them.

Annie removed the canteen cork, wiped off the opening, and took a long sip.

She pushed the cork back in place. "Is it

always so hot here?" It was only March but already it felt like summer.

"It's hot here, all right. Some say God uses this as a backup for below." He chuckled. "Think I'm kiddin', eh? Tell that to the soldier who died out here and was sent below to atone for his sins."

The man evidently liked to talk and for an undercover detective that was a good thing. "So what happened?" she asked, playing along.

Stretch glanced at her sideways before delivering the answer. "He sent back for his blanket."

Annie laughed, mostly to be polite. She needed information — not jokes. "How long have you worked at the ranch?" she asked as they drove out of town.

"Four years," Stretch replied. "Before that, I worked on a ranch in the Panhandle."

"Tell me about Miss Walker."

Stretch shrugged his bony shoulders. "They ain't no words to describe the boss lady," he said. " 'Cept to say she's a tough old bird. Has to be, to run a ranch. Many have tried to run a successful ranch out here and failed, but the boss lady just keeps goin'. I reckon she'll outlive us all."

He then launched into another tall tale and then another, each one more outrageous than the one before. Annie finally managed to steer him back to talking about the ranch.

"We've got two thousand of the finest beeves in the west," he said, with more than a little pride.

The number was consistent with the Pinkerton report. She squinted against the glare of the sun. "But it's nothing but desert."

"I guess that's what you call a blessing," Stretch said. "It keeps most, though not all, competition away. Like I said, many have tried to ranch out here but only a few make it." He slapped the reins against the horse's back and they picked up speed.

She fanned herself with a kid glove. "Who else works at the ranch?"

"Well, let's see. There's Ruckus and Wishbone and Michael. He's our blacksmith and Bessie's nephew. Then there's O.T., short for Old Timer, Brodie our horse trainer, Mexican Pete, and Feedbag."

It appeared that most of the ranch hands went by assumed or "summer" names, which meant they were probably running from something, most likely the law. Though this was not unusual, it made her job more challenging.

"There she is, ma'am," he said at last,

pointing ahead. "The Last Chance Ranch. And for some of us, it really is the last chance."

The note of seriousness creeping into his voice made Annie take a closer look at his hollow-cheeked face. Everyone hid behind something and Stretch hid behind tall tales, jokes, and laughter. Could he be the leader of the Phantom gang? Or was his presence in town during the train robbery simply a coincidence?

She gazed at the ranch house. Nothing in the Pinkerton report prepared her for the size of it. "It's so . . . large." It was by far the largest building she'd seen since arriving in Cactus Patch.

"The boss lady had to rebuild after the '87 earthquake. It's even got inside plumbing."

That was a luxury Annie hadn't counted on. "Thank you for the ride."

"Think nothing of it. Enjoyed the company." He jumped from the wagon, reached for her carpetbag, and set it on the ground. "You sure do travel light, ma'am. You should see how much baggage some of the other heiresses brought."

He held out his hand to help her down. She lifted her skirt to just above her ankles and stepped to the ground.

"Thank you. I can handle it from here," she said.

He swept off his hat and bowed. "Good luck, ma'am."

She thanked him again. He slapped his hat on top of his head and climbed into the seat. Taking hold of the reins, he drove away in a cloud of dust.

With a combination of excitement and nervousness, she turned to face the two-story ranch house. This was it, the moment she'd been waiting for. Her first significant assignment.

A balcony ran the length of the second story, providing shade for the veranda below. The red tile roof shimmered beneath the blazing afternoon sun.

Across the way, the barn and outbuildings were guarded by a tall windmill, all in pristine condition. The sails turned slowly in the unrelenting hot breeze. Horses grazed in the pastures and from the distance came the low mooing of cattle and baying of dogs.

Picking up her carpetbag, she walked through the little courtyard and up the steps to the veranda dotted with wicker chairs. Even the carved oak door looked intimidating.

Annoyed by the tremor in her stomach, she threw back her shoulders and gave the rope a determined tug. A bell sounded inside, seeming to echo through what she imagined were large rooms and a maze of hallways. She waited a moment before giving the rope another yank but still no one answered.

She knocked and the door sprang open a crack, bidding her to enter. She glanced around and, seeing no one, stepped into the dim, cool entry. It felt good to be out of the heat but it took a moment for her eyes to adjust.

"Hello. Anyone here?" She closed the door behind her and called again.

Her voice bounced from wall to wall and was met with silence. She set her carpetbag in a corner out of the way and glanced around, taking careful note of doors, windows, and room layout to familiarize herself with the environment.

She crossed the red tile floor to the large parlor. A stone fireplace commanded one wall, a stuffed steer head guarding the mantel with ferocity. Two walls were lined with bookshelves, each volume lined up with perfect precision. Turquoise and red Indian rugs added bright splashes of color to the otherwise plain adobe walls. A stiff-backed leather couch faced a low dark table and was flanked by two matching chairs.

Annie could tell a lot about a homeowner by how a room was furnished. This particular room with its rigid order and daunting furniture confirmed every negative thing she'd heard about Miss Walker.

One wall opened up to a dining room with a table long enough to seat twelve. A pitcher of water surrounded by several clean drinking glasses was centered on the sideboard. She poured herself a glass and drank, the cool water soothing her parched throat as it quenched her thirst.

A half-open door revealed an office with an oversized desk, more bookshelves, and an Acme safe. Setting her empty glass on a tray, she wandered back to the entry hall.

She glanced up the stairs. She longed to freshen up and use the facilities but didn't want to appear rude or forward.

She waited and when no one arrived after twenty minutes, she decided her need took precedence over good manners. She collected her carpetbag and climbed the stairs to the second floor.

A hall ran the length of the house. Some doors were closed but others stood ajar, revealing empty bedrooms. Only one room seemed to be occupied and she guessed it was the ranch owner's room.

The upstairs furnishings were plain but

adequate and offered a pleasing contrast to the over-furnished rooms in Illinois. She glanced around before darting inside the lavatory and closing the door.

Sunlight streamed through an open window and was greeted by whirling dust motes. The room had a sink, toilet, and portable bathtub. She gazed longingly at the tub but didn't dare avail herself of such luxury until gaining permission from the ranch owner.

After answering nature's call, she washed her hands and face in the sink and opened her purse. Surprised to find her money still intact, she counted her bank notes and palmed the gold coins. The bandit had taken her watch but hadn't bothered with her money. How odd.

The marshal claimed that the train robbers belonged to the Phantom gang. Hard to believe. Shrugging, she dumped the coins back into her purse and tightened the drawstring. She still couldn't get over the feeling that she'd missed something and there was more to the tall bandit than she knew.

She retied the ribbon on her shirtwaist and worked a wayward strand of hair into the bun at the back of her neck. If she held her carpetbag just so, no one would notice the travel stains on her skirt.

Feeling refreshed and more like herself, she cracked the door open and listened. Dead silence. Used to city sounds, she'd never known such quiet. The ranch would take some getting used to on many levels.

Carpetbag in hand, she retraced her way along the hall and decided to wait for Miss Walker in the large room downstairs.

She turned the corner just as a man reached the landing. Startled, Annie gasped and the man jumped, his face twisted in surprise. Much to Annie's horror, he reared back and tumbled down the stairs.

"Oh no!" Annie dropped her carpetbag. She didn't wait for the man to hit bottom before racing down the stairs after him.

He hit the floor with a sickening thump and Annie fell to her knees by his side. "Sir? Are you all right?" She shook him. "Sir?"

Trained to stay calm during emergencies, she quickly worked the string loose from his chin and removed his hat. Staring at the leathery face, she sat back on her heels. A groan confirmed what her horrified eyes had already told her. It was a woman. An older woman dressed in men's clothing.

Please, God, don't let it be true. Please don't let this be her. But it was — she knew it was. The woman lying flat on her back had to be none other than Miss Walker herself. The owner of the Last Chance Ranch.

This was clearly the time to panic. Annie jumped to her feet, rushed to the front door and yelled at the top of her lungs. "Help! Somebody! I need help!"

CHAPTER 4

Sign outside private detective's door: In God we trust; all others will be treated as suspects.

Bessie Adams had seen a lot of changes in her sixty-plus years, some good, some bad, some both good *and* bad. She remembered life before the Singer sewing and ice-making machines, and it was no picnic. Had to sew everything by hand and drink warm lemonade.

She still hadn't made up her mind about the train and telegraph. It wasn't natural to travel at such high speeds and it took three people to put her on the train to Kansas. Telegrams didn't begin to take the place of *real* letters written with pen and ink on fine linen stationery. But nothing amazed her as much as the telephone, not even the doctor's horseless carriage.

When Dr. Fairbanks opened his medical

dispensary, he suggested that Cactus Patch have its very own telephone company. At first, people laughed at him. For what possible reason would anyone wish to talk over a wire? But then poor Mrs. Miller died before the doctor could get to her and people saw the benefit of fast communication.

Bessie's nephew Luke helped raise poles and string wires until all that was needed was an operator, popularly called a "hello girl." At the ripe age of sixty-something, it didn't hurt Bessie one bit to be called a girl. That alone made turning her dining room into a central switchboard worthwhile, but it wasn't the only reason she insisted she was the right person for the job. Who but she could be trusted to listen in to other people's conversations without blabbing all over town?

It's true that at times she lost her patience; not that anyone could blame her. People who wouldn't think of being rude if they saw you on the street thought nothing of being obnoxious and demanding on the telephone. After one such occasion, Bessie gave the offending party a thorough tongue-lashing. This made the man so mad he pulled out all the wires from the telephone pole in front of his house.

After that, her nephew insisted she travel to Kansas for training while he took over in her absence.

The trip was a waste of time. The city manager of the Kansas City telephone exchange insisted that each call be answered "What number?" in a pleasant voice with rising inflection. He made Bessie practice numerous times until she could practically do it in her sleep. He then carried on at great length about the importance of saying "Who is this?" as opposed to the more strident "Who are you?"

He also lectured on ways to turn away wrath with a gentle answer. Ha! Some people didn't know a gentle answer from a turnip.

Knowing her nephew, he probably let people get away with murder during her absence. Calling all hours of the day and night . . . making more than their share of calls in a single day . . . tying up the lines . . . calling to ask the time . . .

As if to confirm her thoughts, the battery-operated light on number sixteen lit up. She plugged the answering cord into the jack, threw the back key forward, and switched her headset into the circuit. "What num-BER?" She spoke into her mouthpiece with her most pleasant and inflected voice.

Jimmy Drake's deep baritone practically blasted her out of her seat. Why did people insist upon yelling into the phone? "Give me Cynthia Noble."

It was all Bessie could do to remain civil. "What do you want with *Miss* Noble?"

"It's none of your business what I want. Now connect me."

"You are a married man," Bessie scolded, "and have no right to call another woman." Politeness and inflection were all well and good but some callers needed to be put in their places.

"I have business with her and —"

"You can take your business elsewhere!" With that Bessie pulled the wire, disconnecting Jimmy midsentence. *"Harrumph!"*

Bessie gave a self-righteous nod. Not only was she the town operator, she was also a fine Christian woman. That made her an authority on proper behavior and good moral standards. As long as she was in charge, the telephone would not be used for reprehensible, unprincipled, or illegal purposes. Proper inflection indeed!

Number thirteen lit up. Now what did that annoying Mrs. White want this time?

"What num-BER?"

"Connect me with Mabel."

"You talked with her not an hour ago."

"So what business is it of yours when I last talked to her?"

Bessie heaved a sigh. What she had to go through. "The telephone is for emergency purposes."

"This *is* an emergency," Mrs. White insisted. "I can't remember how much butter to put in the recipe she gave me."

"Then why don't you go next door like a civilized human being and ask her to her face?" Bessie snatched the wire, disconnecting Mrs. White.

Almost immediately the entire switchboard lit up. "Now what?" she muttered, connecting a line at random.

"What num-BER?" And then, "This better be important, Millicent," she added. "This is the third call you've made today!"

Millicent's excited voice screeched into her ear. "Did you hear about Miss Walker?"

Annie paced outside the closed bedroom door and alternated between wringing her hands and fighting exhaustion. The doctor had been with Miss Walker for hours and it was almost midnight. She paused beneath a softly hissing wall sconce.

Ohhhhhhh. Just wait till Mr. Pinkerton heard what she did this time! Annie's stomach knotted just thinking about it.

64

Causing an old lady serious injury was far worse than shooting a dead man. Not only did she feel terrible, she also felt doomed, her future career as a Pinkerton operative hopelessly in peril. Worse, should Miss Walker file a lawsuit, it could well bring financial ruin to the entire agency.

Miss Walker's angry voice cut through Annie's thoughts. "Doctor, I demand that you leave at once!"

Annie whirled about to stare at the closed door. If the ranch owner suffered pain or shock, it was not evident in her vocal cords.

The doctor's murmurs were steady and calm but too low for Annie to make out his words. She marveled at his patience. As bad as she felt for causing Miss Walker to fall, she felt worse for the doctor.

It took three men to hold the old lady down just so the doctor could stabilize her leg. Never had Annie seen such a commotion. Everything she'd ever heard about Miss Walker turned out to be true.

Something crashed against the door and Annie jumped back. Miss Walker's voice snapped through the air. "How am I supposed to run a ranch with my leg in the air?"

"You're lucky a broken leg is all you have," the doctor said. "A woman your age —"

Another crash. "My age, my age. You make

65

me sound like a fossil."

The door suddenly flew open and the doctor glanced at Annie before looking back over his shoulder. "I'll check on you tomorrow. Now get some sleep."

He stepped from the room and greeted Annie with a weary nod. He held his hat and black leather case in one hand and closed the door with the other.

"I'm sorry we didn't get a chance to talk earlier. I'm Dr. Fairbanks." Even in the soft yellow light he looked young for a doctor, probably in his early thirties. Despite having to deal with a wildcat patient and the lateness of the hour, his demeanor was calm; only his appearance was ruffled. His ruddy brown hair stood on end and exhaustion showed in his watery red eyes. A stubble beard shadowed a firm, strong jaw and his shirtsleeve was torn.

"That's quite all right, Doctor."

"And your name is . . . ?" he asked.

"Annie . . . Annie Beckman."

"Pleased to meet you, Miss Beckman." Something banged against the door and the doctor shook his head. "I should have been a veterinarian."

Another thud made Annie jump but the doctor only shrugged.

"Will Miss Walker be all right?" she asked.

"It's a femur break," he said as if that were answer enough. "Did you know that the femur is the longest and strongest bone in the body?"

"No, I didn't —"

Despite the lateness of the hour, he went on at great lengths about the marvels of the femur bone. Annie was exhausted and in dire danger of falling asleep on her feet. She nevertheless forced herself to listen politely.

Miss Walker would be well within her right to order Annie off the property. If not, then Mr. Pinkerton would probably summon her back to Chicago the moment he heard how she caused the ranch owner's accident. Either way, her days on the ranch, and maybe even hours, were numbered.

Still, she couldn't stop thinking like an operative. For that reason, she was determined to cultivate a friendship with the doctor. If by some miracle she was allowed to stay, anyone who talked as much as the doctor might very well come in handy.

"The femur is perfectly engineered," the doctor continued. "It's also the last bone you want to break. It does, after all, make up a quarter of a person's height."

"Th-then it's serious?"

"Serious enough," he conceded. "Eighty percent of broken femurs result in a patient's demise."

Annie's jaw dropped. Covering her open mouth with both hands, she peered at the doctor over her fingertips. "You mean —"

"Not Miss Walker. She's too stubborn to die. I should specialize in stubborn patients. They're a pain in the gluteus maximus but they seldom die, which does wonders for a doctor's reputation."

Unable to make up her mind whether the doctor was serious or not, Annie pulled her hands away from her face.

He dug in his black bag and handed her a brown vial. "I gave her something to help her sleep. This is for pain. Give it to her in the morning if she's uncomfortable. She should eat something light at first and curtail visitors, at least for a couple of days. The most important thing is to keep her calm. Don't let her get upset."

It seemed a bit late to worry about upsetting her but Annie glanced at the closed door and said nothing. All was quiet, at least for now.

Dr. Fairbanks stalked down the hall toward the stairs and Annie chased after him.

"Wait!"

He turned.

"You want *me* to take care of her?" She was trained to hunt down criminals, not play nursemaid.

"Someone has to. Since her housekeepers have returned to Mexico, there's no one else to care for her but you."

Annie struggled to find her voice. "Surely one of the ranch hands —"

"Miss Walker won't hear of it and probably for good reason. The only way a ranch hand knows to deal with a broken leg is to shoot the unfortunate victim. We can't have that, now, can we?"

"No, but . . . but what if something happens? What if she's in a lot of pain or . . . How do I get hold of you?"

"Send someone into town to fetch me. It's a pity the telephone line hasn't yet reached the ranch but they're working on it. Meanwhile, get some sleep while you can. I have a feeling you're going to need it." He donned his hat and started down the stairs. "Good luck."

It was the second time that day someone had wished her luck.

He paused at the bottom of the stairs and glanced up at her. "One more thing," he called. "When you enter her room, be sure to duck."

CHAPTER 5

An undercover agent is only as good as his (or her) disguise.

Annie's body ached from exhaustion but she still couldn't sleep. Closing her eyes meant having to relive the horror of watching Miss Walker tumble down the stairs time and time again. The deadly sound of the woman's body hitting the ground floor seemed to rise from the very pillow at her head. No matter how much she twisted and turned, she couldn't make the memory go away.

By the time the rising sun turned the desert sands red, she'd been sitting in a chair for hours, a manila folder marked GTF in her lap. Operatives, or Pinks as they were commonly called, were taught to keep detailed records. Every fact had to be recorded with utmost accuracy; every question duly noted, every action scrupulously documented. Notes were to be written on small pieces of paper and attached to reports.

The strict training not only helped professionally, it also impacted her personal life. Some people kept diaries; Annie kept dossiers.

Reverend Jones, the pastor of her church back home, once accused her of treating God like a suspect. She continually bombarded the pastor with questions that even he, with all his seminary training, couldn't answer. It was an odd thing for him to say since he had no idea she was a Pinkerton. Telling anyone, even her pastor, what she did for a living would mean immediate dismissal from the company. The Pinkerton guidelines were clear on that.

"God is bigger than our minds can comprehend," Reverend Jones said on more than one occasion. "Even if we knew all the answers, we wouldn't understand them."

Questions without answers were called enigmas and nothing disturbed a detective more. For that reason, she kept jotting notes in her GTF folder, writing questions, underlining and crossing out words. Today she wrote, *Miss Walker? Why did something so awful have to happen, God?*

She was so well versed in writing in

cryptic that it came naturally to her, even when she wrote something meant to be seen by her eyes only.

She closed the folder with a sigh and put it aside. GTF — for God the Father.

As usual, He offered no answers, only more questions.

Her body stiff, she stood and stretched her arms over her head, then bent to touch her toes.

Anxious to check on the old lady and nervous about meeting her face-to-face, Annie hurried through her morning ablutions and dressed in a dark blue skirt and white linen shirtwaist.

The last thing she did was lift her skirt and strap her leather gun holster around her thigh. The derringer was a gift from her brother Travis, following the successful fulfillment of her first assignment. It was his way of saying she was an operative in every sense of the word, even if their father didn't agree.

At the moment, she didn't much feel like one. This was her first time outside the States and never before had she been required to work in such a remote location. The cattle ranch was nothing like the cities or large towns that offered endless resources for catching criminals.

Even if by some miracle Miss Walker didn't throw her off the ranch, there was still the problem of how to submit the mandatory daily reports to the main office. Annie didn't even know how to contact the marshal in a hurry and she felt very much alone.

She straightened her skirts and could almost hear her father's stern voice: *"You wanted a challenge, Miranda, and now you have one. So quit your complaining."*

Shaking the thought away, she held her head high and shoulders back. With outward confidence and inner doubt, she followed the smell of bacon and coffee downstairs to the kitchen. The man standing in front of the stove had introduced himself the previous night but she couldn't remember his name.

"Mornin', ma'am," he said, wielding a spatula. A crooked-teeth smile flashed against his freckled skin and ginger hair curled from beneath a wilted white hat. His smile made her relax. At least his was a friendly face.

Annie responded in kind. "I'm sorry, you told me your name but —"

"Everyone calls me Able. Got the name when I was a chuck wagon cook." A note of pride crept into his voice. "No cowboy ever

73

went hungry with me around. Wind, rain, snow — you name it — and I was able to whip up a fine meal." He emphasized his words with a nod of the head.

"Sounds like Miss Walker is lucky to have you," Annie said.

He scoffed. "Cooks don't get the same respect they used to." He turned to the cookstove and in a voice barely audible added, "There was a time when being a cook meant something, but those days are long gone."

Not knowing how to respond or even if she was expected to, she glanced around. The kitchen was furnished with the most modern equipment and even had running water. The cooking range was equipped with several burners, a large oven, and a high shelf. On the opposite side of the room, a dry-air refrigerator stood nearly eight feet high.

"Do you want to take up her breakfast or do you want me to do it?" he asked.

She'd rather not face Miss Walker so soon but putting it off wouldn't make it any easier. "I'll take it up to her." She may as well face the music and get it over with. "I feel terrible about what happened."

He wrinkled his nose. "If you ask me, Miz Walker was an accident waitin' for a happenin'. No woman her age should carry on like she does. She can outride and out-rope any man and she ain't slowin' down for nothin' or nobody." He flashed his teeth, his smile as ready as his opinion. "Except for maybe a broken leg."

He turned back to the stove and scooped a hotcake from the skillet. With a flick of his wrist, he added it to a plate already piled high with food.

"Her breakfast is ready."

The plate held enough food to feed a family of four. As if guessing her thoughts, Able chuckled. "Four scrambled eggs, a quarter pound of bacon, a stack of hotcakes, and coffee strong enough to picket a wild horse. Just as Miz Walker likes."

Annie studied the tray. "Perhaps this morning she would prefer something a bit lighter." The doctor had sedated her and it was doubtful that she'd recovered from either her fall or the medication enough to enjoy such a grand feast.

He sniffed and it was obvious by his frown that he took her request as criticism. "That *is* a light breakfast."

"And a very fine breakfast it is. But I'm afraid it's better suited for a cowpuncher than a convalescent. I think some soft-boiled eggs and tea would do quite nicely.

Perhaps some dry toast."

Able looked like he'd been punched in the stomach and his freckles seemed to turn yellow. "Boiled eggs. Dry toast?"

"Yes. And tea. Not too strong."

He shook his head. "This is a cattle ranch, not a tea parlor. We don't even have tea leaves."

"Never mind. We'll use mine." She shot out of the kitchen and upstairs to the room she'd claimed as her own. Having learned the healing powers of tea from her grand-mother, she never traveled without a good supply, all serving a different purpose. White willow was good for pain, calamus for indigestion, and horsetail for bone-knitting. For good measure, she also selected a packet of chamomile. She decided to leave the gunpowder tea for another occasion. Thus armed, she hastened back downstairs.

Able looked even more dubious than before. "Miz Walker ain't gonna take kindly to someone messin' with her coffee."

"I'm not messing with her coffee. I'm simply substituting it with a more favorable beverage. At least while she's convalescing."

His face suffused with doubt, he wiped his hands on his stained white apron. "The only tea I know how to make is Southern sweet tea, and Miss Walker's got no patience

76

for that."

"That's all right. I'll make it. First I need hot water."

"Hot water I can do." He picked up a kettle and carried it over to the sink.

Annie glanced around the kitchen. "Where would I find a teapot?"

Able looked blank. "If we have one, it will be in one of the cupboards."

Annie opened the cabinets one by one. She found a teapot so covered in grime she doubted it had ever been used. Satisfied that she had solved her immediate problem, she scrubbed it clean and dried it. She couldn't find a tea strainer but the cheesecloth found in a drawer would do quite nicely.

She snipped the cheesecloth into little squares with scissors. "How long have you worked here, Able?"

"Almost two years."

While waiting for the water to boil, she picked up a dime novel from the kitchen table and thumbed through it. The rather lurid cover read *Miss Hattie's Dilemma*. Able glanced at her and his face, already red from the heat of the stove, turned another shade darker.

"Yours?" she asked.

He nodded. "That was given to me by the lady writer. She was an heiress just like you.

77

Her name is Kate."

"Really?" She set the book down. "How interesting. What happened to her?"

"She married the blacksmith. Far as Miz Walker's concerned, that's like a hangin' offense." He cut the bread and placed a single slice on the griddle. "Miz Walker won't allow no married woman to inherit her ranch."

Annie, of course, knew the requirements of the job but she let the cook talk. In short order she had a complete rundown on all the women who had tried to be Miss Walker's heiress and failed. It wasn't encouraging. Even without causing the ranch owner's accident, her chance of staying on the ranch long enough to track down the Phantom didn't look good.

"The water's boiling," he said after a while.

"The water must be hot enough to cook a lobster," she said.

"I reckon that water's hot enough to cook a whole rack of 'em." Protecting his hand with a flour sack towel, Able lifted the kettle off the stove.

"You must always start by heating the pot," she explained. He poured a dollop of water into the pot and she swished it around and dumped it out. She then carefully measured out tea leaves and signaled for more water.

"That's it," she said. Curling steam tickled her nose with the smell of tea. Horsetail tea tended to be bitter but a little honey would take care of that. She turned the pot around slowly three times. Something else her grandmother had taught her. "One for the Father, two for the Son, and three for the Holy Ghost," she explained.

"You better add a fourth one for protection," Able said, looking even more dubious. " 'Cause you're gonna need all you can get when Miz Walker takes a sip of that."

Dreading the thought of having to come face-to-face with the ranch owner, Annie shuddered. "Is there anyone we can summon to take care of Miss Walker until her leg is healed?" The doctor insisted that no one was available but she had to make certain. "A friend or relative, perhaps?" According to the dossier, Miss Walker's only relative was an estranged brother whom she hadn't seen in three decades.

Able shook his head. "Miss Walker ain't got no relatives. Least none that anyone knows. She's not big on friends much either, not the kind you're talking 'bout." He picked up a large spoon, scooped the boiled eggs out of a pan, and turned them into a small bowl.

Annie arranged the teapot and cup and saucer on the tray with trembling hands, along with the plate of food, linen napkin, and spoon. Spotting a cowbell on the counter, she added it to the tray as well.

Able grunted. "I want you to know I'm doing this under protest." He arranged two slices of toasted bread on a plate. "Yes-siree, under protest."

Tray in hand, she faced the doorway. The cold knot in the pit of her stomach doubled in size. "That makes two of us."

Annie stood outside Miss Walker's bedroom door. Knock or just walk in? She couldn't make up her mind so she decided to do both.

Juggling the tray the best she could with one hand, she rapped a knuckle against the door. Nothing. Was Miss Walker asleep or . . .

Recalling the doctor's dire statistics for femur breaks, she felt beads of perspiration break out on her forehead. *Please, please, please don't let her be . . . dead.*

Heart pounding, she threw open the door and stared at the bed. Heavy draperies kept out all but the dimmest light.

Miss Walker lay flat on her back with her

leg suspended in midair. Annie walked to the bed on what seemed like wooden limbs. The gentle rise and fall of the older woman's chest told Annie her worst fears had not been realized. *Praise God!*

An apparatus the shape of a large wooden horse loomed over the bed. The sight took her breath away. Now all the lumber delivered to the room, followed by incessant hammering, made sense. If she didn't already feel guilty for having caused the accident, she now felt downright mortified.

"Well? Are you going to stand there all day?" Miss Walker's strident voice made Annie jump and the bone china cup and saucer rattled on the tea tray.

"I thought" — Annie cleared her throat — "I thought you were asleep."

"How am I supposed to sleep with my leg in a noose?"

Annie glanced at the cumbersome splint contraption. A good question indeed.

She set the tray on the bedside table, her gaze lighting on the shotgun next to the bed, butt end down.

The old woman squinted as if trying to see more clearly. Annie walked around the bed and ripped open the draperies. Streams of sunlight poured through the squares of the leaded glass door. The desert that had looked so forlorn and dreary from the train now resembled a master painting in the early morning light. She opened the door and a slight breeze cooled her heated cheeks.

If only she hadn't turned her head toward the eastern sky. The sun's red eye glared down in silent accusation, much like the Pinkerton eye stared at her whenever she was called on the carpet. Even now, three years after her father's death, his blame persisted. Her mother had delivered five bouncing boys and remained in robust health, but delivering one scrawny baby girl had sent her in a downward spiral from which she never recovered. Her father never outwardly blamed her, of course. He was too much of a gentleman for that. It was the elephant in the family that was only mentioned in whispers.

Today the whispers of the past got louder. Annie had put yet another life at risk. Leaving the door ajar, she turned to the bed to find Miss Walker's rigid gaze still on her.

"You!"

Miss Walker didn't appear the least bit fey or soft in the head as Mr. Pinkerton had suggested. Indeed, she looked as bright and alert as a rattler about to strike.

"I can't tell you how sorry I am. I . . . I —"

"Sorry!" Crevice-like lines deepened on Miss Walker's forehead. Her sun-baked skin appeared more ash-colored than tan. The studied gaze offered a contrast to the gray hair falling across her pillow in wild abandon. Had it not been for the vivid blue of her eyes, she would have looked every bit her sixty-five-plus years.

"You near scared the life out of me. Who are you and what were you doing sneaking around my house?"

"I wasn't sneaking. My name is Annie Beckman. I believe you were expecting me."

A shadow flitted across Miss Walker's face as if she was trying to place the name. "That gives you no right to walk into my house uninvited."

"I apologize, but there was no one here when I arrived." The woman's eyes narrowed and she looked about to argue, but Annie continued, "I had a difficult journey. Just before we arrived in Cactus Patch, the train was robbed." When this news brought no reaction, she added, "I needed to use the facilities. I meant no harm. Certainly I never meant to harm you."

"You cause me serious injury and yet you have the audacity to march in here this

83

morning as if you have every right." Miss Walker's nostrils flared and her voice quivered with fury.

Annie hardly marched into the room but she wasn't about to argue semantics. Somehow she needed to get the woman on her side. "The doctor said there was no one else to take care of you."

The older woman's eyes glittered. "So you took on the task yourself."

"It's the least I can do after . . ." Annie glanced at the upraised leg and grimaced. Anxious to fill in the strained silence, she turned to the bedside table. "I brought you breakfast and a bell. If you need anything, just ring."

Miss Walker's gaze flew to the tray. Considering her situation, she was surprisingly intimidating. "You call that breakfast?"

Annie placed a piece of cheesecloth over the cup and poured the tea, careful not to spill it. "Your body is probably still in shock and —"

"Don't tell me what my body is!"

Annie set the teapot down with a clatter. "Are you in pain?"

Miss Walker grimaced. "Of course I'm in pain."

"The doctor left medicine —"

The old lady's curse made Annie blush

but she held her ground. "If you don't want medicine, the tea will do quite nicely."

"Tea?" Miss Walker made it sound like something that crawled from under a rock. "You want me to drink . . . *tea*?"

"This isn't just any tea. It's a special blend that will help knit broken bones." Annie carefully bundled the leaves in the cheese-cloth before adding a dollop of honey to the steaming brew. Turning, cup in hand, she noticed a small book of Shakespeare on the bed.

"What a pity the Bard made no mention of tea in his plays. A terrible oversight, don't you agree?"

Miss Walker frowned. "If the man was as smart as he wrote, then coffee would have been his beverage of choice."

"Like Balzac?" Annie had read somewhere that Balzac was addicted to coffee. "I do believe that Shakespeare wrote with all the sensibilities of a tea man. Balzac, on the other hand, was quite an awkward writer."

"If Shakespeare was a tea man as you say, then perhaps that explains why Hamlet is such an incessant talker. The man never would have survived here in the West."

Annie giggled at the thought, which gar-nered a look of rebuke from the direction of the bed. Miss Walker's expression was every bit as intimidating as the shotgun by her side.

"Well?"

"Oh, I do apologize." Annie slipped an arm beneath the ranch owner's neck and ever so gently lifted the woman's head off the pillow. Miss Walker took a sip of the hot beverage and wrinkled her nose before pushing the cup away.

"Dishwater couldn't taste worse."

Annie straightened and set the cup on the saucer. "It's not my favorite tea, but like I said, it does help heal bones."

"Coffee is the glue that holds these bones together and that's what I want. I want it now and I want it strong."

"The doctor said —"

"Fiddlesticks! I don't care what Dr. Fairbanks said," Miss Walker snapped. "What does he know? A man barely dry behind the ears. Anyone who drives a heap of —"

"I believe it's called a horseless carriage," Annie said.

"I don't care what it's called. Horsepower should be left to horses. It's noisy and smelly and riles the cattle. Anyone with the bad sense to drive around in one has no right to dictate what I should and should not do."

Ignoring the woman's protests, Annie

picked a spoon off the tray and scooped up a bite of soft-boiled egg. She faced the woman with her most determined stance. Miss Walker looked about to argue but apparently thought better of it.

Annie slipped the spoon between Miss Walker's thin, parched lips. The woman sputtered and coughed and pushed Annie's hand away. "Dishwater and lye soap." She spit it out. "Enough of that garbage!"

Annie set the spoon down. She reached for the linen napkin and wiped egg off the blanket. "If you prefer, I'll have Able make you oatmeal."

"Oatmeal?" Miss Walker made it sound like arsenic. "Forget food. Don't just stand there, girl. Get my coffee. And after that you can fetch my foreman." She stopped and grimaced as if in pain but then picked up where she left off. "Tell him I want to see him pronto."

Annie sighed. It appeared that tracking down the leader of the Phantom gang would be easy compared to caring for the old lady. "The doctor said you need to rest."

"I don't have time for such nonsense. I've got a ranch to run! After I finish with my foreman, bring pen and paper from my office. I need to dictate a letter. Then I'll meet with each ranch hand individually. I don't want them thinking they can slack off just because I'm temporarily indisposed. Oh, and make sure Ruckus takes proper care of my horse."

Never had Annie met a woman more stubborn — or demanding. "I'll write your letter for you, but you will be allowed no more than two visitors a day until the doctor says otherwise."

Miss Walker's chest heaved beneath the covers, but then she suddenly surprised Annie by laughing.

Frowning, Annie straightened Miss Walker's pillow and covers. On second thought, perhaps two visitors would be too many.

Miss Walker's expression grew serious. "I guess you'll do anything to prove that you'll make a worthy heiress, even if it means putting up with my demands." She twisted her head to look Annie square in the face. "Don't think I don't know what you're up to."

Miss Walker pushed hard but apparently she liked people who pushed back in kind. Annie met the woman's gaze. "I guess that makes us equal."

Miss Walker narrowed her eyes and snapped her mouth shut. Fearing she might have overstepped the line, Annie picked up the tray and moved away from the bed. "You'd best get some rest." Without another word she left the room, closing the door just in time to avoid the thrown clock.

CHAPTER 6

The path of least resistance often leads to the hoosegow.

Jail fare consisted of hardtack and cold coffee and Taggert didn't have the stomach for either. He marveled at how the other two men attacked the stale, dry biscuits with such relish.

To quench his thirst, he finished the last of the dark brew and spit out the grounds. "So when's the boss gonna spring us?" Grady had talked half the night but said little of any consequence. The man was of no use. He knew a tenth of what he claimed to know, maybe less.

As if on cue, Marshal Morris entered the office and Taggert set his cup on the tray. It was about time.

Morris plucked the keys from a hook by the door and ambled over to the cell. "I decided to give one of you a suspended sentence," he announced.

Grady's eyebrows shot up. "Does that mean you're gonna let us go?"

"Let you go?" The marshal chuckled. "A suspended sentence is just a fancy term for a good ole-fashioned hangin'. Haven't had one of those in a while. Should liven things up a bit. Hangings don't eliminate crime but they sure do stop repeaters."

Squint turned three shades of gray and for once Grady's bravado deserted him, or at least he fell silent.

"You ain't got no right to hang any one of us without a trial," Squint said. "It's the law."

The marshal shrugged. "You know the law and I know the judge. I guess that makes us even." He scratched his belly and studied each man in turn. "Don't feel bad. It's been my experience that outlaws are greatly improved by death."

"So are martyrs," Taggert muttered.

Ignoring his comment, Morris let his gaze travel from man to man. "So who's itching for improvement? You choose or I choose. Don't matter much to me."

"It's gotta be one of them two," Grady said with as much graciousness as a host offering a guest refreshment. "I've got what you call seniority."

"If that's what we're goin' by, then he's the one," Squint said, pointing at Taggert. "He was the last to come on board."

"That true?" the marshal asked, staring at Taggert. "You the last to join the Phantom gang?"

Taggert glared at his two cellmates. "Yes, which means I have less restitution to make."

Grady waved his hand. "This ain't about restitution. It's about feeding the wolves."

"To be fair, we should draw straws," Taggert argued.

"I ain't drawing no straws," Grady said. "He's your man, Marshal. It's two against one."

"Sounds fair to me." The marshal pulled out his Peacemaker. "Now step back, all of you." He waited for the three men to crowd against the back of the cell. Gun in one hand, he unlocked the door with the other, keys jiggling. He motioned to Taggert.

"All right, now move. And keep your hands up."

Hands raised shoulder high, Taggert shuffled out of the cell. The marshal slammed the door shut, locking in the other two. "Turn around and put your hands behind your back."

Taggert did what he was told and the

marshal snapped a pair of handcuffs around his wrists, the iron bracelets cold against his flesh.

"It was nice knowing you," Grady called.

"Wish I could say the feeling was mutual," Taggert muttered, casting a dark look at his former partners in crime.

The marshal pressed the muzzle of his gun against Taggert's back. "Move. Try anything and I'll shoot you full of lead. Makes no difference to me if we improve you here or wait till you get to the gallows."

"If it's all the same to you, I'd rather hang," Taggert replied. "These are the only clothes I've got and they don't need no improving."

Eleanor Walker stared at the ceiling. There wasn't much else to look at when one lay flat on one's back. Of all the ridiculous and aggravating things to happen. A broken leg!

Now that she'd flung the mechanical clock across the room, she didn't even know what time it was. It seemed like hours since that annoying woman traipsed out. It had to be at least noon, if not later. And the pain. The pain!

Where was the doctor? Where, for that matter, was anyone? And where, for pity's sake, was that cowbell?

She ran her hand over the bedside table, knocking the bell to the floor.

She had just about reached the brown glass dropper bottle the doctor left when a tap sounded at the door. It was about time.

Thinking it was her foreman, she moved her hand away from the pain medication and barked, "Come in!"

The door opened and the woman named Annie stuck her head through the crack. "Someone here to see you. A Mr. Stackman."

Robert Stackman was Eleanor's banker and friend — and would be so much more if she would let him. At the moment, he was the last person she wanted to see.

"Tell him I'm occupied," she said.

Robert's voice drifted from beyond the door. "You can tell me that yourself." He walked into the room and bowed to Annie. "Thank you. I'll take it from here."

Even in his sixties, Robert cut an impressive figure with his silver hair as neatly trimmed as his mustache and goatee. Eleanor never saw him when he wasn't impeccably groomed in dark trousers, white dress shirt, vest, bow tie, and polished oxfords. Robert had been after her for years to sell the ranch and marry him. A bad idea on many counts.

He closed the door and stooped to pick up the clock. "I see time's trying to get away from you," he said, grinning. He set the clock on the bedside table. It was a little after 11:00 a.m.

He picked the bell off the floor and set it next to the timepiece. "I see you have a leg up. Trust you to be ahead of the competition."

"I'm in no mood for your jokes," Eleanor snapped. "What did you come here for? To gloat?"

"I heard you had a nasty fall and I came to see how you are. It might surprise you to know that's what friends do."

"If you are truly a friend, I trust you won't say 'I told you so.' "

"I wouldn't think of it." He lifted a chair and moved it to the side of the bed. He then sat, pulled off his straw hat, and balanced it on his knee. "I see you have another heiress."

"Yes, and I plan to get rid of her as soon as possible." If she had her druthers, she would have ordered Annie out of the house that very morning. "Not only is the woman a menace, she's as stubborn as a cornered rattler."

Robert arched his brow. "Then you two should get along quite famously."

95

Eleanor made a face. "She gave me boiled eggs and weak tea for breakfast. Now, I ask you, does that sound like someone who can be trusted around cattle?"

Robert chuckled before growing serious. "Actually, this isn't entirely a social call."

"I should have known." It wasn't like him to travel to the ranch during bank hours just to be friendly.

"I hesitate to mention this while you're . . . indisposed, but I suspect there'll be all hell to pay if you found out I kept something from you."

"Oh dear." She brushed aside a strand of hair. "This sounds ominous."

"I'm afraid it is. I don't know if you heard but the Phantom gang struck again. The train *and* bank were robbed yesterday." Resting his elbow on his crossed arm, he stroked his goatee. "It's odd that two robberies occurred on the same day, don't you think?"

"Odd, but not too surprising." Arizona Territory had gone through many changes since her family settled in the area more than forty years earlier during the '50s. But one thing that never changed was the criminal element. As a ranch owner, she'd battled her fair share of renegade Apaches, cattle rustlers, fence cutters, and water snipers.

She placed her hand on her forehead. She felt groggy and so unlike herself that she had difficulty concentrating. "That annoying girl mentioned something about a train robbery." Or at least Eleanor thought she did. Or maybe it was the doctor. "But the bank too?"

"The marshal apprehended some, but by no means all, of the men responsible."

"Hmm." She studied him. "So how does this affect me?"

Robert glanced at her suspended leg and hesitated.

"Speak up," she snapped. "I will not be treated like an invalid."

"And I wouldn't think of treating you like one." He coughed and cleared his voice. "I don't want to upset you."

"Then stop beating around the bush."

He drew in his breath. "The marshal believes the Phantom is connected in some way to this ranch."

Eleanor stared at him. Did he just say what she thought he said? "How do you mean, connected?"

"Morris thinks the Phantom is using the ranch as a hideout."

"Hogwash!"

He splayed his hands. "I'm just telling you what he thinks."

"That's absurd." She had little regard for the marshal. He hadn't even been able to capture the outlaw Cactus Joe. It took a dime novelist from Boston — and a woman at that — to capture the man. "I'd know if my ranch was being used for nefarious purposes."

"You employ many ranch hands. Any one of whom could be the Phantom."

"I know my men." True, she suspected that some had checkered pasts, but she demanded hard work and loyalty from them and she got it. Anyone caught loafing or breaking the law was immediately dismissed. "No one working at the ranch has time to play outlaw."

He shrugged. "I just want you to be on guard."

"I'm always on guard." One didn't run a successful ranch without due vigilance.

"I will feel a whole lot better once the telephone reaches the ranch. Had you allowed it to be installed when I first suggested it the doctor could have reached you much sooner."

Eleanor made a face. Robert called the telephone progress; she called it an invasion of privacy.

"The day will soon come when the whole country will be connected to a single exchange. Just think, Eleanor. You'll be able to talk to cattle buyers in New York or Chicago as easily as we are talking now."

The thought made Eleanor's head swim. She couldn't imagine talking business through a wire. "The telephone didn't do much for your bank," she pointed out. "You were still robbed."

"But only because someone called to inform Morris that a train robbery would occur. While the marshal was at the station arresting the thieves, someone managed to sneak into the bank vault. Perhaps the Phantom himself."

"It sounds like the criminal element has found a better use for the telephone than you have."

He blew out his breath. "There is one more matter," he said. His hesitation indicated that he was about to broach a touchy subject and Eleanor's gaze sharpened.

"Someone wishes to purchase your property and has made an offer. It's a modest one but, considering the times, quite adequate."

"I'm not selling."

"You're not getting any younger, Eleanor, and this plan of yours to find an heiress is turning out to be a bust, to say the least."

This was an old argument and they had

hammered it out relentlessly in the past. There was nothing more to be said, so she was surprised that Robert seemed intent upon revisiting the subject. He glanced at her elevated leg. "It's time."

"Horse feathers!"

"It's time."

"*I'll* decide when it's time." Eleanor studied him and tried not to think of her throbbing leg. "Just out of curiosity, who is this buyer?"

"I have no idea. The buyer wishes to remain anonymous. It's all being handled by a lawyer back east."

Eleanor frowned. She had no patience for people who hid behind lawyers. "You can tell Mr. Anonymous what he can do with his offer."

Robert heaved a sigh. "So you're still determined to keep the ranch?"

"Why wouldn't I be?"

He studied her with grave concern. "I thought perhaps your fall down the stairs would have knocked some sense into you."

"Sorry to disappoint you," she said.

He raised a silver eyebrow. "Has it ever occurred to you that the good Lord might be trying to tell you something?"

"If that's true, He'll have to speak louder."

Robert's gaze followed the wooden framework that loomed over her. "I shudder to think what He would have to do to get your attention."

She shooed him away with a wave of her hand. "You've had your fun for the day. Now go. I have a ranch to run."

He ran a finger across his upper lip and made no move to leave. "But, Eleanor, you haven't got a leg to stand on."

She glared at him. "Enough of your bad jokes."

"Very well." Robert stood. "I'll let you get back to . . . running your ranch." He donned his hat. "Have a good day, Eleanor."

He walked out of the room and closed the door.

Shrugging away the loneliness that followed his departure, Eleanor reached for the bottle of medicine and rang the cowbell. Where was that annoying girl?

CHAPTER 7

Warning: Peering through a keyhole can give you a private eyeful!

Report #1: Miss Walker is not at all fey or even shy of tongue. She is a formidable woman with a will of iron, the temperament of a mule, and the aim of a charging bull.

Annie looked over what she had written. She would, of course, have to include every detail of Miss Walker's accident, including her own unfortunate role.

The Pinkerton General Order book gave explicit instructions on how to write a report. The reports had to be written in ink or indelible pencil. Descriptions must include all physical traits, clothes, jewelry, and habits. Conversations had to be recorded verbatim with detailed information as to time and locations. All arrivals and departures had to be accurately noted.

The cowbell rang and Annie tossed down her pen. Now what did Miss Walker want? At this rate she would never get her report written, let alone accomplish what Pinkerton had sent her to do.

During the next week, Miss Walker ran Annie ragged. It was hard to imagine that one old lady could require so much care. Annie hardly had time to think about the investigation and her frustration grew with each passing day.

Worse, she had yet to figure out a way to send daily reports back to the main office. Not that she had anything of value to report, but Mr. Pinkerton insisted upon daily updates regardless. He would not be satisfied with the occasional letter Stretch or the doctor mailed for her. She also needed to identify herself to the marshal and collect her watch, but going to town seemed unlikely until Miss Walker had somewhat recovered from her injuries. None of the ranch hands or Able was willing to take care of Miss Walker, even for a few hours.

Adding to her frustration was the constant ringing of the cowbell. Miss Walker insisted upon meeting each ranch hand regular as clockwork and, with the doctor's approval, Annie relented. One by one, she ushered each cowboy into the house and up the stairs.

Each man walked into the ranch owner's bedroom, hat in hand, as if expecting to be hung. Each man came out looking as if he had been.

Even Able had lost his good humor after being closeted with Miss Walker for the better part of an hour. Annie followed him into the kitchen.

"Able, what's going on?"

He slammed a skillet onto the stove top. "Miss Walker thinks that the leader of the Phantom gang is one of us."

Annie was careful not to react. "I don't understand. Who is this gang?"

"They're the ones who robbed the train and bank last week. They've been terrorizing the county for nearly a year."

Annie widened her eyes to feign surprise. "And she thinks that one of the thieves works here? On the ranch?"

"That's what she said. Heard it loud and clear with my own ears."

"Do you think it's possible?" Annie asked.

Able shrugged. "Anything's possible, I suppose. But I know all the ranch hands. I know that Stretch likes his meat cooked all the way through and Ruckus likes his rare. I know that O.T. has a sweet tooth and Feedbag is seriously prejudiced against veg'tables. Wouldn't you think I'd know if one of them was *him*?"

"I don't know if it's possible to completely know another, Able." She couldn't count the times she heard a family express shock and disbelief over a loved one's arrest. "Do you think Miss Walker is in any danger?"

Able's eyes twitched. "Why would you think that?"

"She's an old lady. There's not much she can do, now that she's flat on her back."

"I don't see why anybody would want to do her harm." He frowned. "If so, they'll have to deal with me first."

The ringing bell brought their conversation to an end. Able glanced upward before dipping a measuring cup into a sack of flour. "You better go see what Miz Walker wants this time."

After taking Miss Walker her noon meal, Annie escaped to her room to add to the fast-growing file that included detailed information on each ranch hand. Most of the men went by assumed names, making background checks difficult. Identifying someone solely by physical description was tough, but the agency had successfully done it in the past and she hoped would do so again.

Having learned from Able that the ranch hand going by the name of Ruckus was married with two children, she neatly printed the information on his file. His wife's name was Sylvia. His daughter was married to a rancher and his son attended seminary back east. It was hardly the kind of family one would expect of an outlaw but she wasn't ready to rule him out. He seemed sincere enough and led the others in prayer each morning before starting work, but such religious fervency could be a ruse.

She tossed her pencil down with a sigh and closed her files. She then left her room and hid her files in a vacant bedroom two doors away, where no one would think to look. It was a trick learned from her father and one that had served her well through the years.

Returning to her room, she checked to make certain she hadn't left anything that could provoke suspicion. Something shiny caught her eye and she crossed to the bureau to see what it was.

Her father's pocket watch lay on top of the dresser next to her hairbrush. How odd.

She glanced around. The timepiece hadn't been there that morning, which meant the marshal must have dropped it off sometime between breakfast and the noontime meal.

She picked up the watch and lifted it to her ear. The marshal even thought to wind it.

It bothered her that the lawman appeared at the ranch house without announcing himself. Even worse, he had walked into her bedroom.

She tucked the watch into the top drawer and hastened downstairs and out the front door. No carriage or even a horse was in sight, save the wild mustangs in the corral across the way. Some of the ranch hands had left early that morning and hadn't been seen since.

She walked around the house to where Able tended the vegetable garden. Several small service buildings were located in back. The icehouse and laundry were closest to the main house, the granary and smoke-house a distance away. Next to what appeared to be an unused barn stood an old springboard wagon.

A vegetable garden spread between the buildings, a scarecrow rising from its midst. The soil was kept moist by irrigation ditches.

As she approached, Able looked up and tossed a bunch of carrots into a wicker basket. His freckles looked like orange polka dots in the afternoon sun. "Thought I'd make some gumbo soup," he said. "It's the only dish Miz Walker will eat that's not made with beef."

"Sounds good," Annie said, though it seemed too hot for soup. She watched him pull a bunch of carrots from the soil. Carrots? Already? In Chicago the ground was still frozen.

"Did you happen to see the marshal today?"

Able glanced up. "Marshal Morris? Nah. Is there a problem?"

"Just wondering. I . . . was curious to know what happened to the train robbers."

Able shook dirt away from the carrots. "I reckon they'll spend the rest of their born days behind bars."

"I'm sure you're right." She hesitated. "Anyone else at the house today? Other than Dr. Fairbanks, I mean."

"Just Ruckus and O.T. Why?"

"No reason." She left him and walked around to the front.

She let herself in the house just as Miss Walker's foreman, O.T., descended the stairs. A wiry man with restless, and some might even say shifty, eyes, his sun-baked face placed him in his late forties. He'd removed his spurs before entering the house to comply with house rules but his gun remained and the holster sagged on his hip.

O.T. afforded her a look of pity. "I don't envy your job, ma'am. The boss lady is loaded to the muzzle and ready to shoot."

"I guess we can't blame her," she said. She never meant the old lady harm and felt sorry for her. It must be frustrating, lying in bed day after day, especially for one apparently as active as Miss Walker.

"O.T., something was taken from me during the train holdup — a watch." She studied him as she spoke. If he had placed her watch on the bureau, she didn't want to sound ungrateful, but neither did she want men walking into her room.

"Sorry to hear that, ma'am. You better talk to the marshal about it."

"The watch has been returned," she said. "I just found it on my bureau."

Not a flicker of emotion crossed his face. "Good to hear."

"I was wondering if you happened to see the marshal."

He shook his head. "Nope. Can't say that I have."

"If he's still here at the ranch, I want to

thank him for returning my watch," she said.

"If I see him, I'll tell him you're lookin' for him. Anything else I can do for you, let me know. Soon as the boss lady's on her feet, we'll start learning you the ropes."

She frowned. "What do you mean?"

He tugged on his hat. "If you're gonna be the new heiress, you gotta know how to work a ranch. You ride, right?"

She nodded. Actually, she was a good rider, thanks to her brother's patient tutoring.

"That's something, I guess. You'd be amazed how many women come to this ranch not knowing the front end of a horse from its tail." He narrowed his eyes. "Know anything about cattle?"

"No, but I did stay at a sheep ranch once."

He reared back with a look of disdain. "Well, if you know what's good fer you, you'll tuck that news under your hat and keep it there." He hastened to the door as if she were still carrying the stench of sheep with her.

"Scares me to think what kind of heiress will turn up next," he muttered. With that he left the house.

Annie had no idea whether or not he was the Phantom, but either way, O.T. was a strange one.

She went to secure the door after him but there was no lock. That meant that anyone could walk in day or night. With an uneasy feeling, she headed for the stairs.

CHAPTER 8

A detective without a clue is like a cowboy without a horse; both are in for a lot of footwork.

Annie walked into the bedroom the following morning to help Miss Walker with her usual morning ablutions. The day before, Stretch had ridden into town to fetch the mail and the bed was piled high with correspondence. He also mailed two letters for Annie.

"Time for your bath," Annie said cheerfully.

"Well, get on with it, then." Miss Walker continued to rip through the wax seals one after another with a letter opener. After perusing each letter, she scribbled notes onto the margins with a pencil, presumably to remind herself how she wished to respond.

After giving Miss Walker a sponge bath

and helping her into a clean nightgown, Annie reached for the hairbrush. The best way to contain Miss Walker's long gray hair was to work it into a single plait.

As she interwove the strands, she planned her day. She still hadn't talked to all the ranch hands; the blacksmith, Michael, was first on her list. If he was half as talkative as his aunt, he might have something useful to say.

"Why, the nerve!" Miss Walker's body shook and the bed springs groaned. "That's the second time in two years the county's tried to raise my taxes and I won't have it."

Accustomed to the woman's outbursts while reading her mail, Annie paid little heed as she quickly contained each silvery strand. Reaching for a blue ribbon, she tightly wound it around the feathery-tipped braid.

Annie was about to leave the room when Miss Walker stopped her. "Go to my office and fetch paper and pen. I need you to write letters. And hurry. I haven't got all day."

All day was exactly what Miss Walker had but Annie wasn't about to contradict her. Instead she hastened downstairs to the office.

Able had left earlier to go into town for supplies and she missed the cheerful sound of pots and pans, along with his merry whistling.

Annie walked through the large room but something made her stop. She distinctly remembered leaving the door to Miss Walker's office open and now it was closed. Strange. Ear against the wood, she listened. Nothing. Out of habit, she reached into the false pocket of her skirt to feel for her weapon.

She turned the knob and flung the door open. Curtains fluttered at the window. The wind had evidently caused the door to close. Mystery solved, she headed straight for the desk. The penholder was empty. She knew she had replaced the fountain pen the previous day.

She opened the top drawer, hoping to find a writing implement, but instead found a tintype of a young girl. Odd. The photograph wasn't there when she did a previous search of the office looking for personnel files.

She lifted the image out of the drawer and held it to the light. The picture was dark and faded but not enough to hide the child's pretty face. She turned it over but the back was blank. She discounted the idea that it was a photograph of Miss Walker as a child;

tintypes weren't available until the late 1850s.

Annie replaced the photo and checked the other drawers for a pen. Except for the photograph, nothing else seemed out of order. Still, she had the strangest feeling that someone had searched the desk. The question was why.

A soft scraping sound startled her. "Who's there?"

A man emerged from behind the door and Annie shrank back in her chair. He elbowed the door shut, trapping them both inside the small office.

He poked at the brim of his Stetson and pushed it upward. Cobalt eyes met hers and it was all she could do to catch her breath. She would know those eyes anywhere.

"Wh-what are you doing here?"

No question about it; this was the outlaw who stole her watch on the train. The thief caught her unawares, which gave him the upper hand, but she would relieve him of his advantage as quickly as possible. Surreptitiously, she slid her hand into her false pocket.

Finger to his mouth, he motioned her to stay quiet. "Take it easy. I'm not going to hurt you."

She squeezed the grip of her derringer.

He didn't know it, but it was his own skin in danger, not hers.

"It's Miss Beckman, right? Miss Annie Beckman."

Under normal circumstances she might have been flattered that he remembered her name, but today she felt no such pleasure. "Why aren't you in jail?"

The man flashed a smile, revealing perfect white teeth. He looked different somehow and it took her a moment to figure out why. The last time she saw him, he had a mustache and whiskers. Today he was clean-shaven. His lack of facial hair revealed a previously unnoticed cleft on his fine chiseled jaw and made his eyes look even bluer, if that was possible.

"You're not alone in wanting to see me there," he said. "Sorry to disappoint you."

"It's where you belong." Her legs trembled and that was not a good sign. An operative couldn't afford to be nervous or anxious during a confrontation. To remind herself that she had everything under control, she squeezed the grip of her gun tight.

He narrowed his eyes and studied her. Imagining that most women in her spot would look for an escape or, at the very least, a weapon, she let her gaze fly to the paperweight on the desk.

His gaze followed hers. "Ah, a lady willing to defend herself. I like that." He gave another smile and her heart skipped a beat. The dimple on his right cheek matched the soft impression on his chin. With very little effort, he could probably charm the hide off a steer.

"But you needn't bother," he continued. "If you do as I say, neither of us will get hurt." He moved closer and tossed a pen on the desk. "I believe you were looking for that. A bad habit of mine, I'm afraid. I tend to keep every pen I lay my hands on."

"One of many bad habits, I would think," she said, determined not to let his charming ways or pleasing looks distract her. "What do you want? What are you doing here?"

"I'm the new ranch hand. If we should happen to bump into one another, you are to act like you don't know me."

The nerve of the man. Who did he think he was, coming here and giving her orders? "You're out of your mind."

He arched a brow. "That is neither here nor there. Do we have an understanding?"

The man's audacity might have been amusing under other circumstances but today it was plain unbelievable. "Why would I do the bidding of an outlaw?"

"I believe the lady has a few secrets of her

own that she would prefer not to have known."

She studied him. He couldn't possibly know she was a Pinkerton detective. So what did he think he had over her? She decided to call his bluff. "I have no secrets."

He arched an eyebrow. "None?" He feigned a look of disappointment. "A woman without secrets is like a rose without fragrance."

She smiled; she couldn't seem to help herself. "We can now add bad poetry to your list of crimes."

"And we can add evasiveness to yours. I saw you handing one of our gang members an envelope on the train." He studied her as if measuring her reaction. "So I know you're a member of the Phantom gang too. I'm sure our mutual boss would frown on you turning me in — a member of your own family, so to speak."

Annie's mind spun. He accused *her* of belonging to the Phantom gang? It wasn't just absurd, it was downright laughable. Only her considerable acting skills allowed her to keep a straight face. Still, if she played her cards right this might work in her favor. What better way to pump information from him than to let him think she was one of *them.*

"Perhaps you're right," she said.

"You know I am." Amusement danced in his eyes.

Lord forgive her for thinking it, but he was a handsome, devilish rogue. Had she met him under any other circumstances, well, who knows what might have happened? Dismayed by the thought — and even a little ashamed — she gave herself a mental kick and clenched her jaw. It wasn't like her to let her mind wander when working a case.

His eyes hardened. "You keep quiet about my identity and I'll extend you the same courtesy." He shrugged. "Sounds reasonable, wouldn't you say?"

She pretended to consider his offer. Bright sunshine slanted through the open window, making him look deceptively honest. Thank goodness she had the sense to know it was the lighting and not the man giving the impression of integrity.

"How did you escape?" It seemed like a reasonable question given that he now considered her practically *family.*

He shrugged. "You'd be amazed what you can do if you know the right people."

She wondered if by "right people" he included the marshal. It would certainly explain his release and, unfortunately, she was no stranger to corrupt lawmen.

She matched his frank scrutiny with equal regard. "I assume it was you who returned the watch."

"I had no choice. It doesn't seem right to steal from one's family, so to speak." He hung his thumbs from his bullet-studded gun belt, drawing her gaze down the length of him. He certainly took full advantage of his clothing. His wide shoulders and well-muscled chest stretched the fabric of his well-worn shirt to the limits. His long legs looked as sturdy as tree trunks.

She took a deep breath; she didn't want to think about this.

"So what do you say?" he asked. "Do we have a deal?"

She pretended to hesitate. If she appeared too anxious he might become suspicious. "I'll keep your secret, Mr. . . ."

"The ranch hands call me Branch. Just plain Branch."

"I'll keep your secret, *Mr.* Branch, but if you dare hurt a hair on that old lady's head . . ."

Branch reared back, his face suffused with surprise. "Considering the way she treats you, I can't imagine that you care."

The only way he would know how Miss Walker treated her was by eavesdropping.

120

That was something that the Pinkerton brothers frowned upon, along with offering sexual favors in exchange for information. She would never consider using such tactics, of course, but she wouldn't put it past this man to utilize his considerable good looks to his own advantage any way he could.

"I'll keep your secret," she said. "For now."

His crooked smile made her heart skip a beat. She reminded herself that he was a thief and trespasser and that the two of them were about to embark on a danger-ous, if not altogether lethal, liaison.

"I'm sure our mutual boss will approve," he said.

She moistened her lips. The way his gaze clung to her mouth told her it wasn't just business on his mind. The thought wasn't altogether unpleasant and warmth crept up her neck. She gave herself a mental shake. They were on opposite sides of the law and she'd best not forget it.

Regaining control of her senses, she leaned forward. "I do have a small request."

He raised a dark eyebrow. "Go on."

"I would rather that you didn't mention our meeting to . . . our mutual boss." The moment he mentioned her to the Phantom, the game would be over, for then both men would know she was playing a role.

121

She could almost see the wheels turning in his head. "And why is that?" he asked.

She had to think fast. "It was careless of me to be seen with that envelope. And you know how our . . . mutual boss . . . despises carelessness."

She tried to read the calculating look that flashed across his face. Did he believe her?

"It seems that you have more secrets than a spinster's diary," he said.

Relief washed over her. Confidence restored, she relaxed and pulled her hand out of her false pocket. Elbows on the desk, she steepled her fingers. It was a masculine move learned from her father and one that signaled power.

"I won't reveal who you are, Mr. Branch, but you can be certain I'll watch you like a hawk."

A devastating smile inched across his handsome face. "And I'll watch *you*," he drawled. "In fact, I look forward to it." Without another word, he turned and walked out of the office.

Taggert paused at the gate of the courtyard outside the ranch house. *"I won't reveal who you are, Mr. Branch."*

"No, I don't imagine you will, Miss *Beckman*."

122

Most women would have panicked or fainted dead away upon being confronted by a man perceived to be an outlaw. For the most part the lady remained calm and held her own.

Interesting.

There was something exciting about a woman like that. Enticing, even. Seductive.

One thing was clear: not only did the Phantom know how to hide his identity, but if Miss Beckman was an example, the man also had great taste in women. Such an appreciative eye for the fairer sex could very well lead to the mystery man's downfall.

Taggert intended to see that it did.

Meanwhile, a slew of questions ran though his mind. What was Miss Beckman doing at the ranch? And was Miss Walker's fall really an accident or something more sinister? His guess was the latter, which led to yet another question: For what purpose did the Phantom need the ranch owner incapacitated?

Annie Beckman. He would bet that wasn't her real name but she wasn't alone in that regard. Most of the ranch hands had assumed "summer" names. The unwritten law of the West was not to ask questions. The past was the past. Whatever a man — or woman — might be guilty of was his or her business and no one else's. This made Taggert's task more difficult. Anyone poking around in another's history could well end up riddled with bullet holes.

Yes, Miss Beckman, or whatever her name was, might very well be his key to success, but he must tread with care. She was a complication he hadn't counted on — though admittedly a very pretty complication.

Something made him turn toward the house. Miss Beckman stood on the balcony watching him. A woman of her word.

It didn't seem possible that such a shapely package could contain so much fire. Her raven hair, high cheekbones, and almond-shaped eyes, coupled with her smooth honey skin, gave her an exotic look that was most appealing. No doubt Indian blood ran through her veins. Under normal circumstances, his interest in the lady would be more personal. Fortunately, he knew a deceptive web when he saw it, but that didn't make the temptation any easier to resist. God help him.

He saluted her and, much to his amusement, she returned the favor. A worthy opponent indeed.

Tugging on the wide brim of his hat, he turned and walked away. If things worked out as planned, the lady would point him straight to her leader.

The hunt for the man had occupied him day and night for the last several weeks and he fervently hoped that the chase was close to an end. He had no fondness for cattle and the sooner he could track down the Phantom and leave, the better.

He glanced one last time at the Phantom's woman. Even from this distance he could feel her big, green eyes drawing him in. Ah, but she was a clever one. Cagey. She promised to keep his secret but she would mention him to the Phantom; Taggert would bet on it. That could only make the leader nervous. A nervous criminal made mistakes and that was bound to give him away.

Taggert sucked in his breath. He'd waited this long. He supposed he could wait awhile longer. With this thought, he stomped into the bunkhouse, but not without casting one last look at the pretty woman on the balcony.

CHAPTER 9

Making accusations without proof is like throwing a rope without a loop.

The encounter with the bandit was very much on Annie's mind when she escaped the ranch house the following morning. Walking helped her think and she needed time to plan her next move.

The sky was clear and the sun hot, but after the summer humidity of Chicago, she welcomed the dry heat.

She began her walk just as a gust of wind swept across the desert, carrying with it the smell of sage, cattle, and heated earth. A tumbleweed rolled past and clung to a fence post momentarily before blowing away. The blades of the windmill turned atop the spider-legged tower and the mill rotated as if welcoming a guest.

Horses grazed in a nearby pasture; ears twitched and long tails swished. One mustang lifted its head to gaze at her with soulful brown eyes before burying his nose back into the brown grass.

She followed a trail up a hill behind the horses and came across a little cemetery. Weathered crosses marked four graves. Kneeling by the smallest cross, she wiped away a layer of sand and read the inscription.

Rebecca Abbott, beloved daughter. 01 April 1866 – 21 September 1871.

Annie sat back on her heels. The little girl had only been five when she died. That was about the same age as the little girl in the tintype. So who was she? A family member?

Annie stood and examined the other graves. *Mary and Harold Walker* — Miss Walker's parents. The fourth and newest grave was marked Ralph Abbott, who died two years ago. The little girl's father, no doubt.

She straightened and turned slowly, surveying the land and buildings that made up the ranch. Miss Walker was a force to be reckoned with but she knew her business. Knew how to run a cattle ranch — no one could deny that. She probably also knew her ranch hands like no one else. Miss Walker dictated business letters and issued orders but she wasn't given to idle gossip.

Getting her to talk was a challenge but Annie had to keep trying.

She started down the hill and stopped. A strange, unsettling sensation came over her, as if she was being watched. But no one was around. Shaking the feeling away, she hurried to the ranch house.

Later that same day she questioned Able about the little grave.

The cook pushed a rolling pin to the edge of the pastry dough spread across the wooden table before replying. "That was way before my time, but I heard talk that Miz Walker lost her daughter to smallpox."

Annie frowned. "I didn't know Miss Walker had any children." Nothing like that had shown up in the Pinkerton file.

He sprinkled flour on the dough and rolled again. As he worked, his white floppy hat rocked back and forth in a sea of ginger curls. "Far as I know, she just had the one. Her husband's buried up there too."

"Miss Walker was married?"

"And divorced," Able said. "But you didn't hear that from me."

Annie blew out her breath. Divorced. Great Scott! That must have raised some eyebrows. "Stretch said Miss Walker rebuilt after the earthquake."

"From what I heard, the quake flattened pretty near everythin' within miles. What was left standing was destroyed by fire, except for the barn and stables. Most people around here left after that, but not Miz Walker."

"I can't imagine what she must have gone through."

Able set his rolling pin aside and reached for a tin biscuit cutter. "She's a tough old bird, that's for sure." He dipped the cutter into flour and pressed it into the dough. "But if she likes you, consider yourself one of the lucky ones. If not, watch out."

No doubt Able spoke the truth, but given her present predicament, Miss Walker would have a hard time finding another caretaker.

Annie had questions galore but that was all Able knew, or at least, all he was willing to talk about. Obviously there was more to Miss Walker than met the eye.

Less than a week after her confrontation with the train robber who called himself Branch, she stood on the balcony of her room waiting for him to leave with the other cowpunchers. It was just after dawn but Annie was dressed and ready to search the bunkhouse the moment the cowpunchers left for the day.

129

The horses were saddled and ready to go. The air was perfectly still. Already it promised to be another hot day and the men were eager to get an early start. They stood in a circle while O.T. laid out the chores for the day.

She could hardly take her gaze off Branch and it had nothing to do with his pleasing looks, although admittedly that made her job more agreeable. No, the reason for such close observation was that something about him kept nagging her. He reminded her of a wolf in sheep's skin. Careful observation told her he could ride a horse and lasso a steer with the best of them. Then again, he had looked equally confident robbing a train.

His lazy smile and studied gaze belonged on a ranch, but he walked and moved with a city swagger. His clothes were worn in all the right places but hardly seemed to go with his long, lean form. Cowpunchers had a tendency to tilt forward when they walked, but not Branch. Instead he walked tall and straight, as if he had a broomstick for a spine or perhaps even military training.

Ruckus led the morning prayer. Even Branch took off his hat and looked respectful. Anyone not knowing his true identity could easily mistake him for a man of faith.

She curled her hands at her sides. "You might fool the others, but you can't fool God," she muttered. *Or me.*

Ruckus finished the prayer and yelled, "Let's go!"

The cowpunchers broke away from the circle and hastened to their horses with jingling spurs.

Branch mounted with one fluid move. Instead of taking off with the other men, he lingered behind and glanced at the balcony where she stood. She didn't bother to duck. He knew she watched him and even seemed to derive perverse pleasure from her doing so.

She couldn't see his face in the early morning light but she didn't miss the hand touching the brim of his hat. The simple gesture made her heart flutter. Never had she known an outlaw so brazen or cocky, or a man who exuded such charm. Like a woman sending her man to war, she returned his salute with a wave. The expression in his eyes was hidden, but not the flash of white teeth. She returned his smile. She couldn't help herself.

He turned his horse toward the rising sun and galloped off, leaving her bereft and more than a little shaken. Her papa once said that a person had only one important decision to make in life and that was whether or not to follow the Lord; everything else was secondary. Branch had chosen crime and that put them on opposite sides no matter how much she might wish otherwise.

Sighing, she waited until the horsemen were out of sight before leaving the house and walking to the empty bunkhouse. Her heart could flutter all it wanted, but she had a job to do and she'd best not forget it.

The smell of saddle leather, alcohol, adobe, and sweat greeted her as she opened the bunkhouse door. The building was divided into two rooms. One room was for sleeping and the other, judging by the large wooden table, was mainly for eating.

There wasn't much in the large room except a stack of old newspapers and some dime novels, including *Miss Hattie's Dilemma* by the local author. The book made her laugh; who said men didn't read love stories?

A stuffed steer head hung over the stone fireplace. The skin of a rattlesnake draped from the mantel and saddle blankets were scattered about the floor for rugs.

The second room was furnished with bunk beds. According to Able, only the single men lived here. Married men like

Ruckus had their own places. Able, of course, slept in the ranch house in the room next to the kitchen.

Knapsacks hung haphazardly from the backs of chairs or hooks on the wall. She stood in the middle of the room considering each bunk in turn. It was always the details that tripped a person and today it was the bedroll. Only one was rolled military-style and had been placed at the bottom of the bed. No cowpuncher worth his salt would leave such a tidy space. But a military man would.

"Got you, Branch!"

A thorough check of Branch's mattress, bedroll, and knapsack revealed nothing remotely useful or even personal. No photographs, no letters, no notes, no paper — but lots of pens. The man hoarded pens like a dog hoarded bones.

A quick search of the knapsacks belonging to the other ranch hands revealed nothing of any interest. A couple held photographs of pretty young women. Chips of wood on the floor marked Wishbone's bed. She never saw the man when he wasn't whittling.

After rummaging through each man's belongings, she stood in the center of the room. Hands on her waist, she turned slowly, regarding each man's space one by one. Had she missed something?

"Kin I help you?"

Startled, Annie spun around. Wishbone stood in the doorway staring at her from beneath a ten-gallon hat. His knees were so far apart a cow could walk between them and turn around. His knife and ever-present piece of wood was in hand. He greeted her with a nod of his head and then resumed whittling, chips of wood falling to his feet.

Trained to have an explanation handy for just such an occasion, she quickly explained her presence. "Miss Walker is in need of a new housekeeper and asked me to check to see how much work was needed."

Wishbone's steer-horn mustache twitched. "No housekeeper ever set foot in here," he said with a worried glance around.

She wrinkled her nose. "Yes, I can believe that."

He slid his knife down the length of his wood. "I've worked my share of ranches and I ain't never known a housekeeper to step foot in the ranch hands' livin' quarters."

She forced a smile. "I reckon there's a first for everything."

His brows slanted downward. "I don't think the boys will cotton to someone re-arranging their stuff."

She couldn't decide if that was a warning or a general statement against housekeepers. "Then perhaps it would be best if the housekeeper's job is confined to the main house."

"Maybe so." He looked relieved. "Maybe so."

"I'll suggest that to Miss Walker." She tossed a nod at the stick in his hand. "What are you making?"

"Makin'?" He held the stick up. "I'm not makin' anything. The point of whittlin' is to enjoy the journey and not worry about the dest'nation." He looked at her with squinty eyes. "You ought to give it a try sometime. The way you zip around, you'd think there was a hangman on your tail. A little whittlin' would do you a world of good."

"Maybe I'll try it sometime." It was hard to imagine doing something just for the sake of doing it. She had always been goal oriented, even as a child. Everything was done with a purpose in mind, mostly in an attempt to gain her father's approval.

Following an awkward silence, she started for the door. "I'd better go. It's time for Miss Walker's breakfast."

She brushed past him and he didn't try to stop her. Outside she filled her lungs with morning air. Could Wishbone be the Phantom? She glanced over her shoulder but the ranch hand was nowhere in sight, no doubt still enjoying his journey to nowhere.

Able greeted Annie that afternoon with less than his usual exuberance. His honor had been questioned and he took it hard. He wasn't the only one. None of the ranch hands liked being suspected of being the Phantom.

"Hmm. Something smells good," she said.

"Gingerbread cookies," he said. "Fresh out of the oven."

She helped herself to one and sank her teeth into the still-warm confection. It tasted every bit as delicious as it smelled.

"Where did you learn to cook like this?" she asked between bites. She had never tasted so many delicious desserts. The ranch was a sweet tooth's paradise.

"I grew up on a farm with three brothers. After my ma died, we drew straws to see who would take over as cook."

"And you won."

"At the time I thought I'd lost." He shrugged. "I left home at eighteen, came west, and landed a job as a chuck wagon cook." He paused, his face lit with a wistful expression. "That was the life. My wages were twice what the cowpunchers earned and everyone knew to treat me right, even the wagon boss. I was the king of the range."

"What happened?" she asked.

"What happened?" His eyebrows disappeared beneath the band of his hat. "I'll tell you what happened. The train!" He practically spit out the words. "It's now cheaper to send cattle to market by train than herd them there. Now I'm nothing but a kitchen lackey."

"That's not true." She helped herself to another cookie. "I think if you asked any of the ranch hands they would say you're still king."

He shook his head. "Nah. These men don't 'preciate good cooking. As for Miss Walker, all she wants is beef, beef, and more beef!" He shook his head.

He obviously objected to being confined to such a limited menu. Perhaps that explained why he put so much culinary energy into his desserts. It was the one area where he was given free rein.

She finished the last of her cookie and brushed the crumbs off her hands. "Have you met the new ranch hand?"

"Branch? Yep. He likes his meat cooked medium. You can tell a lot about a man by how he eats his meat."

It was an interesting thought. The Pinkerton brothers preached the importance of details but never asked how a suspect liked his meat cooked. "And what does that tell you about Mr. Branch?"

"It tells me he's a nonviolent man."

Interesting if true. "What about Wishbone?" she asked.

"What about him?"

"How does he like his meat?"

"He don't eat meat at all," Able said.

"Like Shelley," she said.

"Who?"

"Never mind." Able read dime novels but she doubted he had much use for poetry. "It's hard to believe that someone can work on a cattle ranch and not eat meat."

Able shrugged. "Probably why he looks like he's on a horse even when he ain't."

She giggled. "How long has Wishbone worked on the ranch?"

"Awhile. He was here long before me. At least five years."

"Hmm." She reached for another cookie. "I think I'll take some to Miss Walker, along with a pot of lovely tea."

Able made a face but he put water on the stove to boil. "Gingerbread and tea," he muttered. "That's like mixing sheep and cattle."

"You'd better not let O.T. hear you mention sheep in the same sentence as cattle." After arranging a cup and saucer on a tray, she put several cookies on a plate and brewed the tea.

She was halfway out of the kitchen when he called to her. "I almost forgot. Happy All Fools' Day."

She glanced at the Hood's Sarsaparilla calendar on the wall next to the icebox. Was it April already?

Able glanced at the calendar too. "Time sure does fly."

"Yes, indeed it does." In little more than two weeks it would be Easter. Time was whizzing by and she had yet to figure out a way to send daily reports back to the home office. Mr. Pinkerton would have her head.

"Do you have a small candle?" she asked.

He pointed to the china cabinet. "In the middle drawer."

Annie set the tray on the counter and opened the drawer he'd indicated. She pulled out a thin candle and stuck it into a cookie's soft dough. She then pocketed a box of safety matches.

Able shook his head. "If it's her birthday, you best not mention it. Women can be mighty touchy about their ages. Miz Walker ain't no different."

She lifted the tray. "It's not her birthday.

It's her daughter's. I always light a candle on each of my parents' birthdays and I find it very comforting. I hope this comforts Miss Walker."

His freckles seemed to fade beneath his doubtful expression. "Miss Walker don't like to think about the past. What's gone is gone and that includes people."

Annie hadn't been able to get the little grave on the hill out of her mind. She thought about her dear mama's grave. Her papa's. The past wasn't something you could remember or forget at will; it stayed with you, was part of you. Unless she guessed wrong, it was part of Miss Walker too.

The old lady was reading when Annie walked into her room. "It's about time." She laid her book facedown on the bed. "What is that?"

Holding her hand around the lit candle to protect the flame, Annie set the tray on the bedside table. "Tea time." She crossed to the window to adjust the draperies against the hot afternoon sun.

Miss Walker slumped back against the pillow and rolled her eyes. "Dishwater time, more like it." She regarded the lit candle as one might eye a coming storm. "So what are we celebrating? Your birthday?"

"My birthday is in October." Annie turned from the window. "It's a memorial candle."

Miss Walker grimaced. "And what are we memorializing?"

"It's April first," Annie said quietly. She waited and when Miss Walker showed no reaction, she wondered if perhaps Able had been right.

"It's your daughter's birthday."

Miss Walker's eyes bored into Annie like two burning coals. "How dare you!" she sputtered. "What gives you the right to poke your nose into my business?"

"Please don't be angry. I happened to come across the little grave and —"

"Get out!" Miss Walker pointed at the door. Veins stuck out from her neck and her face turned an alarming red.

Annie held her hands up, palms out, in an effort to calm the ranch owner, but the woman only grew more agitated.

"Get out and don't come back! And take your dishwater with you!"

Not wanting to upset her any more than she already had, Annie fled the room without the tray. *What have I done, God? Oh, what have I done?*

CHAPTER 10

Suspicion ain't proof unless you're married.

Annie rushed down the hall to her room, biting back tears. Now she'd done it.

The assignment of a lifetime; her chance to prove that she could do a man's job and honor her father's memory, and she'd failed. Miserably.

First she caused Miss Walker's accident and now this. The ranch owner had every reason to throw her out on her ear.

Even worse, she had let William Pinkerton down. He had trusted and believed in her when no one else would. Wait till he heard what a mess she'd made of things. The thought cut through her like a knife. Odd as it seemed, she also felt like she'd let her father down. Not even death had severed the need to try to please him.

She reached for the door handle and just

as quickly pulled her hand away. It was no time to get careless. Since finding the watch on her bureau, she never left the room without first inserting a thread between the door and casing. It was a trick from her father.

She ran her hand down the length of the crack but could find no thread. She checked again to make certain but there was no mistake. The thread was gone and that could only mean one thing. Someone had entered her room during her absence.

Hand in her false skirt pocket, she curled her fingers around the gun. She pressed her ear to her bedroom door but heard nothing. Whoever had entered her room was probably long gone, but she couldn't afford to leave anything to chance.

She placed her hand on the brass handle, silently counted to three, and threw the door open.

Branch looked up from her desk. "Ah, Miss Beckman." He looked so relaxed it was almost as if he belonged there or, at the very least, was invited.

"What are you doing here?" she demanded. Her GTF file was open in front of him and her cheeks flared. She rushed to the desk. "What gives you the right to go through my private papers?"

He didn't even have the decency to look apologetic. Instead he closed the file. "You went through my things and I was simply returning the favor."

She studied him with wary regard. She had taken special care to leave everything exactly as she found it in the bunkhouse.

He grinned. "You might have fooled Wishbone with all that nonsense about a housekeeper but you didn't fool me. You were nosing through my things. Admit it."

She lifted her chin. "Why would I be interested in anything of yours?"

"Why indeed? Unless, of course, our leader put you up to it. Ah!" He pointed his finger at her and practically yelped with certainty. "He did, didn't he?"

"Why don't you ask him yourself?"

He gave a nod of satisfaction. "I'll do that."

"Good!" And make it soon! The only chance she had of redeeming herself after the fiasco with Miss Walker was if Branch led her to the Phantom. "Now if you would kindly leave my room —"

"Not until I'm ready." He tapped his finger on the manila folder. "GTF? Give to Phantom?"

"You really ought to work on your spelling," she said.

He shrugged. "I get by. So what does GTF stand for?"

"It's none of your business."

"I might be a poor speller, but I know *business* starts with a *b.*"

She grabbed the file but he stayed her hand with his own. Pressing her palm against the desk, he rose from his chair, his nose practically in her face. He stared at her with bold regard and a fiery charge shot up her spine.

"Why is it coded?" he demanded. He was so close she could feel his warm breath. He smelled of bay rum, leather, and hot desert sands. The heady fragrance complemented his strength and power.

"So that people like you can't read it," she retorted.

"You're lying, Miss Beckman."

She returned his stare with equal boldness. "So are you, Mr. Branch." It looked like neither of them would back down. Certainly she had no intention of doing so.

He finally released her hand. "Stay away from my things."

She stepped back, but the disturbing memory of his touch remained. "And of course you'll show me the same courtesy."

For several moments he held her gaze and she would have given anything to know what thoughts went through his head. Finally, he touched the brim of his hat in a one-finger salute. "Always a pleasure," he said and headed for the door.

"The pleasure is all yours," she called after him.

A grin flashed across his face before he left the room.

Shaken by the worrisome power he held over her, she paced the floor. Why had he gone through her things? What could he possibly be looking for? But those weren't the only questions on her mind.

The feeling that something about him didn't register refused to go away. If only she could figure out what it was. Perhaps then she would be better able to fight the worrisome hold he had on her.

He was a puzzle in more ways than one. Most criminals breaking out of jail took off quicker than a hound with a tail afire but Branch stayed. Except for cutting off his mustache and availing himself of a haircut, he didn't even bother disguising himself. It was hard not to admire a man that sure of himself, that bold. Was that what had turned her head? Surely not.

"He's a sneak and a thief," she said out loud.

He was also the most pleasing-looking

man she'd ever set eyes on, if not the most arrogant.

"He's nothing but a crook and a liar."

Still, there was definitely an attraction. Not that such a thing was all that unusual; some Pinkerton operatives did forge a bond with criminals. Even the agency's founder befriended criminals he'd once pursued and had been known to loan money to some who promised to toe the straight and narrow.

The trouble was, Branch hadn't shown the least inclination to change his reprehensible ways. She had no business being attracted to such a man — God forgive her — none.

It was late that afternoon by the time Annie braced herself enough to enter Miss Walker's room again. The tray was still on the bedside table where she'd left it. The candle had burned to the nub and the cookies and tea had not been touched.

Thinking Miss Walker was asleep, she tiptoed into the room and picked up the tray. She was wrong. One cookie was missing on the plate but she wouldn't have noticed had she not counted. Even more surprising, the cup wasn't quite as full. Smiling, she turned and traced her way back to the door.

Miss Walker's voice stopped her. "No one ever remembered my daughter's birthday." After a moment she added, "Only you." The normally strong, strident voice had been replaced by a hoarse whisper.

Annie turned. She could handle the woman's wrath and biting tongue. Could manage Miss Walker's obstinate ways but this . . . this was something altogether different. This was the voice of a grieving mother. Had Annie known the depth of the woman's pain, she never would have lit that candle.

"Forgive me," she said. "I lost my mother and father. I always light a candle on their birthdays."

The ranch owner said nothing; she only stared into space as if looking at something that only she could see.

Annie guessed that something was a pretty little girl with light-colored hair.

The day Annie lit the memorial candle for Miss Walker's daughter marked a change in the old lady's demeanor. The ranch owner was still her usual demanding and difficult self, but without the same critical air or harshness. Or maybe Annie simply had grown used to the ranch owner's ways.

Miss Walker made no mention of that day

and neither did Annie. But it was as if the candle still burned, binding them together in an invisible glow. Never was this more evident than during afternoon tea.

Today Miss Walker greeted Annie with her usual snide remark. "What poison do you have planned this time?"

"Darjeeling," Annie replied. "From India."

Annie had just finished pouring their tea when the peaceful quiet was interrupted by angry voices.

"What in the world?" Miss Walker turned her head to stare at the open door leading to the balcony.

After setting the teapot down, Annie hurried outside and leaned over the railing. Wishbone and the man she recognized as Feedbag stood practically nose to nose. Feedbag's square-cut beard did indeed look like a nose bag worn over a horse's muzzle.

"When I get through with you, you'll be scratchin' the back of your neck with your front teeth," Wishbone yelled.

"And I'm gonna turn your Adam's apple into cider," Feedbag shouted.

Wishbone stepped back and rolled up his sleeves. Head down, arms windmilling, he barreled into Feedbag's middle.

"Oomph!" Feedbag tried to fight him off

149

and the two men fell to the ground and rolled.

Annie shook her head in disgust and stepped inside. "It's Wishbone and Feed-bag."

A flash of annoyance crossed Miss Walker's face. "Well, don't just stand there. Make them stop at once! I will not have my men fighting."

Annie left the room and rushed down the hall to the stairs. Having grown up in an all-male house, she'd done her share of making peace. But the sibling blackmail that had worked so well on her brothers would have no effect on the cowhands.

By the time she reached the courtyard, more men had entered the fray and the sickening sound of pounding fists made her flinch. Stretch swung his arm in a wide arc and his fist just missed the man wearing a black leather apron. No doubt he was the blacksmith, Michael, who also happened to be Bessie Adams's nephew.

One man fell backward and another jumped on top of him.

"Stop it!" she yelled. "Please, please stop it."

Branch walked up from behind and held out his Peacemaker. "Politeness is more ef-fective when combined with a gun." His voice in her ear was as smooth as silk, and chills slithered down her spine.

She pushed his gun away. "Don't tempt me."

The sharp report of a shotgun split the air and Annie jumped. The men on the ground froze and all heads turned in the direction of Miss Walker's balcony.

A grayish-brown prairie falcon fell to the ground, dead.

"Well I'll be a beaver's uncle." Still flat on his back, Stretch stared at the bird, which was mere inches from his head. He stood and brushed himself off. "The boss lady still is the best shot in the terr'tory."

Branch holstered his gun, his gaze still on the balcony. "Miss Walker did that? But isn't she still confined to her bed?"

Annie couldn't help but laugh. "Yes, but she keeps her shotgun by her side." Anyone who thought the old lady helpless would be sadly mistaken.

The blast brought Ruckus and O.T. running and even Able rushed outside to see what all the racket was about.

"What's going on?" O.T. demanded.

Wishbone held his jaw. "Feedbag accused me of being the Phantom."

"I did no such thing," Feedbag said. "I said you looked like him." He pulled a

151

circular out of his pocket, unfolded it, and held it up for all to see. The word *WANTED* was written in bold letters across the top of the handbill. "These are posted all over town."

The image was dark and fuzzy. The man pictured might or might not have a mustache and maybe even a beard. It was hard to tell.

Wishbone read out loud, "Twenty-five-hundred-dollar reward for the capture and conviction of the Phantom."

O.T. whistled. "That's a lot of money."

"Does it say how tall he is?" Stretch asked.

Wishbone scanned the paper in his hand. "It says he's between five foot eight and six foot two."

Stretch made a face. "Heck, that can be any one of us."

"Yeah, but you and Branch are the only ones taller than six feet," Wishbone argued.

Everyone turned to Branch and the air crackled with tension.

He gave a casual shrug. "That makes the odds in our favor."

Stretch laughed and gave Branch a friendly slap on the back. "You got that right."

Ruckus held up his hands and his crooked nose twitched. "Enough with the accusations. If a member of the gang worked here, the boss lady would know about it. She don't miss nothin'. If the good Lord ever needed help keeping track of his flock, Miz Walker would be a good candidate."

One by one the men wandered away, some limping, some grumbling.

Annie kept her gaze on Branch while he walked to the barn with the others.

Next to her Able said, "What a shame."

She swung her head around to face him. "What?"

Able tossed a nod at the dead falcon, his white cook's hat flopping back and forth like a building about to topple. "That bird ain't good for nothing. Tough as doornails and tasteless as paper. It's a shame Miz Walker didn't down a bird we could eat."

CHAPTER 11

Old gumshoes never die; they just escape detection.

It was early Tuesday morning when Annie stepped out on Miss Walker's balcony to shake out a feather duster. Her hand froze the moment she set eyes on Branch. Today, instead of riding out with the men, he and Ruckus stayed behind. Curious as to why, she stood watching the two of them.

How Branch fit into the scheme of things she didn't know, but somehow he held the key to the mysterious man behind the train and bank robberies.

He was easy to pick out even at night since he stood taller than all the other ranch hands save Stretch and sat straighter in the saddle. He also walked with long, easy strides, head held high, shoulders back. The long days in the saddle chasing cattle had yet to take their toll as they had on the other cowhands.

As if feeling her gaze, Branch turned his head to look over his shoulder. He smiled and tipped his hat as if they were playing some sort of game. She refused to back down and forced him to break visual contact first.

The Pinkerton eye never slept, but in this case, neither did it see. For no matter how much she tried, no matter how much she asked for God's guidance, she was no closer to identifying the Phantom than on the day she arrived and her frustration grew daily.

Though she had little to report to the Chicago office, every piece of correspondence from Mr. Pinkerton held the same terse orders: continue investigation.

Easier said than done.

Most of the men were gone all day except for the blacksmith, Michael, and horse trainer, Brodie. The men's absences didn't make her job any easier. She needed to get on a horse and ride the range with them. That was the only way she would ever get to know them, but that would mean leaving Miss Walker alone all day.

Branch walked into the stables behind Ruckus. Moments later Branch appeared with his horse in tow. The steed limped slightly and Branch headed toward the blacksmith shop. One mystery solved.

Feeling oddly depressed and out of sorts, she walked back into the bedroom.

Miss Walker was quick to sense her change of mood. "What's wrong with you? You look like your horse died."

Denying it wouldn't do any good, so Annie said what she thought any fledgling heiress would say. "All this talk about the Phantom has upset me."

"It's a good thing you weren't around when renegade Apaches terrorized the area." Miss Walker got a faraway look in her eyes, as if traveling back in time. "I shot three right from that very balcony."

Annie shuddered. She had been thoroughly trained to fire a gun but had never shot anyone, other than a man already dead. She hoped she never had to. "Weren't you scared?"

Miss Walker made a face. "Who has time to be scared? You do what you have to do and get on with it."

Annie flicked the feather duster across the chiffonier and washstand. Earlier, Stretch and Feedbag had lifted Miss Walker off the bed while Annie smoothed clean sheets over the mattress.

"What you need is a housekeeper," she said. The ranch's former housekeepers had returned to their native home just prior to Miss Walker's accident and she didn't seem in any hurry to replace them. Annie had assumed some of the chores herself, but keeping up a large house and taking care of the old lady cut into time needed for her investigation.

Miss Walker scoffed. "I don't need anyone else gawking at me. And I certainly don't have time to conduct proper interviews."

"I'll do it for you, if you like." She slid the feather duster into the pail of cleaning supplies.

"And what do you know about hiring a housekeeper?" Miss Walker regarded her from beneath a knitted brow. "Have you ever hired one?"

Annie folded an extra blanket and laid it in the oak chest at the foot of the bed. "No, but I don't imagine it would be that hard."

Miss Walker narrowed her eyes. "Just exactly what did you do prior to coming here?"

"Do?" Annie fluffed an extra pillow and slid it under Miss Walker's head.

"To support yourself."

"I worked in a bakery," Annie replied.

"A novelist, a dance hall girl, and a woman barber all tried to persuade me that they had what it takes to run a ranch. And now a baker."

"I didn't say I was a baker. I said I worked in a bakery." That part was true. What she didn't say was that she was only twelve at the time and the bakery was run by her English grandmother on her father's side. "That's where I learned the fine art of tea."

"Art and tea should never grace the same sentence," Miss Walker muttered, and Annie laughed.

Odd as it seemed, she had grown quite fond of the old lady and had a sneaking suspicion the feeling was mutual. Normally, the rapport between them would bring her pleasure. Instead it filled her with guilt, and that made her job that much harder. She hated having to lie to the woman about who she was and her reasons for being at the ranch. Hated having to measure every word, every thought, and every action for fear of revealing more than was wise.

"Was your grandmother Indian?" Miss Walker asked.

"No, she was my paternal grandmother." It was the truth. Her Pinkerton training had taught her to answer as honestly as possible without giving too much away. This made undercover agents sound credible and helped avoid inconsistencies.

"So your mother was Indian. But you said you lived in Chicago."

Annie nodded. "Her tribe was moved to Indian Territory in the '70s, but since she was married to a white man she stayed behind." She didn't mention Kickapoo. Had Miss Walker pressed for the name of the tribe, Annie would have told her Chickasaw or Shawnee. Sometimes even truths had to be kept vague or wrapped in fabrication.

When Miss Walker made no comment, Annie asked, "Does my being a half-breed bother you?"

"Why should it?"

"It bothers some people." Actually, it bothered many.

Miss Walker discounted this with a wave of her hand. "So does being divorced."

Annie appreciated Miss Walker's open mind but she resented the comparison. A divorce wasn't noticeable at a glance but her Indian heritage was the first thing people saw. Many didn't bother looking for anything else.

"Enough idle chatter," Miss Walker snapped. "Let's get to work. Bring me my checkbook so I can pay my men, and don't forget pen and paper."

Annie welcomed the change of subject. "We're out of stationery." That wasn't entirely true but she needed an excuse to go to town. Not only did she need to telegraph headquarters, but her talk with the marshal was long overdue.

Miss Walker flung up arms. "Well, don't just stand there. Ride into town and purchase some."

It was exactly what Annie hoped Miss Walker would say. She hadn't wanted to leave her, but anyone able to shoot a bird out of the sky from her bed wasn't as helpless as Annie imagined.

As if to guess her thoughts, Miss Walker added, "While you're there, tell the marshal to get off the stick and find the Phantom before my men kill each other. And don't you dare say one thing about my condition. As far as anyone need know, I'm on the mend."

"Of course you are," Annie said, gathering the pail of cleaning supplies. "I'll ask Able to bring your lunch. I'll be back in time for afternoon tea."

"Good heavens, I hope not."

Dressed in a rust-colored skirt and lace-trimmed shirtwaist, Annie donned her white gloves as she walked into the barn and called to Ruckus. "I need to go into town."

"He's not here."

160

The smooth, easy drawl made her heart flutter even before its owner stepped into view. "They had some problems with one of the windmills." Branch leaned against the post, arms crossed. "Perhaps I can help."

"I doubt it," she said. Turning, she walked out of the barn.

He followed her. "I could drive you to town. In fact, I insist."

She spun around to face him. "What makes you think I would go anywhere with you?"

He tilted his head. "Since you seem to derive such pleasure in watching my every move, I thought I'd make it easy for you."

She angled her gaze. Irritated that she had to keep reminding herself that the handsome and yes, even charming, man was in fact an outlaw, she glared at him.

"Aren't you afraid someone might recognize you in town? Perhaps the marshal?"

"Everyone will be too busy looking at you to pay any heed to me."

"And why is that?" she asked. Too late she realized she had fallen into his little trap.

"You look mighty fetching today, ma'am. All decked out like that." He tugged on the brim of his hat as his gaze traveled the length of her. The approval on his face obviously had less to do with her attire than the way the fabric followed the peaks and valleys of her feminine form.

She blushed but nonetheless managed to keep her composure. "I'd be more than happy to call attention to you."

"Ah, but you won't. Loyalty to *family* and all that. I'm like a brother."

She almost laughed in his face. No brother ever affected her the way he did — or made her feel so womanly. "You seem very certain of what I will or will not do."

He shrugged. "So what's the big rush to get to town?"

"Miss Walker needs stationery."

"Ah, so that's your excuse. For your information, I happen to know that there's plenty of stationery in Miss Walker's office."

"How thoughtful of you to keep track of our office supplies," she said lightly. "Speaking of which, that wouldn't happen to be Miss Walker's pen, would it?"

His hand flew to his vest pocket. "I do believe it is." He pulled it out and handed it to her. Their fingers barely touched but it was enough to send warm ripples shooting up her arm. Hoping he didn't notice how he affected her, she took her time tucking the pen into her drawstring purse. Only when she had contained her rampant emotions did she dare lift her head.

His mouth twitched with humor. "I have a tendency to walk off with pens."

"Among other things," she said. He lifted an eyebrow, which she took to be acknowledgment.

He shifted his weight. "Now that we've established an adequate stationery supply, perhaps you would care to enlighten me as to your real reason for going to town."

"I don't owe you an explanation as to my comings and goings." Too late she realized that the way her eyelashes fluttered could be misinterpreted as perhaps a bit coquettish. It had been purely unintentional, of course, but the knowing look on Branch's face was not.

"It seems to me that we gang members should stick together," he said, a smooth, suggestive tone in his voice. "You never know when an unwanted lawman might pop up."

"I don't need your help." She was careful to keep her expression perfectly composed and did not blink or otherwise appear flirtatious or compliant. The last thing she needed was him looking over her shoulder while she sent a telegram to headquarters.

"I'm perfectly capable of taking care of myself." She walked away.

"Yes, I can see that," he called after her.

She stopped. "What exactly do you mean by that?"

When he failed to answer, she glanced over her shoulder. He was gone. The way he tended to appear and disappear without notice kept her on her toes, but not as much as her traitorous heart.

Annie got a later start to town than she intended. It was after eleven by the time Ruckus returned and hitched up a wagon. So much for making the journey before it grew unbearably hot.

Her meeting with Branch was still very much on her mind. Nothing disarmed a targeted victim more than good manners and charm, and most criminals had made an art form out of both. But none had mastered charm better than Branch. His smile alone had probably relieved more women of their jewelry than any weapon ever could.

Still, for an escaped criminal, he didn't seem particularly worried about being caught. Come to think of it, he acted more like a hunter than the hunted. Why else would he search her bedroom or even Miss Walker's office? Or listen in on private conversations?

When she reached town she planned to

send a telegram inquiring as to whether anyone matched Branch's description. She couldn't imagine what was taking Pinkerton so long to find a file on him. It had been weeks since she sent full descriptions of Branch and the other ranch hands and she'd received nothing in return.

The sky was clear and the air shimmered with heat. Wiping her damp forehead with the back of her hand, she shook the reins, forcing the horse to pick up speed. Branch wasn't the only cause of her frustration. She still didn't have a clue as to the Phantom's identity. Her report to headquarters would be mighty sparse indeed.

It was this thought, along with the relentless sun, that kept her company as she drove into town.

Main Street fairly bustled with activity, forcing her to park her wagon several buildings away from her destination. She was positive she hadn't been followed but even so, she glanced around and carefully weighed each individual before dashing into the marshal's office.

The marshal looked up and tossed what looked like a wanted poster onto his desk. His crossed feet were perched on the desktop, the worn soles of his boots plainly in sight.

He greeted her with a nod. "Miss Beck-man, isn't it?"

"Yes," Annie replied. It was normal proce-dure for operatives to identify themselves to local lawmen when on assignment, but something made her proceed with caution. She glanced at the empty jail cell. "I notice the train robbers are gone."

He dropped his feet to the floor, sat forward, and folded his hands on his desk. "Not to worry. They were safely delivered to Tombstone where they will stand trial."

"All of them?" she asked.

"Just the train robbers. I still don't know who robbed the bank."

Annie studied him. Was it possible that he didn't know that one prisoner had escaped? She doubted it and, for that reason, decided it best to keep her true identity secret.

"I came to thank you for returning my watch." His mustache twitched but other-wise he was without expression. "I found it on my bureau," she said with emphasis.

He pushed his chair back and stood. "That was all that was taken from you, right? Just your watch?"

"Yes." She hesitated. Obviously he had no intention of volunteering information. "You did say *all* the train robbers were in Tomb-stone, right?"

"Yep."

"That's a relief," she said.

The marshal rubbed his nose, which meant that he either had an itch or was lying. She guessed the latter. The question was why. She tried another tactic.

"There's talk that the Phantom himself might be hiding at the Last Chance. I'm sure you can understand my concern."

"Rest assured that we're doing everything possible to check out the rumors," he said.

As far as she knew, neither the marshal nor his deputy had questioned anyone at the ranch, so she doubted he had done *everything.*

He plucked his Stetson off a wooden peg. Donning his hat, he tugged the brim low on his forehead. "Speaking of the Last Chance, how's the old gal doing?"

"*Miss Walker* is doing very well, thank you."

"Be sure to give her my best. Now if you'll excuse me, I have business to attend to." Moments earlier he hadn't seemed all that concerned about business, or anything else for that matter. Now he all but hustled her out the door. He couldn't seem to make his escape fast enough. He untied his horse from the hitching post, mounted, and galloped away.

167

Annie stood on the boardwalk and watched him with a sense of unease. She could think of only one reason why the marshal would lie: he was involved in some way with the Phantom. Perhaps was even the Phantom himself. It was a good thing she hadn't revealed her true identity.

Unfortunately, corruption in law enforcement agencies was not that unusual. Her father often spoke of the fraud that ran rampant in the Chicago Police Department in the '70s, but the problem existed in almost every large city. The agency had taken much criticism for using harsh methods, especially during all that union trouble, but Pinkerton operatives were honest and never took a bribe. Too bad the same couldn't be said for some lawmen.

She went over every word she and the marshal exchanged. He had to know she had seen Branch and still he lied. That made her job even more difficult. Now she had to work without the support of local law enforcement.

After leaving the marshal's office, she checked her post office box and eagerly fingered the letter waiting for her. She'd sent careful descriptions of every man working at the ranch to the main office and

168

hoped the letter would offer answers.

Tearing the seal on the envelope, she perused the neatly ciphered handwriting. A man matching Wishbone's description had served time for forgery. No other matches were found in the Pinkerton Rogue Gallery.

She folded the letter and tucked it into her handbag. Pinkerton's criminal photograph file was the largest collection in the country but it was nowhere near complete. Still, she'd hoped for more — a lot more.

Most criminals started small, committing petty crimes before advancing to more serious transgressions. It was hard to believe that the Phantom didn't have some sort of criminal record.

Had Wishbone gone from forging checks to robbing banks? Possibly. Still, it was hard to imagine that the most wanted man in Cochise County was really the slow-paced whittler.

No one was in the telegraph office when Annie arrived except for the youthful operator. She stepped to the counter and he looked up from beneath his visor. Unlike the well-dressed telegraph operators in the East, he was dressed shabbily in canvas pants and a wrinkled shirt rolled up at the sleeves.

"What can I do for you, ma'am?"

"I wish to send a telegram."

He pulled a yellow sheet of paper from a low shelf and handed it to her. He was an awkward-looking lad who appeared to be all legs and arms and pimply skin. He pointed an ink-stained finger at the pen and inkwell.

She thanked him and set to work. The telegram she addressed to Octavo at Napthia, cipher for Principal William at Pinkerton. As concisely as possible, she explained that she was suspicious of the marshal and then asked for another file check on Branch, giving the same description as before.

She signed the telegram Unicorn, her cipher name.

CHAPTER 12

For a job that supposedly doesn't pay, crime has no lack of employees.

The battery-operated switchboard lit up like a Christmas tree and Bessie Adams shuffled to the dining room. *Now what? Can't a body have a moment of peace?* Never would she have agreed to have the switchboard installed in her home had she known people would take advantage of her good nature.

Planting her generous form on the stool, she donned the headphones and stuck a peg in number twelve. "What num-BER?" Her voice might not have passed Bell Telephone standards for pleasantness but she remembered to inflect her voice at the end.

"This is Agnes." Agnes worked in the assay office.

"I know who you are. What number?"

"I don't want any number. I called to tell you that Miss Walker's new heiress is in

171

town. You told me to let you know. I saw her walk into the marshal's office."

Bessie pursed her lips. Hmm. No doubt she was collecting the belongings taken from her during the robbery. "Let me know when she leaves."

"You're planning to match her with your nephew," Agnes announced. "Admit it."

"All right, but don't go blabbing it all over town." Now that her older nephew, Luke, was married, finding the right wife for his brother, Michael, was of prime concern.

"I wouldn't think of blabbing, but it seems to me that a man should pick his own wife," Agnes said, her voice sharp with disapproval.

Bessie sniffed. What an absurd thing to say. "A man picking out a wife is like asking a cow to pick out a farmer."

"And you think you can do better, of course," Agnes said.

"With a little help from the Lord." Fine Christian woman that she was, Bessie didn't like to take *all* the credit.

Numbers seven, three, and fifteen lit up. "I've got to go." She pulled the peg to disconnect Agnes and blinked. Mercy. Cactus Patch only had sixteen telephones. How did operators in large cities like Boston or Chicago manage thousands of them?

172

During the next several minutes, every light lit up — and every call was in regard to Annie.

"What num-BER?"

"I thought you'd want to know that Miss Walker's new heiress just left the telegraph office."

For the next fifteen minutes the switchboard was quiet except for the hypochondriac spinster, Miss Whitehead, calling with her latest organ recital.

Finally number eight lit up.

Bessie placed the cord into the jack and threw the back key forward. "What num-BER?"

Mrs. Daniel's voice crackled over the line. "I just saw Miss Walker's heiress walk into the mercantile. Thought you'd want to know."

Bessie smiled. Now they were getting somewhere.

While waiting for Mr. Green to fill her order, Annie happened to look outside and spotted someone who looked like Stretch on the opposite side of the street.

She walked to the window to get a better look. It was Stretch, all right. She'd recognize that tall, awkward form anywhere. The ranch hand looked around as if making

173

certain he wasn't seen before dashing into the barbershop.

Annie frowned. What was he doing in town on a Tuesday? Stretch was the only cowpuncher she knew who had been in Cactus Patch during the robberies. That made him a suspect from the start. Still, unless he was planning to hold up the barbershop, it didn't explain his presence in town today.

No sooner had Stretch vanished than she spotted Wishbone. He, too, dashed into the barbershop, followed by Feedbag. What was everyone doing getting a haircut at the same time?

The door flew open, followed by a woman's hearty voice. "Why, Annie Beckman. Imagine meeting you here."

Annie smiled. "Nice to see you, Mrs. Adams."

"My friends call me Aunt Bessie. If surviving a train robbery together doesn't make us friends, I don't know what will." She lifted a bar of Pear's soap from the counter and sniffed it. "And how is Miss Walker these days?"

"She's on the mend," she replied carefully. Annie eyed the jars of hard candies. With all the desserts she'd eaten lately, she didn't dare avail herself of more sweets.

Mr. Green returned from the storeroom with a box of stationery. "The finest we have," he announced in a nasally voice. He set the box on the counter and glared at Bessie. "Shouldn't you be manning the phones?"

"I can take a break if I want to," Aunt Bessie snapped. It was obvious that no love was lost between the two.

"I'd better take two boxes," Annie said, purposely sending the store owner scurrying away.

Wanting to take full advantage of his absence, Annie wasted no time. "How well do you know the marshal, Aunt Bessie?"

Bessie looked surprised by the question. "Fairly well. Why do you ask?"

Not wanting to seem overly interested, Annie picked up a tin of gunpowder tea and examined it before setting it on the counter next to the other items she wished to purchase.

"I was just curious. If I recall, you said something at the train station about it being time he earned his keep."

Bessie made a face. "Let's put it this way. If I were an outlaw, the last person I would be afraid of is Marshal Morris."

"He did catch the train robbers," Annie said.

"Yes, but through no fault of his own. He got an anonymous tip that the train would be held up. While he was at the station, someone robbed the bank. I'll bet my feathered hat that it was the Phantom." She lowered her voice and her eyes grew wide as wagon wheels. "Some think the gang leader is hiding out at the Last Chance."

Delighted that Aunt Bessie mentioned the Phantom first, Annie asked, "Is that what you think? That one of the ranch hands is the leader?"

"Ranch hands, my foot," Aunt Bessie muttered, looking self-righteous. "I think the old lady herself is the gang leader."

Annie stared at her. "You can't be serious. Miss Walker?"

"It wouldn't be the first time a ranch owner became known for duplicity. Several years ago the owner of the Redfield ranch turned out to be the leader of a group of highwaymen. And he was a *respected* ranch owner."

Aunt Bessie didn't come right out and say it, but her meaning was clear: Miss Walker was held in no such esteem. Bessie held up her hand and crossed two fingers. "She's this close to the bank president, which means she probably has inside information."

"But from what I've been told, Miss

Walker seldom ever comes to town," Annie pointed out.

"That's true. Far as I know, she's only been to town once in twenty years. She conducts all her business in Tombstone."

"Why is that?" Annie asked. Cactus Patch was so much closer and didn't have Tombstone's bad reputation.

"I don't remember all the details, but she got into some sort of hassle with the church ladies' auxiliary over her divorce. But that isn't to say she wouldn't send others to do her dirty work." The older woman sniffed. "It makes perfect sense, when you think about it."

Could Miss Walker be the Phantom? The idea was ridiculous. Crazy. Still, Annie hadn't been able to think of anything else since leaving town.

Certainly female criminals and gang leaders were not all that rare. Hell-Cat Maggie came to mind, as did river pirate Sadie Farrell. Still, Annie had a hard time imagining someone as blunt-spoken as Miss Walker doing anything underhanded.

The moment Ruckus stepped out of the barn to unhitch the horse from her wagon, she bombarded him with questions. "Did you know that some of the ranch hands are in town?" she asked.

"Shh." Finger to his mouth, he glanced around. He was a compact man with a horseshoe mustache and a quiet, modest demeanor. No swagger here. Not like some men she knew and immediately a vision of Branch came to mind.

"Don't say anything to the boss lady. They're pretty riled up about the acc'sations flyin' around. I sent them to town to blow off steam. Maybe then we can get some work done around here."

She nodded. "That makes sense." Though the barbershop seemed like a strange place to blow off steam.

She waited for Ruckus to unbuckle the reins before broaching the topic foremost on her mind.

"How is Miss Walker managing the ranch? Financially, I mean?" She had gone through the ranch ledgers and had seen nothing amiss, but that didn't necessarily mean anything. If Miss Walker was stealing to support her ranch, there could well be a second set of ledgers somewhere, perhaps locked in the safe.

Ruckus lowered the shafts to the ground and glanced at her sideways. "Many have shown up hopin' to be the boss lady's heiress but you're the first to inquire 'bout finances."

"I hope you don't think I'm being forward."

He straightened and removed the horse's bridle. "Nah. It just tells me you got a good head on your shoulders." Holding the horse's mane, Ruckus let his gaze wander for a moment. "We've had our share of tough times," he said. "Kind of makes me think of Job in the Bible. Ranching makes 'Jobs' out of us all. But you ain't finding any better than the boss lady. She's run this ranch for forty years. And if she can find the right heiress, I don't doubt it will go on for another forty."

"Even though beef prices have dropped and you're going through a drought?"

He shrugged. "Prices go up and prices go down. Rain comes and rain goes. But the Good Book tells us that no matter what happens, we need to store our trust in God's stables instead of our own. And that's what's gonna keep this ranch goin'."

Ruckus struck her as a true man of faith and she felt guilty for suspecting him. Suspicion was like walking through the desert at night. Everything that moved was suspect, even one's own shadow.

"Has she no family to take over the ranch?" Annie asked.

"I heard talk that she had a brother. From what I gather, he was more interested in gamblin' than in running a ranch."

"Do you believe the rumors? Do you think the leader of the Phantom gang is here somewhere?"

He shook his head. "Don't take much stock in rumors. If the Phantom was on the premises, I'd know about it. But out there . . ." He tossed a nod toward the distant mountains. "That's a mighty big desert. Anything's possible."

A pall had fallen over the ranch. At no time was it more evident than that night as Annie made her way to the bunkhouse with a tray of Able's sweet cakes.

She had taken up the habit of bringing the men nightly dessert. It was a good way to get to know them better and build up a rapport. For the most part, she liked the cowhands and enjoyed their teasing banter. She enjoyed even more the occasional slip of the tongue that revealed a man's background or history. Still, she resisted forming any sort of friendship — ultimately, she would have to betray one if not more of them.

Tonight the bunkhouse was eerily silent. No laughter. No whining sound of a fiddle or mouth organ. Nothing.

Feedbag greeted her at the door and for a moment she didn't recognize him. His square black beard was gone, leaving his face two-toned, the upper half the color of leather and the lower half white as a frog's underbelly.

He wasn't the only one sporting a clean-shaven face. Stretch and Wishbone had shaved, too, and not a beard or a whisker was in sight, though plenty of pockmarks had been uncovered. Now she knew what they were doing at the barbershop earlier that day.

"What do you think?" Feedbag ran his hand over his clean-shaven jaw. "Did you notice that my whiskers and face have parted company?"

"I'd have to be blind not to notice." Her gaze traveled over Feedbag's shoulder to Branch. Their eyes locked for a moment before he winked. Cheeks flaring, she quickly turned her attention back to Feedbag.

"You all look so . . . different." Strange, more like it.

Feedbag grinned. "That's the idea." He took the tray of confections from her and motioned her inside with a toss of his head. No sooner had he set the tray on the long wooden table where Aunt Bessie's nephew Michael sat writing in a notebook than the men all helped themselves to sweet cakes.

"Careful," Wishbone muttered, brushing the powdery sugar off the table with a feather duster. "We don't want the boss lady sending a housekeeper over here."

"So what's going on?" she asked. "Why no beards or mustaches?"

Even Ruckus had changed his appearance since that afternoon. His crooked nose twitched above the ghostly white outline left by his mustache.

Feedbag lowered his voice. "Friday night when we were all in town we heard a rumor that Wells Fargo is sending a detective to snoop around. We decided none of us best resemble any of those wanted posters hangin' in the post office."

Annie clenched her fists. Just hearing the words *Wells Fargo detective* made her stomach turn. If the rumor was true, her job had just gotten that much harder. She had a very personal reason for detesting Wells Fargo detectives, but today her alarm was purely professional. The presence of one would no doubt force the Phantom deeper underground.

"Yep. Every outlaw has himself face cover," Feedbag said. "Beards and mustaches go with the terr'tory."

Stretch wiped crumbs off his mouth with the back of his hand. "We decided to make things easier on the detective by cutting off our facial hair. That way the real outlaw would stand out like a sore thumb."

Annie frowned. "Are you sure that's the real reason and you don't have anything to hide?"

"Ain't got nothing to hide," Feedbag assured her. "Least not that I know of." He helped himself to another cake. "That's why I had myself a good shave. If you have something to hide, you grow a beard. If you're not hiding anything, you cut it off."

Wishbone set the feather duster on the mantel and reached in his pocket for his whittling knife. "Simple as that."

Her gaze shifted to Branch, who was watching Wishbone too. As if sensing her gaze, he looked her way and the corners of his mouth quirked upward. Whether he was amused at the rather odd logic or something else, she couldn't say.

She walked back to the ranch house with a feeling of unease. Of all the bad luck! A Wells Fargo detective. That was all she needed. *Please, God, don't let it be true.*

CHAPTER 13

Outlaws are so prevalent in some western towns you can walk from one end to the next without leaving the scene of a crime.

"What poisonous brew have you cooked up this time?" Miss Walker asked when Annie walked into her room with a tray.

Today Annie had chosen Earl Grey. She poured the hot tea and handed a cup to Miss Walker. "This was created especially for Charles Grey, the second Earl Grey and prime minister of England. I heard that it's Queen Victoria's favorite tea." She then poured a cup for herself and took a sip. "Hmm. I love that citrusy taste, don't you? The bergamot orange is what gives it that taste."

Miss Walker took a sip of her own tea and made a face. "Perhaps if the queen drank less citrus she would be less of a prude."

Annie sat on a chair next to the bed. "How

prudish can one be with nine children?"

Miss Walker grunted but said nothing. She would never admit it but Annie suspected the old woman looked forward to afternoon tea. On more than one occasion, Annie caught her staring pointedly at the clock whenever tea was late.

The other operatives laughed at her habit of serving tea when interviewing suspects or witnesses. They could laugh all they wanted, but it worked. Something about tea made people lower their guards. Perhaps that's why tea and gossip were synonymous. Miss Walker didn't gossip but she did reminisce.

Today she talked about the beginnings of the Last Chance. "My mother nursed an Englishman to health and he repaid her with a heifer. My mother saw it as her last chance to take care of the family. Instead of butchering it to feed us, she started a cattle ranch."

"What about your father?" Annie asked.

"He was a drunk, a gambler, and a philanderer, and those were his good qualities. Unfortunately, they were also the qualities my brother inherited." Miss Walker made a face. "Enough about me. What about you?"

"Me?"

Miss Walker arched her brows. "I know so little about you."

"I'm afraid you'd find me quite boring."

"I doubt that." The old woman studied her. "You do know that I require an heiress to sign a legal document agreeing not to marry."

"I'm aware of that," Annie said.

"So why would an attractive woman like yourself agree to such a thing?"

Annie expected the question and had a ready answer. "I'm a follower of Miss Nancy Rosewell."

"Never heard of her." Frown lines deepened at her brow. "Don't tell me she's one of those — what do you call them? Suffragettes?"

"Not exactly. She believes that women have the right and, indeed, the obligation to adapt nontraditional roles if they so choose. That includes remaining single."

"Hmm. Since I require that of my heiress, it appears that I was a woman before my time."

"Indeed." Annie set her cup on the tray and rose to straighten the bed. "Perhaps you'd like to take a nap."

Miss Walker protested. "That's all I do, eat and sleep."

"And dictate letters," Annie teased.

Annie took the cup from Miss Walker's leathery hands and set it on the tray next to her own. Today the ranch owner had finished half a cup. Perhaps Annie would make a tea drinker out of her yet. "It won't be for much longer."

Miss Walker narrowed her eyes. "Since you refuse to talk at any great lengths about yourself, could you at least answer me one question?"

"I'll try," Annie said, drawing the sheet up to Miss Walker's shoulders. "But then you must rest."

"Very well." Miss Walker's gaze impaled her. "Do you think one of my men is the Phantom?"

Annie kept her face perfectly composed. "Do you?"

"I asked you."

Annie debated how to answer. Sometimes the best way to glean information from someone was through surprise. "There's a rumor in town that *you* are the Phantom."

Miss Walker stared at her, incredulous. "Me?"

Annie nodded.

The ranch owner's eyes crinkled and she laughed so hard that Annie feared she would pull the leg apparatus down. "Why, that's the most absurd thing I ever heard," she said between guffaws.

Annie laughed too. "I quite agree."

■ ■ ■ ■

Robert arrived at the ranch the next day bearing a bouquet of spring flowers.

Eleanor waved the spray away. "Flowers are for funerals and I'm not in my grave yet."

Accepting the rebuff with his usual good humor, Robert laid the flowers on the dresser. "I'm happy to see that you're in pleasant spirits."

"I'm always pleasant." She eyed him with curiosity. "To what do I owe this visit?" She raised a hand. "Don't tell me. Another offer to purchase my ranch?"

Robert moved a chair to her bedside and sat. "Actually, it's the same one as before. Only this time the interested party has increased the offer." When she made no response, he asked, "Don't you want to know by how much?"

"I'm not interested," she said. "Did you not convey my message?"

Robert ran his finger along his silver mustache. "I conveyed your message, though not in your precise words."

"Ah, that explains it, then," she said. "This time I trust you'll tell the party in no uncertain terms what they can do with the offer."

"If that's what you wish," he said, his voice thick with disapproval.

"I do have some other business I wish you to take care of." She hesitated. "I don't want you to think you came all this way for nothing." In a lower voice she added, "That girl, Annie . . . She's up to something."

He leaned forward. "How do you mean?"

"I don't think she's who she pretends to be."

"What makes you think that?" he asked.

"Just a feeling. For one thing, she refuses to talk about her family or background. That's always a bad sign." It pained her to say it. The truth was, she really liked the girl and felt a kinship with her she'd not felt with anyone in years, save Robert. After being disappointed by so many people in the past, she had to make sure that Annie was someone she could trust. The future of the ranch depended on it.

Robert sighed. "So what do you want me to do?"

"Her last name is Beckman and she says she's from Chicago. I want you to find out whatever you can about her."

He sat back in his chair and crossed one leg over the other. "Eleanor, you've entertained several women during the past couple

189

of years and never once did you bother checking their backgrounds. Why now?"

The answer was simple: she felt vulnerable. She hated to admit the truth even to herself and certainly had no intention of taking Robert into her confidence. Perhaps even more worrisome, she felt scared. Through the years she'd fended off more enemies than a dime novel heroine and now she could barely fend off a fly. Shooting that bird from the sky was pure luck, nothing more. The truth was that she had never felt so helpless.

"The timing bothers me," she said. That part was true. "She breezes into town on the very same day there's both a train and a bank robbery."

Robert's eyebrows rose. "You think she was involved with the robberies in some way?"

"Who knows? There's a rumor in town that *I* may even be the Phantom."

"You?" Robert chuckled.

"I guess it stands to reason. You told me yourself the marshal suspects the outlaws are connected to the ranch."

"So I did." He pulled a gold fob out of his vest pocket and flipped the hinged case cover open with his thumb. "I'll see what I can find out. A bank detective is in town.

I'll ask him to look into this." He closed his watch and slipped it back into his pocket. "As for the offer . . ."

"You can put it in the trash along with the flowers."

CHAPTER 14

During surveillance, a detective must
remain inconspicuous.
No loitering sober in a saloon or reading a
newspaper on a horse.

Annie stood outside the corral watching
Brodie put a palomino through its paces.
The wrangler didn't talk much but he had a
way with horses. His long sandy hair, tied
back with rawhide, swung back and forth
like a mare's tail. A scraggly beard made
him look older than his years, which she
guessed was probably early thirties.

A shadow drew her attention away from
horse and trainer. Branch had sidled up
next to her. He hung his hands over the top
fence rail and rested a boot on the lower
one. "I trust you enjoyed your trip to town."

She peered at him from beneath the brim
of her hat. "Yes, very much so. I dropped by
the marshal's office." After a moment she

added, "It's always nice to drop in on other gang members."

He looked momentarily surprised but quickly recovered. "Yes, isn't it?"

He neither confirmed nor denied the marshal's involvement, but what she didn't understand was his surprise. Did he think her so dumb that she couldn't figure out how he escaped jail?

The palomino bucked past them. Kicking his hind legs, he whipped up a cloud of dust.

She brushed the dust away with a wave of her hand. "What do you think about the rumor that there's a Wells Fargo detective in town?"

Branch turned to face her, his elbow hooked over the railing. "I don't take much stock in rumors." His eyes shone with amusement as if playing a game. "Are you worried?"

"Wells Fargo detectives don't worry me in the least. I'd be more concerned if it was . . . say . . . a Pinkerton." She was treading on dangerous ground, but playing it safe had gotten her nowhere.

"Would you now?" His voice was calm, yet rife with challenge.

Had she expected a reaction, she would have been sorely disappointed. "Most definitely. And you? Are you worried?"

"The only ones who worry me are mysterious women," he said. With that, he pulled his arm from the fence and walked away.

Taggert walked with long strides to the barn. *Other gang members?* What did Miss Beckman mean by that? Certainly she couldn't have meant the marshal. He knew she went to the mercantile, but the question was, where else did she go?

"Branch!"

At the sound of his name, he slipped into the barn and out of sight. Men were needed to oil windmills but he had no intention of riding out to the range. Right now his main concern was sending a message, but slipping away from the ranch unnoticed was never easy.

The solution came moments later when Michael Adams walked by with his saddled horse. He was usually dressed in a leather apron and covered in black soot. Today the blacksmith wore a neatly pressed shirt and pants, his shoulder-length hair oiled and combed, his chin newly shaved.

Taggert stepped out of his hiding place. "Are you going into town?"

Had Michael been sneaking out of a married woman's bed he couldn't have looked guiltier. He hesitated before answering.

"Yeah, why?"

"I need to get a message to the bank." By way of explanation he added, "My folks are having some financial difficulties."

"Who isn't?" Michael said.

Taggert pointed to the pencil and notebook in Michael's shirt pocket. "Do you mind?"

"Yeah, sure." Michael pulled the writing tablet out of his pocket and handed it to him. The pencil needed sharpening and Taggert used the pen in his vest pocket instead.

After scribbling his message in code, he tore the sheet of paper out of the tablet, folded it, and handed it over, along with the pencil and notebook. "Much obliged."

Michael slipped all three back into his pocket. "Tell your folks not to worry. President McKinley's only been in office since March. He'll get the economy booming again."

"Sure hope you're right," Taggert said. Hard times generated more crime and Wells Fargo could hardly keep up with the number of stage, bank, and train robberies in recent years as it was.

Michael mounted his horse and rode away like he couldn't leave the ranch fast enough. Had they been in the city, Taggert would already be on his tail, but without buildings and vehicles to hide behind, the territory made it impossible to trail anyone unnoticed.

Frustrated by the physical limitations the desert presented, he considered everything he knew about the blacksmith. Bessie and Sam Adams had raised Michael and his brother, Luke, after the death of the boys' parents. Michael went to church every Sunday the preacher was in town but that could be part of his cover. He was also a fiction writer and hoped one day to give up the smithy business and write full-time. Taggert had read one of his published stories and had all but discounted him as a crook. It didn't seem possible that a man who wrote with such emotion could be the Phantom. Now Taggert wasn't so certain.

Cleaned up and hair combed, Michael wasn't half bad to look at. A woman might even think him handsome. Taggert couldn't remember seeing Miss Beckman and the smithy together, but that didn't necessarily mean anything.

He turned and there she was, standing by the windmill. Speak of the devil. Never had a woman affected him more or made him feel more like a man.

From this distance it was hard to tell if she was watching him or Adams. The thought did nothing for his presence of mind. As much as Taggert hated to admit it, he sincerely hoped she was watching him.

Ruckus drove Annie to church early that Easter morning in his wagon. It had been more than a month since she first arrived at the ranch and she felt restless and out of sorts. Miss Walker's demands were many; between caring for the old lady and working on the case, Annie hardly had a moment to herself.

At first she had declined his offer to drive her to church. Miss Walker's spirits seemed low of late and Annie didn't want to leave her. Then Ruckus's wife, Sylvia, offered to stay home and check in on her.

Still, as they pulled away from the ranch house, Annie couldn't help but cast an anxious glance over her shoulder.

"Quit your worryin'," Ruckus said. "Sylvia can handle the boss lady. If she needs any help, Wishbone and Stretch are in the barn."

"Don't they go to church?" she asked.

"Everyone tries to go whenever the circuit preacher is in town and, of course, today, being Easter." He shrugged. "But we got a calf about ready to pull."

"Pull? As in deliver?"

He tossed a glance in her direction. "If you're gonna be the boss lady's heiress, you gotta learn the language."

"You're right," she said. "Pull." She focused her attention on the wagon up ahead carrying the other ranch hands. She strained her neck trying to pick out Branch. She was curious to know if he would chance showing his face in town.

Rough voices rose up in a heartfelt though tuneless rendition of "Rock of Ages," but all she could make out over the back side of the wagon were bobbing hats.

After a while they pulled up behind a long line of buckboards and wagons. A crowd gathered outside the adobe church building. Children dressed in their Sunday-go-to-meeting clothes chased each other while the adults greeted each other and chatted.

No sooner had she climbed out of the wagon than she spotted Branch and an unwelcome jolt of womanly awareness rushed through her.

"Annie!" Aunt Bessie's voice rose above the murmurs of the crowd. "How nice to see you."

Annie turned. "Nice to see you too." Bessie was painted to the hilt and her blue eye shadow and red lip rouge clashed with her yellow-green frock.

She took Annie by the hand. "I have someone I want you to meet." She led Annie over to a pretty blonde, who greeted Bessie with a radiant smile.

"This is my daughter-in-law, Kate Adams," she said. "She's so important she not only has a married name, she also has a pseudonym."

Kate laughed. She was in a family way and her carefully draped shawl did little to hide her expanded waist.

Annie and Kate shook hands.

"Ah, so you're the new heiress I've been hearing so much about," Kate said.

"Yes, and I've been hearing a lot about you too," Annie said. "I see your books everywhere."

"You absolutely must read them," Aunt Bessie said. "Especially the one banned in Boston."

Obviously used to Aunt Bessie's outrageous statements, Kate gave her husband's aunt a fond pat on the arm. "I wanted to stop by and see Miss Walker, but Dr. Fairbanks won't let me travel that far." She rubbed her extended middle. "He thinks it's twins."

"How exciting. Congratulations," Annie said, surprised to feel a flash of envy. Marriage and family were out of the realm of possibility for a female operative. No man would put up with the demands of her occupation and she could never give up the work she loved so much.

"Please give Miss Walker my best," Kate said.

"Come along." Aunt Bessie took Annie by the arm and guided her through the crowd. "I want you to meet another former heiress." They walked up to a raven-haired woman whose pretty green eyes matched her bright emerald dress.

"This is the doctor's wife, Molly Fairbanks."

Like Bessie, Molly wore face paint, but with a lighter touch that enhanced her delicate features. "My husband speaks highly of you. I understand you're doing a great job taking care of Miss Walker."

"And so is the doctor," Annie said.

At mention of her husband, Molly's rouged lips spread into a wide smile. "How do you like the ranch?"

"I love it there," Annie said. She always considered herself a city girl and she was surprised by just how much she had come to like the ranch.

"I meant to stop by and see Miss Walker, but I'm afraid she's never forgiven me for getting married."

"Molly was once a dance hall girl but now she sings in the choir," Aunt Bessie explained. She lowered her voice. "She sings better when she's allowed to wiggle her hips."

Molly gave Aunt Bessie an affectionate tap with her folded fan. "Shh, don't tell Reverend Bland."

Aunt Bessie pointed to a nice-looking young man in a wheelchair who was in animated conversation with the preacher. "That's her brother, Donny. He's also Dr. Fairbanks's assistant. And Molly here works in the dispensary."

Molly smiled. "I'm better suited to caring for patients than herding cattle."

"We might have something in common in that regard," Annie said. She hoped to identify the Phantom soon and avoid having to work with cattle altogether.

"I'd better go," Molly said. "It was nice meeting you." She hurried to join her husband as he wheeled her brother into the church.

Aunt Bessie waved to her sister. "Lula-Belle, look who's here."

Lula-Belle hobbled over, the feathers on her hat doing a wild dance above a pinched face. "What is that ghastly color you're wearing?"

201

Annie looked down at her floral rust skirt before she realized that Lula-Belle was addressing her sister.

Aunt Bessie arranged her frilly neckline. "It's chartreuse and it's the latest rage."

"It makes you look like a seasick cow." Lula-Belle rolled her eyes and added, "If you want a good seat, you'd better come." She shuffled away without another word, the outlandish feathers on her hat keeping time to the ringing of the church bells.

Aunt Bessie didn't seem the least bit put off by her sister's rudeness, but Annie couldn't remember meeting a more unpleasant person. It was hard to believe that the two women were related.

"I think you look quite lovely," Annie said.

Aunt Bessie's rouged cheeks turned a shade redder and she quickly changed the subject. "I've been meaning to invite you to the church bazaar. It's only a couple of weeks away."

Annie didn't want to promise something over which she had no control. She didn't even know if she would be around that long. It all depended on how successful she was in tracking down the Phantom.

"I'll try," she said.

Aunt Bessie seemed satisfied with her answer and didn't press further. Instead she exclaimed, "Well, count my stars, look at that!"

Annie followed the older woman's gaze to Lula-Belle, who was actually laughing. Even more surprising: she was laughing with Branch.

Aunt Bessie squinted as if to get a better look. "Do you know the man talking to my sister?"

"His name is Branch." Apparently Aunt Bessie didn't recognize him from the holdup but that wasn't too surprising. He looked quite different without his whiskers. "He's new at the ranch."

"What a nice-looking man. He really must be something for my sister to take a liking to him."

"Oh, he's something, all right," Annie said. If only Aunt Bessie knew the half of it.

CHAPTER 15

An honest thief is about as rare as clean socks in a bunkhouse.

Annie settled Miss Walker down for the night and retired to her own room. Seated at her desk, she went through each man's profile one by one. She crossed off the words *beard* and *mustache* next to every description and wrote *none.*

She studied her notes for some previously unnoticed clue as her mind recalled a verse from John 9. *"I was blind, now I see." Oh, God, if only I could. There's got to be something here I missed . . .*

Snatches of dialogue she'd carefully recorded, word for word, revealed nothing of value. Cross-referencing each man's schedule, she looked for odd patterns, unexplained absences, and inconsistencies.

Seeing nothing new or enlightening, she tossed her pencil on the desk and walked out to the balcony. Though it was only a little after nine, already the bunkhouse was dark.

The wind had died down and after the heat of the day, the cool air felt refreshing.

Stars winked merrily from a black velvet sky and a full moon bathed the desert in a silvery glow. Cattle mooed and dogs bayed. From the distance came the wail of wolves.

Annie sighed. It was beautiful outside, so serene, like a church meeting. Perhaps a little walk would help her sleep. She hadn't slept well for several nights. She kept waking up and mentally reviewing her notes, pondering the many questions that kept her twisting and turning. Yes, a walk would do her a world of good.

She returned to her room and reached for her shawl. Wrapping it around her shoulders, she hastened to the door.

The hall was dark except for a gas wall sconce that lit the way with a flickering light. Soon it would run out of fuel like the other sconces and the hall would be cast in darkness. She paused in front of Miss Walker's room, but all was quiet.

Something — she couldn't say what it was — made her pause at the top of the stairs. For the longest while she stood in place, not daring to move. She had just about decided she was imagining things when a man stepped out of the shadows on the floor below and into a beam of moonlight slanting through a narrow window. Holding her breath, she drew back. She'd caught only a glimpse of the intruder but she knew it was Branch, no question. She would recognize his tall, straight form anywhere.

But what was he doing here? Going through Miss Walker's office again, no doubt. She could barely hear the front door open and close over the pounding of her heart.

Curiosity directed her feet down the stairs. She opened the door a crack and peered outside. Not a soul was in sight. Stepping onto the veranda, she closed the door behind her ever so quietly. Soundlessly she walked down the steps and through the courtyard. She pulled the shawl tight around her shoulders, more for comfort than for warmth.

She spotted Branch walking away from the bunkhouse on the main road. Certain he was about to meet the Phantom, her breath grew ragged with anticipation. Ducking behind the adobe wall, she waited until he had moved a distance away before hurrying to the gate. The moonlight was both a help and a hindrance. She would have to take special care not to be seen.

She clutched her shawl and followed at a discreet distance. Saguaros rose from the desert floor, arms twisted in grotesque shapes. She made good use of the oddly shaped cacti, pausing behind each one until certain she had not been spotted. Something moved and she jumped. A rabbit.

No longer able to see Branch, she stood perfectly still. A wolf's howl rolled from the hills and the lonely cry sent cold shivers down her spine. She crept forward.

Suddenly she heard a man's voice. Branch was no longer alone but she couldn't tell how far away the voices were. With so few obstacles to muffle noise, sounds carried in the desert. They could be close or some distance away. It was impossible to tell.

Heart pounding, she darted behind a tall, hat-rack-shaped saguaro, her boots sinking into the soft soil. The voices grew louder. It sounded like an argument but the actual words escaped her.

Hidden behind a thick pleated stem, she peered beneath a spiny arm. Branch stood next to a man on horseback. They were about forty or fifty feet away. One of the other robbers? Bent at the waist, she moved closer and ducked behind yet another tall cactus.

"The timing's not right." The sound of Branch's voice snapping through the air made her jump. "This can't be rushed."

"Get it done, Taggert," the other man growled. "Now!"

She recognized the second voice at once as belonging to Miss Walker's friend, Mr. Stackman, the banker. Eyes wide, she covered her mouth with her hand. What was *he* doing here?

She moved closer and gravel crunched beneath her foot. She froze and waited, not daring to breathe. The argument continued and relief flooded through her. "I'll handle Miss Beckman," Branch said. "The last thing we want to do is show our hand."

"See that you do before it's too late," the banker shot back.

Annie's jaw dropped. Branch and Mr. Stackman were arguing about her!

Their voices faded away, but she'd heard enough to know that Branch was reluctant to do the banker's bidding, whatever that might be. Stackman's abrupt departure spoke volumes and she sensed Branch's frustration even though she couldn't see him.

Was Mr. Stackman the Phantom? It was hard to believe but not all that surprising. It wouldn't be the first time that a bank had been robbed by a trusted employee.

The pounding sound of horse's hooves faded away but she didn't dare move. Branch would have to pass by on the way back to the bunkhouse and she couldn't take a chance on being seen.

And so she waited. Minutes passed. What was taking him so long? The air was still and even the wolf had fallen silent as if sensing danger.

Had Branch walked in the opposite direction? It didn't seem likely but it was possible. She peered around the cactus. The cool desert sand seemed to glow beneath the bright full moon. She couldn't see anyone. No moving shadows. Nothing out of the ordinary.

She backed away, careful to avoid the gravelly patch, and stopped to listen again. She had just about decided to head back to the ranch house when someone grabbed her by the waist. It happened so quickly she barely had time to think.

"Let go of me," she cried.

Branch spun her around in his steel-like arms and she pounded on his chest with her fists.

She was no match for his strength. He quickly pinned her arms to her sides and her shawl fell away. He held her so close that no defensive move was possible; she couldn't even reach for her weapon. Perhaps it would be better not to fight him. Maybe then he would let her go.

He didn't and that caused yet another problem. No longer struggling, she was now extremely conscious of his strong body next to hers. An unwelcome surge of warmth coursed through her.

"What are you doing here?" His voice was low but held an iron-hard edge.

"I . . . I was taking a walk," she stammered, drawing in a breath. She deliberately tried to ignore her awareness of him and frantically drew on her years of training as a detective.

"You were eavesdropping."

"That's your specialty, not mine." She forced herself to stare up at him without flinching. "Is that what you were doing in Miss Walker's house earlier? Eavesdropping?"

He didn't even bother denying it. "Spying on me is a habit with you." His voice was less harsh, the dangerous edge less sharp.

"I told you I intended to watch your every move." She managed to speak with the slightest of tremors, which belied her quivering insides and paid tribute to Pinkerton's thorough training.

Something passed between them. A shadow? A light? Whatever it was, it was more than awareness, more than attraction, and more than a physical response.

As if he, too, felt something, he inclined his head, his moonlit face suffused with indecision. His quick intake of breath sounded as if he were battling for control.

"And what have you discovered about me so far?" His low baritone caressed her ears with velvet smoothness.

The slight but masculine scent of bay rum hair tonic was intoxicating and a shiver rippled through her. "You mean other than the fact that you're an arrogant outlaw?"

"You say this even after I returned your watch and have shown you nothing but the utmost courtesy?"

She laughed, but more out of nervousness than humor. "Is this what you call courtesy? Holding me hostage?"

His fingers dug deeper into her flesh. "You probably wouldn't like the alternative."

She didn't like the sound of that but refused to back down. "It would take a great deal more than the return of stolen property for me to change my opinion of you."

Their bantering had taken on an intense air but the verbal wall failed to counter his nearness. She was aware of every flex of his muscles, every flicker of expression, every inhaled breath.

He angled his head and their gazes locked. The pale moonlight made his eyes look more amber than blue. Surely if he intended to do her harm, he would have done so by now. The thought gave her little piece of mind.

"What a rarity. A woman slow to change her mind."

She moistened her lips and immediately regretted it, for the action only drew his gaze to her mouth. It was only a glance but it felt like so much more; it felt like the beginning of a . . . kiss.

"I . . . I wish I could return the compliment," she stammered. "But there's nothing rare about a common thief."

"I wonder what it would take to change your opinion of me." His hands moved slowly up her arms and the sensation sent warm shivers racing along her flesh.

"There's n-nothing you can do to change my opinion," she said, her denial sounding false even to her own ears.

"Ah, now that's a challenge too good to pass up."

He pulled her so close his breath on her face felt like a warm ocean breeze. Her pulse skittered. She closed her eyes. If he was going to kiss her, she wished he would hurry up and do so.

A warm chuckle filled the air. "Ah, an easy conquest if I ever saw one."

She opened her eyes and glared at him. "I wouldn't be so certain of that!"

His grin broadened and he let her go. "What did you hope to find out when you visited the marshal?"

She scooped her shawl from the ground, shook away the sand, and wrapped it around her shoulders like armor. Having regained her professional state of mind, she answered his question with one of her own.

"Why were you discussing me with Mr. Stackman?"

Round and round they circled, hammering away at each other like dueling lawyers.

"What were you looking for in the bunkhouse?" he asked.

"What were you doing in the ranch house earlier?" she countered.

They weren't getting anywhere and she soon grew tired of the game. The feeling was apparently mutual because he stopped moving. They stood a good ten feet apart but it felt much closer.

"Why are you really here, Miss Beckman?"

"To make your life miserable, Mr. *Taggert*!"

213

The use of the name spoken by the banker seemed to stun him — or at least render him speechless. When she turned to leave, he didn't try to stop her.

By the time Taggert got over the shock of hearing Miss Beckman call him by his real name, she had long disappeared. He could have followed her, of course, and easily caught up with her, but he decided to let her go. For now.

Drat! What had Stackman been thinking, to use his real name? He kicked a rock, but instead of relieving his frustration, he hurt his toe.

He gritted his teeth. Stackman wasn't the only one to put him in a foul mood. The woman was a problem in more ways than one. After holding her in his arms, he now knew she packed iron, but that was the least of it. Never had a woman attracted him more.

The sheen of her shirtwaist paled in comparison to the glow that came from the woman herself, but that wasn't all; a man could get lost in those vibrant eyes of hers. Never had he seen such thick, long lashes. And those full, sweet lips had parted just for him . . . Thinking about them quickened his pulse. It had taken a great deal of willpower not to answer the invitation so plainly written on her finely sculptured features.

The woman obviously felt the same attraction.

Not good, not good at all. The last thing he needed was a diversion, especially one as fetching as Miss Beckman.

Business! Must concentrate on business. So far, his time on the ranch had turned up nothing in the way of useful information. He was no closer to blowing the Phantom's cover now than when he had first arrived. Stackman was running out of patience and Taggert couldn't blame him.

His reputation as a Wells Fargo detective was on the line; Taggert needed answers and he needed them now.

He didn't start out as an investigator. Had it not been for his father's violent death, Taggert probably would have pursued a law degree. Not that he was complaining. Working under Chief Special Officer James B. Hume, Taggert had the privilege of catching desperadoes from San Francisco to St. Louis and recovering enough stolen loot to keep the company solvent. The same dogged determination used to track down ten-thousand-dollar bandits was utilized to hunt down fifty-dollar embezzlers.

215

He meticulously avoided distractions whenever he was on assignment. Some even said he had a one-track mind. That and his powers of observation made him a force to be reckoned with. But to tell the truth, he was sorely out of practice. His gut feeling wasn't all that sharp, not like it used to be. No surprise there. For more than two years he did nothing but push paper around a desk. A man's skills could get mighty rusty from lack of use.

After what happened with the Vander case, he never thought he would be in the field again. He no longer had the stomach for it. But that was before his best friend and Wells Fargo detective Paul Lester disappeared without a trace while working on the Phantom case. Not only did Taggert intend to uncover the outlaw's identity, but he wouldn't rest until he found out what had become of his friend.

That was easier said than done. None of his previous assignments had been as challenging as the current one. The Phantom was either exceptionally clever or exceptionally lucky. Cleverness only went so far and luck always ran out, and that was what Taggert counted on.

Miss Beckman might hold a clue to the man's identity or simply be an innocent bystander. Whatever the answer, he could not, *would not* permit himself to be further distracted by the lady's considerable charms.

He started for the bunkhouse with long, even strides. He was so deep in thought and the moon was so bright that he almost missed the flash of light on the distant range.

Running most of the way, Annie finally reached the courtyard, chest rising and falling beneath her labored breathing. She rested her hand on the gate and glanced back. No sign of Branch.

She lowered her shawl and fanned her face with a flick of her hand, trying to calm her rebellious emotions.

Try as she might, she couldn't shake away the memory of being held by Branch. A gal could get lost in those strong arms of his. And what about those shoulders and that chest? Although he hadn't kissed her, it wasn't hard to imagine his lips pressed against hers and her mouth quivered as if in anticipation.

Appalled at the direction her thoughts had taken, she pressed her fists to her forehead. Stop it! What was wrong with her? She was here for one reason and one reason alone. She had no time for foolish notions.

"Get it done, Taggert. Now."

The memory put her thoughts back on track. Why was the banker interested in her? Had Miss Walker said something?

She didn't know whom to trust. The ranch hands? Could she trust any of them? Normally when she worked a case, she was in constant contact with the Pinkerton home office or, at the very least, local law enforcement. Neither was possible out here and she felt isolated and very much alone. She tried to think what her father would have done had he been assigned to the case. When no answers came, she said a silent prayer.

Okay, God. What am I missing? What am I not seeing?

She finished her prayer with a sigh and stepped through the gate. A flash of light caught her eye and she stopped to take a closer look. The light was barely larger than a corn kernel. It glowed for a moment and then went out.

Odd. She thought all the ranch hands had returned after sundown, but maybe not. Or maybe she was simply imagining things. With a backward glance, she hurried into the house.

CHAPTER 16

The only person to get into trouble for following a good example is a counterfeiter.

Annie peered out of the glass door that afternoon as she pulled gray hair from the bristles of Miss Walker's hairbrush. Still shaken by last night's encounter with the man she now knew as Taggert, she tried to calm her rampant emotions.

The rumbling sound of Dr. Fairbanks's horseless carriage offered a welcome relief from her wayward thoughts. The doctor's vehicle pulled in front of the house with a boom that shook the glass panes.

"Good heavens," Miss Walker called from her bed. "It's not bad enough that you make me wear this confection. Now I have to put up with Sawbones and his old clunker. Can't a woman be left alone?"

Annie turned away from the door. "You look very pretty today." Earlier she had washed Miss Walker's hair in a basin, brushed it, and tied it back with a blue ribbon.

What Miss Walker called a confection was in reality a nightgown Annie found tucked in a bureau drawer in her room. Miss Walker denied it was hers and said it had probably been left by one of her failed "heiresses." No matter, the gown was a vast improvement over the plain nightshirts Miss Walker favored. The blue brought out the color of her eyes.

Miss Walker was still grumbling when Annie left the room and hurried downstairs to let the doctor in. Chatting amiably, he followed her up to the second floor and into Miss Walker's room.

He greeted his patient with a cheerful smile. "Good morning." He set his black bag on the floor. "How are we today?"

Impatience crossed Miss Walker's face. "*We* should only be used by politicians, expectant mothers, and people with tapeworm."

"I'll keep that in mind," Dr. Fairbanks said good-naturedly. He pulled off his hat and tossed it onto a chair. "I have some good news. We can get rid of this apparatus."

"That's wonderful," Annie exclaimed. It

was the news she had been waiting for.

"Does that mean I can also be rid of this annoying cast?" Miss Walker asked.

"The wooden horse goes but the cast remains," he said. "At least for a couple more weeks."

"Weeks!"

Fairbanks shrugged. "It takes a good twelve weeks for a bone to heal properly, and at your age —"

"What are you talking about?" Miss Walker glared up at him. "Like any woman my age, I'm not a day over fifty!"

The doctor chuckled. "I'll let you and your bones argue that point."

Annie gave Miss Walker's shoulder a reassuring squeeze. "Just think. You'll be able to sit up and move around."

"I want to do more than sit." Miss Walker threw off her covers. "Don't just stand there," she snapped at the doctor. "Get on with it."

Without further ado, Dr. Fairbanks unhooked the leather straps attached to the cast and gently lowered her injured leg onto the bed. "There you go. You're not ready to dance yet, but it's a start."

"I don't want to dance," Miss Walker growled. "I want to get out of bed."

Fairbanks scratched his head. "Very well.

I have a pair of sling-top crutches in my office. They were designed for wounded soldiers but I've yet to find any crutch safer."

"Now! I want to get out of bed now," Miss Walker insisted. "And I want to go downstairs."

Fairbanks considered her request for all of two seconds. "In that case we'd best get some help. Miss Beckman, would you be kind enough to fetch a ranch hand or two?"

"Yes, of course."

Moments later Annie found Ruckus, Stretch, and Branch sitting in the shade of the veranda. It was unusual to find the ranch hands sitting around so early in the day, but then, it was exceptionally hot.

"We just got through pulling twin calves," Ruckus explained.

Stretch mopped his forehead with his kerchief. "It was like pulling a locomotive uphill." Ruckus grinned. "They're in the barn if you want to see them."

"I do," she said. "But first we need help carrying Miss Walker downstairs."

"Downstairs, eh? She's making progress." Ruckus stood. "Come on, Stretch. You too, Branch."

Her heart skipped a beat. "Oh no, I mean . . ."

Ruckus looked from Branch to her. "Is there a problem?"

Branch's face darkened dangerously and he looked ready to pounce. What was he so afraid she would say? His real name? Or that he and the banker were in cahoots?

"Two of you should be enough," she said. She gave Branch a meaningful glare. *We won't be needing you.*

Oblivious to the undercurrents, Ruckus persisted. "We might need an extra hand taking that apparatus apart."

Branch's gaze remained on her face. "Let's not keep the boss lady waiting," he said with a few visual daggers of his own.

Seeing that it would do no good to argue, Annie spun around and led the way into the house and up the stairs.

Leaving Stretch to dismantle the apparatus over the bed, Branch and Ruckus carried Miss Walker down the stairs and planted her on the leather couch in the large room.

Dr. Fairbanks lifted her injured leg ever so carefully and propped it upon a footstool. The plaster cast encased the entire leg, leaving only her toes showing.

Annie placed a pillow behind her back. "How's that?"

"Fine, fine," Miss Walker snapped, though

she sounded out of breath. "Now stop fussing, all of you."

Dr. Fairbanks arched his brows. "You do know you'll have to go through the same ordeal tonight when you retire?"

Miss Walker ran her hand over the pillow by her side. "I'll sleep down here if necessary."

Annie felt Branch's gaze and her face burned. Avoiding his eyes, she kept her focus on the doctor. "Do you know if Mr. Stackman will be coming to the ranch?"

Dr. Fairbanks shook his head. "I heard he's in Tombstone on business. Won't be back for a day or two."

This time she did glance at Branch but his closed expression revealed nothing. Her mind scrambled. She couldn't be certain if Mr. Stackman was truly the Phantom, but she now knew that he and Branch were in cahoots. For that reason alone, it would be interesting to know the nature of the banker's business.

As if to guess her thoughts, Branch's gaze sharpened and his eyes grew dark. The visual warning to watch what she said couldn't have been clearer had he spoken aloud.

Annie quickly looked away.

"Ruckus, how's my horse?" Miss Walker

asked. She never failed to query her ranch hands on her horse's care.

"Like I told you, Miz Walker," Ruckus said. "Baxter has been groomed and exercised every day."

Miss Walker gave a brusque nod. "I should hope so."

Stretch walked into the room. "I took all the wood down and carried the lumber outside. Anything else you need me to do?"

"That's it." Ruckus turned to Miss Walker. "If there's nothing else, me and the boys will mosey on back to work."

"Not so fast." Miss Walker's demeanor had improved considerably now that she was downstairs and she took full command of the room. "What's going on?"

Ruckus and Stretch exchanged glances. "Goin' on?"

"You both look like you've been attacked by a hay cutter."

Ruckus wiped a hand across his clean-shaven face. "There's a Wells Fargo detective on the loose and word is he's looking for a man with a beard and mustache."

Miss Walker's eyes narrowed. "Why should a detective be of any concern to you?"

Ruckus clutched his hat to his chest, his face as red as an overripe tomato. "The truth is . . . I haven't always been picking grapes in the Lord's vineyard. As a lad, I stole tobacco from a general store."

"Oh dear." Miss Walker pushed a strand of hair away from her face. "A hanging offense if I ever heard of one."

"And when I went to the owner's house to make amends, he thought I was seeing his wife." Pointing to his crooked nose, he continued, "I didn't even see his fist coming." He lifted his gaze to the ceiling. "As God is my witness, I swear I never even thought about smoking after that."

Miss Walker leveled her gaze at Stretch. "And what dreadful crimes are you guilty of, pray tell?"

Stretch cleared his throat, his Adam's apple bobbing up and down like a rubber ball. "I'm a wanted man, but it's all a misunderstanding. All I did was walk into a bank and a woman teller thrust a bag of money at me."

Miss Walker narrowed her eyes. "Why would she do that?"

"She mistook me for an outlaw. That's 'cause it was a windy day and I wore a kerchief over my face to keep from swallowing dust. I tried to explain but everyone in the bank dropped to the floor." He shrugged. "I figured, heck, if they're gonna throw money around, who am I to argue?"

226

Annie couldn't make up her mind if Stretch spoke the truth or was simply weaving one of his tall tales. Probably a little of both.

Miss Walker waved her hand in dismissal. "Who indeed?"

Dr. Fairbanks began examining Miss Walker, asking her a series of questions. Stretch and Ruckus left but Branch stayed.

"You can go now," Annie said, keeping her voice low. "Unless, of course, you also have a confession to make."

"Confession might be good for the soul but it doesn't do much for one's reputation," he whispered back. "What about you? Anything you dare confess?"

"I have a perfectly clear conscience," she said.

His gaze settled on her mouth. "And not so much as a wayward thought ever crossed your mind?"

She refused to let him intimidate her. "Not a one."

His eyes met hers. "What a pity."

He moved away. Shaken, she stared at his back. How did he do that? One look from him and she was a quivering mess inside. She tightened her hands into fists. Whatever his little game, it had to stop. Now!

Dr. Fairbanks finished checking Miss

Walker's pulse and blood pressure. He folded his stethoscope and stuffed it into his black bag. "See that she doesn't overdo. I'll be back in a day or two."

"Thank you, Doctor." Annie fingered the envelope in her pocket, which she hoped he would mail for her. She wrote to ask Pinkerton to check the files for the name Taggert. "I'll see you out."

"You needn't trouble yourself," Branch said, stepping between her and the doctor. "I'll be more than happy to do the honors."

"Don't rush off." Miss Walker arranged a pillow behind her back. She looked tired, her face strained, but she showed no sign of giving in. "Stay and join us for afternoon tea. You too, Branch. I haven't had a chance to get to know you." She swung her gaze to Annie. "What poison do you have planned for today?"

Annie stared straight at Branch. "Gunpowder."

He grinned. "Sounds lethal."

It took every bit of willpower not to be charmed by his crooked smile. "Not lethal enough."

Dr. Fairbanks donned his hat. "Thank you, but I'm due back in town. I have patients scheduled for this afternoon. Come along — Branch, is it? I'll show you how to crank up the car."

The two men walked out of the room.

Annie wanted to scream. Branch knew she wanted to be alone with the doctor. It was as if he could read her mind.

"Well? Don't just stand there." Miss Walker waved Annie away. "Go do your tea thing. We've got letters to write."

Able shook his head as Annie set cups and saucers on a tray. The kitchen was hot and beads of sweat battled with the freckles on his forehead. Even his cook hat seemed to droop more than usual.

"Pity sakes, Miz Annie. You're hoppin' around like a mad toad. The way you're taking it out on the dishware, we ain't gonna have none left." He pointed to a bowl on the counter covered with a moist cloth. "Why not put all that fury to good use and knead my dough?"

Feeling guilty for taking her frustration out on Able, she apologized. It wasn't his fault that Branch flustered her the way he did. She washed her hands and sprinkled them with flour. She then lifted the cloth and worked the soft mound of dough with the heels of her palms. Her efforts probably did wonders for the bread but failed to calm the knot of emotions churning inside.

Able covered the bowl with the cloth. He attended his dough like a mother with a newborn babe. "So what's got you so riled up?"

"Nothing. I'm just anxious to get back to Miss Walker. She's no longer in traction but she still has a cast."

"Sounds like your days as a nursemaid are numbered." He poured boiling water into the teapot, swished the pot around, and emptied it.

He waited for her to measure out the tea leaves before filling the pot with hot water.

"Gunpowder tea from China," she said. The tea was rolled by hand to protect the fragile leaves. She loved the little popping sounds the pellets made as they unfurled.

Able set the kettle on the stove and added a plate of freshly baked cookies. "Do you want me to do the hocus-pocus thing of yours?"

"I'll do it." Hocus-pocus indeed! She placed her hands on the teapot and turned it slowly. She inhaled the smoky smell that drifted from the spout and thought of her grandmother, whom she still missed after all these years. "In the name of the Father, Son, and Holy Spirit. Amen."

Feeling more in control, she carried the tray out of the kitchen and down the hall.

The sound of Miss Walker's laughter was followed by what sounded suspiciously like the whinny of a horse.

What in the world . . . ? Annie stepped into the entry hall, her mouth open. Miss Walker's red roan, Baxter, stood in the middle of the large room.

Branch was the first to speak. "I thought Miss Walker would like to see for herself how her horse was doing in her absence."

The man never failed to surprise her and was unlike any criminal she'd ever pursued. Why would a man capable of such kindness to an old lady choose a life of crime? He was like two separate people rolled into one.

Miss Walker smacked her lips and ran her hands along her horse's withers. It did Annie's heart good to see the ranch owner looking contented and less like an invalid.

The horse dipped his head and buried his nose in her hand. Laughing like a schoolgirl, Miss Walker stroked his muzzle. "You old crow bait. They been taking good care of you?" Right on cue the horse's head bobbed up and down.

Annie was still staring at the horse and its owner when Branch stepped in front of her. "May I?" Without waiting for a response, he took the tray from her hands and set it on the low table. The chairs had been moved aside to make room for the animal.

She sidled up to him. "What you did for Miss Walker . . . it's very thoughtful of you." She kept her voice low.

"Yes, wasn't it?"

She frowned. His mocking tone made her wonder if perhaps he had an ulterior motive for seeking Miss Walker's favor. Like a mother shielding her child, she felt a protective surge rush through her. Whatever his game, he'd better not involve the old lady.

"I'm surprised she didn't give you a tongue-lashing about damage to her floors," she said, though it was doubtful that anything could harm the red terra-cotta tiles.

"Considering the company she keeps, the floors should be the least of her worries," he whispered back.

"I quite agree," she replied coolly, or at least as coolly as her trembling limbs would allow.

"Did you recover from your late-night outing?" he asked.

No. Aloud she said, "Yes, thank you."

"A woman shouldn't wander about the desert at night." The dark look in his eyes belied the concern in his voice. "It could be . . . dangerous."

"So I discovered," she said.

"Can I take that to mean we're in accord

and that from now on you will confine your walks to daytime?"

No such accord prevailed. "Is that an order?" she asked. What was he afraid she'd discover? She'd already caught him with the banker. Who else might she find him with?

He folded his arms and regarded her from beneath a furrowed brow. "Just a bit of friendly advice from one *family* member to another."

A warning if she ever heard one. "Your advice is . . . well taken," she said. *Over my dead body.*

Seemingly satisfied with her answer, he glanced at the tray. "Do you mind if I help myself to some of that . . . what did you call it?"

"Gunpowder tea." She picked up the teapot. "Oh dear, you'll have to forgive me. I only brought two cups."

"He can have mine," Miss Walker called from the couch.

The man whose name she now knew was Taggert cracked a crooked, heart-pounding smile. "Care to join me, Miss Beckman?"

That night Annie couldn't sleep and after hours of twisting and turning, she finally gave up. She checked her watch in the light of the moon. It was a little after 3:00 a.m.

Sighing, she walked out onto the balcony. The night air was brisk but felt good against her fevered brow.

If only she could quiet her raging thoughts. Names ran through her head like sand through a sieve. Stretch, Ruckus, Feedbag . . . could any of them be the Phantom? Then there was Wishbone and —

Before she could run through the entire list of suspects, the sound of galloping hooves alerted her. The horse came to a stop and the rider slid from the saddle.

Who was out riding at this time of night? She leaned over the railing to get a closer look but horse and rider had disappeared into the stables.

She rushed into her room, quickly threw on her clothes, and grabbed a shawl. Moments later she crept through the courtyard. Light shone through the cracks between the wooden boards. The night rider had lit a lantern.

She peered through a knothole. Michael!

She drew back. What was he doing out so late? Aunt Bessie's nephew was the one person she hadn't seriously considered a suspect, which was why she hadn't pursued him. She didn't want to consider him even now.

It was moments like this when she hated her job.

The light went out and Michael emerged. She stood perfectly still while he headed in the opposite direction toward the bunkhouse. A strong smell of bay rum drifted toward her and her nose twitched.

He vanished into the building. Moving away from the barn, she hurried to the house. She paused at the gate to glance around and a cold shiver ran down her spine.

The strangest feeling came over her and hairs stood up on the back of her head. A dark form standing a distance away told her that someone else stood watching too.

CHAPTER 17

A con artist is usually a man of many convictions.

Mr. Stackman stopped at the ranch house on his way home from Tombstone, bringing with him the Sunday *Epitaph.* He also had other news to share: The buyer from the East was determined to purchase the ranch and had increased his two previous offers. Again, Miss Walker refused to consider selling.

After the banker left, Annie sat on a chair opposite Miss Walker and broached the subject with care. "It sounded like a generous offer," she said, though she couldn't imagine why anyone would want to purchase a cattle ranch in the current economy.

Miss Walker glanced up from the newspaper. "My daughter is buried here and so are my parents." She said nothing about her former husband. "One day I will be buried here too."

As if to announce the subject closed, she turned back to her newspaper and groaned. "There they go again, suggesting that we ranchers build fish ponds."

Annie frowned. "Fish ponds?"

"It's the latest madness. Not long ago it was all about barbed wire. That was going to save us ranchers. Now it's farming fish. That's all we cattle ranchers need to worry about. Fish!"

"Is there anything in the paper about the train robbers?" Annie asked.

"Nothing," Miss Walker said. "Not a thing."

Annie hesitated a moment before venturing forth with the next question. "How well do you know Mr. Stackman?"

Miss Walker lowered the newspaper. "Robert? I've known him for years. He's a good friend. Why do you ask?"

"I was just . . . curious." *Curious* hardly described Annie's interest in Mr. Stackman. He now topped her list of suspects.

Miss Walker folded the newspaper and tossed it aside. "If he had his way, I would have married him years ago."

"Why didn't you?" Annie asked.

"The ranch." Miss Walker sighed. "It's my life and no man wants a wife who puts her work first."

Annie knew from experience that what Miss Walker said was true. Every man who'd ever courted her had soon grown weary of her sudden disappearances and long absences. Of course, it didn't help that she had to keep her occupation secret. After a while, she ran out of excuses for having to leave town. One man decided she had too many "sick" relatives for his liking and ended the courtship. Another beau accused her of seeing someone else.

"Is that why you insist that your heiress sign a spinster pact?" she asked.

Miss Walker chuckled. "Never thought of it in those terms, but yes. It's either the ranch or a man. You can't have both."

"Lots of male ranchers are married," Annie said.

"Yes, but that's only because most women are fools. They'll take whatever a man dishes out, even neglect. Men are far more demanding and far less forgiving."

Annie wondered if any of the Pinkerton operatives would agree. The nature of the detective business made it impossible to have any sort of normal life, even for men. Many who ventured into marriage ended up divorced or estranged — her father the exception, though who knew how long her parents' marriage would have lasted had her mother not died of consumption at such a young age.

"Do you think that's true of all men?" she asked.

"All that I've ever met." She studied Annie. "As you no doubt know, I was married once. Years ago. Once you go through a divorce . . . trust me. You don't ever want to go through that again."

"It must have been very difficult," Annie said.

"You have no idea, but Ralph gave me no choice. He said it was either him or the ranch." Her gaze sliced through Annie like a bullet. "Having second thoughts?"

Annie frowned. "About what?"

"About the stipulations that will prevent you from marrying, should you become my heiress."

Annie couldn't imagine anyone signing such a document but her job required her to play her role to the hilt. Such deception was, after all, for the greater good. Wasn't that what she always told herself? Only this time it didn't work; she hated being dishonest, especially with the old lady.

"Well, are you?" Miss Walker snapped. "Speak up, girl."

"No. No second thoughts," Annie said,

239

but the words tasted like acid on her tongue.

Miss Walker gave her a piercing look. "You seem to be on friendly terms with the new man, Branch."

Annie's face blazed. "I was just thanking him for bringing your horse to you."

"Hmm. Makes me wonder which of us he was trying to impress. Me or you."

"It would do him no good to impress me," Annie said. "The man's a —" She caught herself just in time. Revealing that he was an outlaw would serve no real purpose at this time, and might even hinder her investigation.

"Go on," Miss Walker said. "You were saying?"

"I was just going to say he strikes me as a . . . ladies' man," Annie said.

Miss Walker greeted this news with raised eyebrows. "In that case, I'd better watch my step." Offering no clue as to whether she was joking, Miss Walker abruptly changed the subject. "Would you mind asking Able to help me upstairs before he turns in?"

"Yes, of course." Annie rose and thought of something. "I meant to ask you, what's on the range east of here?"

Miss Walker stifled a yawn. "What do you mean?"

"Occasionally I see a light at night and I

was just wondering what was out there."

"Nothing's out there, just desert and cattle. Perhaps what you saw was a windmill. Sometimes moonlight bounces off the steel blades."

"That must have been it," Annie said, though she was almost positive that it wasn't.

The following morning Annie crossed to the barn looking for Ruckus. She found him sitting on a stack of hay, his crooked nose buried in a letter.

Ruckus shook his head but didn't look up.

She sat on the hay by his side. "Bad news?" she asked. It was unusual to see him look so serious.

"My son. He's now officially an ordained preacher."

"Why, that's wonderful, Ruckus. You must be very proud." She studied him. The skin that previously supported a mustache was now sunburned. "So why do you look so downhearted?"

"I counted on him settling down in Cactus Patch and preaching at our church. We need a new preacher. Don't get me wrong; I like Reverend Bland, but he's a circuit rider and can only make it here every other week or so. We need a full-timer."

"Where does your son plan to preach?" Annie asked.

"Africa. Would you believe such a thing? His mother will have a conniption." Ruckus folded the letter and tucked it into his vest pocket. "I don't know why he has to preach the gospel in a foreign country. We got all the sinners a body could want right here in Cactus Patch."

Annie patted his arm. "Have you told him how you feel? Perhaps if he knows how much you want him to preach here, he'll change his mind."

"It don't matter how I feel. It's not my son's job to please me. It's his job to please God, and he told me plain out that this is what God means for him to do."

She drew her hand away and said nothing. She didn't know what to say. She'd spent nearly her entire life trying to please her father. As the only girl, she'd had to work ten times harder than her brothers to gain her father's attention. Old habits died hard. Even now, three years after his death, she never stopped trying to earn his approval. Not once in all that time had she thought to ask whether God had another plan.

His eyebrows met. "Sorry," he said. "Don't mean to bother you with my troubles. You look like you got enough of your own. The boss lady giving you a hard time?"

She shook her head. Miss Walker was the least of her troubles. "I guess all this talk about the Phantom has made me nervous," she said, though in reality she was frustrated by her lack of progress in tracking him down.

"You don't have to be nervous. Me and the boys won't let anything happen to you or the boss lady."

She smiled. "It's hard not to worry. Maybe if I was able to lock the ranch house doors, I could relax more. As it is, anyone can walk in."

"If it's locks you want, then it's locks you'll get. I'll have Michael take care of it today."

She had no idea it would be that easy. "Thank you, Ruckus. I feel better already."

He grinned, his normal good humor restored.

She gave careful thought to what to say next. As much as she wanted to believe that Ruckus was as honest and forthright as he seemed, she couldn't take a chance. It never paid to underestimate a criminal, especially one as cunning as the Phantom.

"Another thing . . . the other night I saw

lights on the east range. I was just wondering what was out there."

She studied him, but his only reaction was a shrug. "Not much of anything. Cattle, cactus, and old bones. Far as I know, none of them carry lanterns."

She smiled. "Miss Walker suggested it was moonlight glancing off a windmill."

"Could be." He cocked his head. "You weren't thinking it was the Phantom roaming the desert?"

She shrugged. "I don't know what I was thinking."

"That's the problem with suspicion. Once it takes root there ain't no stoppin' it. Colors everythin'. Suspicion makes every rock look like a monster."

What Ruckus said was true; it was an occupational hazard.

"Reminds me of a story my son told me," Ruckus said after a while. "A traveler stopped by a church and inquired as to the kind of people who worshipped there. Said the people at his former church were a bunch of hypocrites.

"The old minister shook his head and said, 'You won't find any different here,' and the traveler moved on. A little while later, another traveler stopped by and inquired as to the kind of people belongin' to the church. He 'xplained that his former church was filled with warm and carin' people and it saddened him to move away. The minister shook the traveler's hand and said, 'You'll find the same kind of people here.' "

She eyed him thoughtfully. "Are you saying we should all don rose-colored glasses?"

He shook his head. "What I'm sayin' is that we see what we want to see. Some of the boys see the Phantom in everyone, and that's asking for trouble."

"They're not alone. Aunt Bessie even suggested that Miss Walker was the Phantom."

Ruckus chuckled. "That's about as dumb as settin' a milk bucket under a bull. You better not let the boss lady hear that."

"She already knows and she thought it was a fine joke." She picked up a piece of straw and twirled it in her fingers. "It's hard to know what to believe or whom to trust."

"It's times like this that you best put your trust in the Lord." Ruckus slanted a glance at her. "God's as trustworthy as an old bloodhound."

Annie smiled at the image that came to mind. "You still feel that way? Even though He called your son to Africa?"

Ruckus nodded. "I still feel that way. Oh, I rant and rave sometimes 'bout God's will, but in the end it always works out for the best."

She wished she had Ruckus's trusting faith. Hers was a questioning faith. At times she interrogated God like He was one of her suspects. *If You're so good, God, why do You allow so much evil to exist?* Her job required her to mingle with criminals, and after a while it took its toll. Even her father made that complaint and said it was the thing he hated most about being an operative; after a while you saw nothing but bad in people.

She tried to combat the problem by constantly reminding herself of all the good in the world, but it was hard and sometimes even impossible.

She brushed pieces of straw from her skirt. "So do you think the Phantom is on the ranch?"

"Nah. I'll vouch for each and every one of the boys."

"Even the new man, Branch?" she asked.

Before he could answer, a voice rang out, "What about me?" Taggert stepped into the barn.

Her pulse skittered and suddenly she couldn't breathe. Somehow his very presence seemed to suck the air out of every space he entered.

Ruckus stood. "She was just asking me if I thought you were the Phantom."

Branch's brows lifted. "And how did you plan to answer?" He asked the question of Ruckus but he kept his gaze squarely on her.

"I was about to say that if you were an outlaw, I'd eat my hat." Ruckus stretched out his arms and sauntered away, spurs jingling. "Come on, we have work to do."

Taggert stared at her a moment, a puzzled look on his face, before turning to follow Ruckus.

"I'd hate to think that a fine Christian man like Ruckus should have to eat his hat," she called after him.

Taggert stopped, his back to her. "Perhaps we should suggest a straw hat." He cast a glance over his shoulder, his hooded eyes impossible to read. "They're easier to digest."

CHAPTER 18

To a pickpocket, the world is at his finger-tips.

Taggert kept a detailed log on all the ranch hands. He knew what time each man left in the morning and how they spent their days. He'd searched Miss Walker's office and had even managed to open her safe one night, but could find no personnel files.

Having no written records, he had to depend on astute observation and an attentive ear. It was a slow but effective process. He knew where each man had started on the road of life and had a pretty good idea how each wound up at the Last Chance.

It was possible to tell where a cowpuncher came from by the way he rode his horse. Those from the northern country of Montana and Wyoming sat back on the rig with stirrups in front. Cowboys from the South sat straight up from head to feet. The differences between northern and southern cow-boys showed up in all areas of ranch work, from the way a man roped a steer to the way he rigged his horse.

He knew which cowpunchers were quick to anger and which were even-tempered. He could pretty much guess who went to church with a faithful heart and who went to socialize.

He'd narrowed the suspects down to three, four if he counted Old Timer. Stretch, Wishbone, and Michael headed his list.

The question that plagued him was where Miss Beckman belonged on his list of suspects. The woman was like a butterfly flitting from bloom to bloom. In the last twenty-four hours alone, Taggert had found her laughing with Stretch, discussing politics with Wishbone, helping Brodie calm a skittish mustang, and discussing family and God with Ruckus.

Taggert even caught a glimpse of her the night Michael returned home in the wee hours of the morn, and it wasn't the first time he'd seen the two of them together at odd times.

She seemed perfectly at ease around men and didn't so much as blush when one of the cowpunchers forgot his manners and used a curse word in her presence. Either she was raised with brothers or had spent a great deal of time around males.

Though she remained perfectly ladylike in speech and manner, the intensity in her eyes at times puzzled him. It was as if she was out to prove herself to someone or something. The Phantom? It was hard to know.

At other times she gazed at him with what could only be described as sadness. Was it sadness for him or for herself? Either way, he had to resist a nearly overwhelming urge to take her in his arms and comfort her.

No question, the lady had gotten under his skin. The thought made him wince. *Not good, not good at all.*

Ruckus was as good as his word. By late that afternoon, Aunt Bessie's nephew Michael had installed locks on the ranch house doors.

"There you go," he said, handing Annie two keys. "One is for the front and one for the back. You only need the keys to open the door from the outside." He showed her how to turn the inside bolt to lock and unlock the door.

"Are these the only keys?" she asked.

"Yep, so you better not lose them." He stooped to gather his tools and dumped them into a wooden box one by one.

Dressed in overalls, his hair uncombed and a two-day growth of stubble on his chin, he looked nothing like he had the other night. He even smelled different; instead of bay rum he smelled of tobacco, horses, and heated iron.

"Michael, I couldn't help but notice that you sometimes keep rather late hours."

He looked up from beneath the brim of his hat, his cheeks stained red. His scarlet face spoke volumes in Michael's favor. Certainly no one as daring as the Phantom would blush.

"Did Miss Walker say something?"

"No. She doesn't know you've been keeping late hours."

Michael studied her. "I didn't mean to disturb your sleep."

"You didn't. I was already awake. But I am curious as to who is keeping you up all hours of the night. A young woman, I imagine."

He gave her a shy grin. "What makes you think that?"

"I can't think of any other reason why a man would wander around at night doused in bay rum."

He rubbed the back of his neck. "Her name is Charity, Charity Chase. I'm sure you'd recognize her if you saw her. Not only is she the prettiest gal in church, she reads all my stories and poems."

Annie couldn't help but smile at his enthusiasm. "I would like very much to meet her."

A frown erased his silly grin. "I'd rather you not mention this to my aunt. She's not particularly fond of Charity and doesn't believe a man is capable of picking his own wife."

That sounded like Aunt Bessie, all right. "Don't worry. I won't say a word."

He tossed a screwdriver into his toolbox with a clunk and snapped the lid shut.

"Michael, when you come home late at night, have you noticed anything strange?"

"Strange?" He stood with his toolbox in hand. "No. Can't say that I have. Why? Have you?"

"Every so often I see a light east of here, but everyone tells me there's nothing out there."

"Far as I know, there isn't." He shrugged. "The desert can sure be deceiving at times. I've found some quartz out there. Some copper too. Could just be moonlight reflecting off rocks."

"Yes, that's a possibility," she said.

"Anything else you need?" he asked.

"No, Michael. Thank you. That's all."

■ ■ ■ ■

Annie's official training began early that Monday morning. Miss Walker insisted she no longer needed a nursemaid and that it was time Annie learned the ropes if she had a mind to ever become a rancher.

Annie was given a brown mare named Caper. The horse had a thick mane and a star on her forehead. She also had a gentle disposition.

"We'll see how you do with Caper before we put you on a horse with more gumption," Ruckus said.

"I can handle any horse you give me," she said.

"I'll be the judge of that." He stood over her like an old mother hen while she saddled her horse and mounted.

"Well, what do you know?" he said with a nod. "You'd be surprised how many women are helpless as a cow in quicksand around horses. One of Miz Walker's past heirs didn't know how to ride nothin' but side-saddle. A steer sees you on one of those cockeyed saddles, he's likely to laugh his hide off."

Holding on to the reins, she grinned down at him. It felt good to be on a horse. Riding with the ranch hands afforded her a chance to observe and perhaps get to know them better. A person could tell a lot about a man when he didn't know he was being watched.

She adjusted her hat's stampede string. Miss Walker insisted she dress properly in a divided skirt and man's shirt, and told her to take whatever she needed from the wardrobe.

It took needle and thread to make Miss Walker's clothes fit and a snip with scissors to create a false pocket for her weapon. Though all the ranch hands packed guns, she had no intention of letting anyone know she did too.

Ruckus raised his arm and gestured for Branch. Branch rode over on a black steed.

"Miss Beckman," he said with a slight dip of his head.

"You two stay with me," Ruckus said. "Still got some soon-to-be mamas out there. Keep your eyes and ears open for any of 'em in distress and we'll pull 'em in. Let's go."

Stretch and Wishbone took up the lead and the others fell in line. They followed cattle trails across the desert, kicking up dust and sending prairie dogs diving for cover.

Ruckus explained the different cattle.

"That's a weaner," he said, pointing to a young grazing bovine. "He and his mama recently parted company. And that there is a first-calf heifer." He pointed to a brown-and-white animal whose sides stuck out like saddlebags. "Looks like she's about ready. Heifers about to give birth are called spring-ers."

Ruckus's depth of knowledge amazed her. He knew his cattle like most people knew their children. He had the observation skills of a private eye and only his trusting nature made him unsuitable for the job.

"What you see out here is God's hand at work," he said.

She glanced at his profile. "Do you ever have doubts?" she asked. "About God?"

He glanced at her. "I reckon everyone has doubts."

"There's so much I don't understand. Like, for example, why God allows evil to exist."

Whenever she asked such questions of her pastor in Chicago, he made her feel guilty. *"You must have faith, child."* That was his answer for everything.

"If God was small enough to understand, I reckon He wouldn't be big enough to wor-ship," Ruckus said.

She smiled. "You should have been a

preacher, Ruckus."

His expression grew serious. "I would have been if it weren't for my feet."

She blinked. "Your feet?"

He nodded. "Years ago I appeared before a church committee in Texas and asked to be considered for the preacher job. Back then you didn't need no special training. All you needed was a call from God. The committee quoted Romans 10:15, which talks about the beautiful feet of those who preach. Then they made me take off my boots, took one look at my ugly dogs, and sent me on my way. Fortunately, my son has his mother's feet."

Annie shook her head. "I never heard anything so ridiculous."

"Ignorance of God and the Bible ain't unusual. The world is full of misinformed Christians." Ruckus shrugged. "Anyway, who needs a pulpit to preach? I can do all the preachin' I want from right here in my saddle."

He sounded optimistic but she detected a note of regret. "Maybe this is what God wanted you to do all along."

"Maybe so. Maybe so," he said, his voice wistful.

Stretch called to him and Ruckus galloped away. Without Ruckus's ongoing commentary, it was even harder to ignore Taggert, who rode just ahead. Her gaze swept across his broad shoulders and strong back. He looked perfectly relaxed and in tune with his horse, yet he managed to exude a restless power that both excited and intrigued her.

He looked over his shoulder. Heat rushed to her face but she forced herself not to look away. He reined in his horse, allowing her to catch up to him.

"How are you enjoying the . . . scenery so far?" he asked.

She glared at him. He couldn't possibly read her thoughts, could he? "I've seen better."

He grinned and her heart skipped a beat. There should be a law against handsome thieves.

"Are you referring to GTF?" he asked.

The reference to her "God the Father" file startled her. If only he knew . . .

"No one can even come close to GTF," she said. "Especially you."

Ruckus stopped ahead next to an enormous steel windmill. "All right, men. Spread out."

Taggert flashed his white teeth. "I believe he means the lady too."

"I know what he means." Tugging on her

reins, she pulled away from him and turned her horse in Stretch's direction. If anyone could still her rampant thoughts, it was the lanky cowpuncher and his tall tales.

Away from the others, Caper showed more spunk, but the mare had a smooth, even gait and needed very little direction.

Annie pulled alongside Stretch's gelding. He gave her a nod and pointed to a calf wobbling on spindly legs. "Can't be more than an hour or two old," he said.

She had no fondness for cattle, but the young ones never failed to make her smile. The mother eyed them with suspicion, then nuzzled her calf with her nose as if trying to steer him away from them.

Annie waited until they were a distance away from mother and babe before asking her question. "I heard that some of the married men live in cabins."

"That's right. Why? You planning on getting married?"

"No, it's just that sometimes at night I see a light." She pointed in the general direction.

"Ruckus is the only married man, and his cabin is that way." He pointed a thumb over his shoulder.

"Then what do you think I saw?" she asked.

He gave her a lopsided grin. "Maybe you saw the Red Ghost."

She should have known Stretch would launch into one of his tall tales. "I'm serious."

"So am I. Years ago there was something called a U.S. Camel Corps. The army imported the animals to help forge a way to California. After the war, the camels were sent to carnivals and zoos, but some have been spotted roamin' this here desert, including the Red Ghost."

She glanced around. Camels in Arizona? Could that possibly be true? "Why is it called the Red Ghost?" she asked.

He spit out a wad of tobacco juice. "Because of its red fur. Some farmer supposedly shot him dead a few years ago. 'Course, there're still camel sightings from time to time, but I haven't seen any myself."

"That still doesn't explain the lights," she said.

"I reckon not." He tugged on his reins to study a group of cattle peacefully grazing. None appeared to be distressed.

Spotting Feedbag ahead, she pressed her knees in her horse's sides and took off in his direction. Something caught her eye, a movement. She veered off the trail and over to a patch of sage.

A bovine staggered around dragging its hind legs. The animal appeared to be blind, or maybe just confused. Pressing her head against a boulder, the critter threw her head back, teeth grinding. She then fell to the ground with a strange strangling noise.

"Oh no!" Annie waved frantically for help and Taggert was the first to arrive. He quickly dismounted and leaned over the fallen animal.

He pulled off his hat and grimaced. He didn't say a word. A shake of the head said it all.

Annie and the cowhands stood in a circle around a fly-covered carcass while Ruckus checked it over. Hats had been removed out of respect and everyone spoke in low tones.

So far that morning, sixteen dead cattle had been found, all within a short distance from the windmill the men called Job, after the biblical figure.

O.T. dipped his finger in the water trough and raised it to his lips. "Salt!" He spit out the word with a stream of saliva.

Annie looked from one man to another. No one moved and she was the first to speak. "What does that mean?"

Stretch slammed his hat on his head. "It means that someone poisoned the cattle on purpose."

Poisoned? Annie felt sick to her stomach. "I don't understand. Don't cattle need salt to live?" They had passed several salt licks so far that morning.

"Yeah, but too much salt will kill 'em," Feedbag explained.

"Who'd want to go and do a thing like that?" Taggert asked. He looked every bit as shaken as she felt.

"I don't know, but let's stop jawing and get to work." O.T. spun around and walked away, issuing orders. "Bury these bodies and keep the live ones away from that water."

Stretch thrust a shovel in her hands. The sound of spades hitting the soil reminded her of the day her father had been buried. It had been cold and rainy that morning, a fitting atmosphere for a sorrowful event.

Today, in contrast, the sun blazed merrily overhead and the unrelenting heat made her feel lightheaded.

"Here." Taggert held out a canteen of water. "Better drink this."

Perhaps it was the shimmering air rising from the desert floor, or maybe it was the stench of death all around her. Suddenly she had the craziest feeling that Taggert wanted to take her in his arms. She was equally positive that had he done so, she

261

wouldn't have objected.

It was a dangerous notion and not one she could afford to entertain. She did not dare think about anything but putting him and his cohorts away for good.

She stood her shovel upright and took the canteen. The water soothed her throat but did nothing to banish her dark thoughts.

"Thank you," she said in a shaky voice and handed the canteen back.

"Maybe you'd better sit," he said.

She shook her head. An operative never backed down from a job, no matter how unpleasant. Right now her job was to make the others believe she was capable of becoming Miss Walker's heiress. "I'm all right."

He stepped away without a word but the concern on his face spoke volumes. Looking at him, she felt as if her breath had been cut off.

He hung the canteen from his saddle, rolled up his sleeves, and reached into the back of a wagon for a shovel. From beneath lowered lashes, she watched him dig, admiring his power and strength.

Stop it, she screamed silently. Swallowing hard, she tore her gaze away.

A glance at a nearby carcass turned her stomach. She gripped the handle of her shovel tight. It was times like this that she wished she'd followed her father's wishes and had become a teacher. Or married what's-his-name, the law student her father liked so much. She hesitated momentarily as she remembered something Ruckus said. *"It's not my son's job to please me. It's his job to please God."* Why his words came back to her at that particular moment she had no idea.

With grim determination, she plunged her spade into the soft sandy soil and tried to put her troubled thoughts to rest.

CHAPTER 19

Wells Fargo Detective Agency: We never forget.

A half-moon lit the nighttime sky, but it was warmer than in previous weeks. For this, Annie was grateful. She shifted in her saddle and Caper nickered. She had been sitting on her horse for the last two hours, waiting. Stakeouts were her least favorite part of the job. She preferred action to sitting around and hoping for something to happen.

Of course, stakeouts in the city were far different from stakeouts in the desert, where there were so few places to hide. She stayed in the shadow of the barn so as not to be seen from the bunkhouse, but should Miss Walker happen to look out the window, she might well wonder what Annie was doing.

It had been a horrible day. It was late afternoon by the time the corpses were buried, the salt water replaced with fresh, and the other water outlets checked.

Miss Walker had taken the loss of cattle in stride. She blamed the other ranchers in the area. "I install and maintain windmills and they want my water," she said by way of explanation.

It didn't seem that far-fetched to think that some mean-spirited rancher might have dumped salt into the water trough. The fight for water rights was not new and the recent drought had made things progressively worse.

Still, something about the whole affair didn't sit right with Annie. For one thing, the location of the windmill seemed all wrong. An outside rancher would have had to pass two windmills before reaching the one called Job. It made no sense. Why not poison the water closest to the property line? Why take a chance on trespassing and being caught?

Her guess was that the perpetrator was someone from the Last Chance and she intended to find out who that person was — if it killed her.

A light flashed in the distance and her thoughts scattered like field mice. Feet pressed hard into the stirrups, she rose half out of the saddle. Another light flicked on and off, followed by a steady glow. She lowered herself. Someone was out there.

The question was, did that same someone poison the water? And if so, what, if anything, did it have to do with the Phantom?

Mr. Pinkerton's voice echoed in her head. *"I mean it — you're to take no unnecessary chances."*

She hesitated, and as if sensing her indecision, Caper whickered and bobbed her head.

The pinpoint of light beckoned like a beacon and the temptation grew too strong to ignore.

Making up her mind, she jerked on her horse's reins and kicked her sides. "Gidup!" Caper sprang forward and carried her swiftly along the dusty trail.

She traveled for about a mile before the light went out. "Whoa." She brought her horse to a standstill, her gaze focused straight ahead. Caper gave a low whicker. "It's okay, girl."

The stars were bright, the half-moon orange, and the air still. The lone cry of a wolf broke the silence, followed by a cattle's long lowing as if to warn the herd of danger.

At first, she thought the pounding was her heart. She then realized the sound was coming from behind. Stretch's tale of a red camel came to mind but she quickly pushed the thought away. Unless camels wore iron shoes, the racing hooves belonged to a shod horse.

Not wanting to be caught out at this time of night, she slapped the reins and Caper took off. The light in the distance flashed again and she headed straight for it.

She urged her horse to go faster but the horse behind her still gained. Spotting the dark outline of a windmill a short distance away, she made a quick decision. She veered off the trail and made her way through the milling cattle and reached the windmill without mishap. Dismounting, she hid in the shadow of the water tank, though it probably wasn't necessary since several cattle stood between her and the trail. With luck, the horseman would whiz by too fast to notice her or her horse.

She got her wish. The black steed shot past, and though she only got a glimpse of the rider's dark form, she knew it was Taggert. No question.

So what was he doing out here this time of night? Who was he in such a hurry to meet?

She slid her gun into the holster at her thigh and mounted. She then followed in Taggert's wake.

■ ■ ■ ■

Taggert dismounted and pulled his Peacemaker out of his holster. This was where he thought he saw the light, but maybe not. It was hard to tell. Distances could be deceiving at night, especially in the desert. He staked his horse and circled the granite wall rising from the desert floor. The jagged spires stood out against the star-pocked sky. The shadows of the lower buttes looked like animals ready to spring.

He crept forward slowly, cautiously, stopping from time to time to listen. Every desert creature seemed to be holding its breath. He stayed in the shadow of the granite peaks and was just about to turn back when he heard something: the slow, steady drip of water.

He holstered the gun and reached into his pocket for safety matches. Striking a match on the sole of his boot, he held it shoulder high. The flickering flame revealed what looked like the mouth of a cave. It was hard to tell how deep the cave went, but he guessed it was deep enough for a hideout. Was this where the Phantom lived? He would know more tomorrow when he checked out the cave in the light of day.

He blew out the match before it burned his fingers.

The crunch of gravel made him reach for his gun again. Something or someone was coming from behind. He pulled his Peacemaker from his holster and whirled about.

Staying close to the rocky wall, Taggert walked ever so slowly. Something snapped beneath his boot and he froze. Whoever was on the trail had obviously heard it, too, and stopped moving.

Taggert's ears strained to pick up the softest sound. From a distance came the muffled beat of hooves. Someone was getting away but there was nothing he could do about it. Someone else stood between him and his horse.

He gripped his gun, but otherwise didn't move a muscle. *Come out, come out, whoever you are.*

At long last the shadow moved forward and stepped into the stream of moonlight.

Taggert practically dropped his gun. "Miss Beckman?"

She froze, her gun pointed straight at him. "Hello, Taggert."

They stared at each other like two wily animals meeting at a watering hole.

He drew in his breath. "I didn't expect to see you here." She was, in fact, the last person he expected to see. The moonlight bounced off her weapon but it was too dark to make out much more than its pocket size. "Plan on shooting anything with that toy?"

"John Wilkes Booth managed and his was a Deringer with one *r*. This one has two."

She was right in that regard. The original derringers were spelled differently and had only one shot. Imitations such as hers had two shots. "You might be interested to know that this is a Peacemaker — with one *r* — and I've got a good mind to arrest you. I believe that's two *r*'s."

She surprised him by laughing. "You're joking, right?"

"No, I'm pretty sure that's the correct spelling," he said.

"You have no authority to arrest anyone."

He hadn't expected to blow his cover so soon, but his investigation was going nowhere, fast. He didn't know how Miss Beckman fit in the scheme of things, but he meant to find out and there was no time like the present.

"I'm working undercover. As you unfortunately know, my name is Taggert. Jeremy Taggert. I'm a Wells Fargo detective." He held up his badge with his free hand.

Even in the pale moonlight the shock was evident on her face. It took her a full moment to recover or at least lower her weapon.

"Th-that still gives you no authority to arrest me," she stammered.

She was right, of course, but he had no intention of letting such a small detail deter him. "We can remedy that by a trip to town. The marshal has all the authority we need. Not only are you a nuisance, but your presence here tonight allowed someone, perhaps even the Phantom, to get away. So I suggest you start talking and begin by telling me your real name."

"Arresting me would be a grave mistake," she said, "even if you could."

"Really. Suppose you give me one good reason why."

She reached into her waistband and held up her palm, revealing a shiny shield. "I'm also working undercover. Pinkerton National Detective agency."

That was a good reason, all right, but a blow to the head couldn't have stunned him more. "A Pinkerton?" He could barely get the words out. "You're kidding, right? But . . . but you're a woman."

"Yes, that has been brought to my attention," she said.

Of all things, a woman detective. Great guns! What an unexpected turn of events.

He holstered his weapon. "Okay, I take it back. I won't arrest you."

"How considerate of you." She tilted her head. "So that's how you escaped jail. Am I right in assuming that the marshal knows your true identity?"

"He does." The hanging was a setup from the start and it worked like a charm. "And so does the bank president."

"Mr. Stackman." She frowned. "It seems like everyone knew your true identity but me."

"I consider it a compliment to my skills that you didn't figure it out," he said. No doubt she was just as annoyed as he for failing to pick out a fellow detective.

"No one told me there was a second undercover agent."

She sounded angry and he couldn't blame her. It was imperative that a detective be aware of any other agents in the environment. A lack of such information could result in embarrassment or even tragedy. He knew that from painful experience.

"Did you inform the marshal of your presence?" he asked. Notifying local law enforcement was the first order of business for a Wells Fargo detective. He would be willing to bet Pinkerton operatives were required to follow the same procedure.

"I suspected you and the marshal were in cahoots, but never did I imagine the possibility that you were working on the right side of the law."

He raised his eyebrows. "You thought Morris was a crook?"

She shrugged. "You were walking around free. What else could I think?"

He blew out his breath. "It seems like we've been working at cross-purposes."

"Yes, haven't we?"

He still couldn't believe he'd been so easily fooled by her. "Miss Walker's accident? That wasn't planned?"

She gasped. "You don't think that I —"

He shrugged. "The thought did occur to me."

"I would never —" She angled her head. "So how did you manage to work your way into the Phantom gang?"

"With a golden tongue and a loose purse. You can talk your way into anything if you ply others with enough drinks."

"I see. And what exactly are you plying out here in the middle of the night?"

Thumbs hooked onto the belt of his holster, he considered how to use this rather surprising development to his own advantage. "If you're who you say you are, then you already know the answer to that."

"You saw the lights too."

They eyed each other and he noted that she still held her gun. Was that because she didn't want him to know where she kept it, or did she still not fully trust him?

"Who do you think the Phantom is?" he asked.

"Do you think I would tell you?" She paused a beat. "A Wells Fargo detective?"

Competition between the two agencies led to hard feelings and the Vander affair made relations even more strained, but Taggert suspected another reason for her reticence.

"In other words, you haven't the vaguest idea."

She lifted her chin. "I didn't say that."

"Didn't have to. If it'll make you feel any better, I haven't got a clue either."

She considered this for a moment. "What makes you think the Phantom is here, at the Last Chance?"

"One of our detectives sent a telegram to the head office telling us he'd tracked the Phantom to the ranch following a holdup. That was the last we heard from him." It was the disappearance of his colleague and friend that had brought Taggert out of semi-retirement. He tilted his head. "And you? What makes *you* think he's here?"

"Mr. Pinkerton mapped out the robberies

and this seemed to be the most centralized location."

"Ah. An admirable deduction." His mind raced. "What do you say we combine resources?"

"Sorry, not interested." She turned and quickly walked away. He followed.

"Think about it." They reached the horses and he prevented her from mounting with a hand on her arm. Her gun was no longer in sight.

"Two heads are better than one. If we help each other, we'll capture the guy in half the time. Then we can both go home." He didn't mind detective work, but working with cattle was pretty near killing him.

She looked up at him. In the soft moonlight her eyes sparkled like stars and her skin looked as smooth as fine silk. He still couldn't believe she was a Pinkerton.

"And Wells Fargo will take full credit," she said.

Of course it would, but somehow he had to convince her that the benefits of working together far outweighed the negatives. He lowered his head and her warm, womanly fragrance momentarily made him lose his train of thought.

"That's negotiable." Over his dead body. "So what do you say?"

Stars blazed like fire in her eyes. "I say forget it."

Her voice sounded almost as husky as his. He didn't need his detective skills to know that she was affected by his nearness. Of course, he'd be in a better position to negotiate if her nearness didn't muddle his own thoughts as well.

Nevertheless, he moved closer. Mere inches separated his mouth from the soft curve of hers. He inhaled her sweet, warm breath. Her lips trembled and he could sense her quickening pulse.

"We're both working on the same side of the law." He kept his voice low, smooth, persuasive.

"What a pity," she said. "I was so looking forward to turning you in."

"If that's a no, you'll regret it, I promise you."

She flashed a smile. "I don't think so." She moved away, breaking the strange spell that held him in its grip.

She mounted her mare with one smooth move and stared down at him. "It's been most enlightening."

"Yes, hasn't it?"

She turned her horse in the opposite direction and trotted away.

"Good luck," he called after her. "And may the best man — or woman — win."

CHAPTER 20

Turning temptation into opportunity is what a thief does best.

Annie returned to the ranch in a daze. *A Wells Fargo detective.* She still couldn't believe it. Why hadn't she figured that out before now or at least suspected it?

She knew from the very beginning that Taggert didn't fit the picture of a criminal, but a lawman? That never even entered her head.

I was blind.

We never see things as they really are, her brother once said. It was his way of explaining why her father was so against her being a detective. *"In Pa's eyes you'll always be his little girl and in need of protection."*

People didn't only see what they wanted to see; they saw in others what they needed to see. As long as Taggert was an outlaw in her eyes, he was off limits. She could then more easily control the worrisome feelings his nearness invoked. Now it was going to be a whole lot harder to ignore the way he affected her, if not altogether impossible.

She unsaddled Caper and one by one checked each stalled horse. None were overheated or gave any other indication of having been recently ridden. Odd. She distinctly heard someone ride away while she and Taggert were tracking each other.

Moments later she stood in the courtyard with only the night sky for company and tried to make sense of her ambiguous thoughts. Taggert wasn't an outlaw but he worked for Wells Fargo, and the very thought made her cringe.

Wells Fargo detectives were Pinkerton's biggest competitors, but that wasn't why Annie harbored such contempt for them. Her reasons were far more personal and ran deep as the ocean. It was a Wells Fargo agent who had caused her father's death.

Shivering against the memory, Annie slipped into the ranch house, surprised to find Miss Walker downstairs on the couch surrounded by thick ledgers.

"What are you doing here?" Annie asked. She had made certain that the ranch owner was settled in her room before leaving. "You didn't come downstairs by yourself?"

Miss Walker waved away her concern. "I couldn't sleep. I wanted to add up the loss of those cattle." She stared at Annie. "Where were you, and why do you look all flushed?"

Annie flopped in a chair opposite her. "I needed some air." That part was true at least.

"Hmm." Miss Walker exchanged one ledger for another. "You now have an inkling what it means to be a ranch owner."

Only an inkling? Annie drew in her breath at the memory of dead cattle. It had been a strange day on many accounts. "Aren't you worried that whoever poisoned the water will try again?" she asked.

Miss Walker shrugged. "All we can do is keep checking the water supply and hope we catch the culprit."

"You don't suppose it's the Phantom?" Annie asked.

"What earthly reason would he have for doing such a thing? It makes no sense." Miss Walker made a notation with a pen. "I hope your unfortunate experience hasn't discouraged you. Are you still interested in learning the ranching business?"

Annie wanted to tell Miss Walker her real reason for being on the ranch, but that would be grounds for immediate dismissal. Mr. Pinkerton was clear on that. "Of course."

Miss Walker didn't pursue the matter, and for that Annie was grateful.

She hated lying, especially to the old lady. God forgive her. It was the thing she hated most about her job.

She was only ten when she attended a Christmas party with her father as he worked undercover. That was when the agency was at its peak. Some of the guests were militant mine workers suspected of being Molly Maguires and her father posed as a sympathizer.

She complained at having to pretend to be something she wasn't and her father told her that everyone at that party was wearing a false face. The hostess pretended not to notice her husband flirting with a younger woman. The stuffy bank president acted as if he were having a good time. The man drinking too much and laughing too loudly wanted everyone to think he was successful and not about to lose his job.

"The only difference between an operative and the rest of the world is that we get paid to pretend," her father told her.

Miss Walker worked on her ledgers, making notations, checking bills of sale, and adding figures. Even with her leg in a cast, she looked determined, businesslike, commanding, content. No doubt she was pretending too.

All night long Annie chided herself for missing the boat as far as Taggert was concerned and she didn't sleep a wink. The time wasted watching him could have been better spent elsewhere. She might have already figured out the identity of the Phantom had it not been for the distraction.

It was still dark when she gave up any hope of putting her troubled mind to rest and catching some shut-eye. Instead she rose and stood on the balcony waiting for the sun to appear. At long last, golden rays of light trickled down the distant hills like warm honey over freshly baked rolls. Sage and some aroma she couldn't identify seasoned the cool morning air.

From the distance came the crow of a rooster and the barks of dogs waiting for their morning meal. Normally she wasn't an early riser, but the desert mornings had become her favorite part of the day.

She sighed and tried to concentrate on the task at hand. One by one, she considered each ranch hand.

She was pretty certain Ruckus wasn't involved. Stretch? She hated to think that might be true. She liked the tall, rather gawky, always affable man. How could she not? Feedbag? Possibly. O.T.? And what about the horse trainer, Brodie, who kept pretty much to himself?

She had no proof that the gang leader was anywhere near the ranch. The principal Pinkerton had simply based his theory on a map and Wells Fargo based theirs on one man's word. Both agencies could be wrong and that meant she and Taggert might very well be on a wild-goose chase.

That, basically, was what she had written in her latest report. Pinkerton wouldn't like it but she had to report the truth. Either the evidence was there or it wasn't.

She was just about to go inside when she spotted Taggert riding away, headed in the same direction as the lights. She should have known he would check out the area at daybreak. "Oh no, you don't!" she yelled out.

She flew into her room, dressed quickly, and strapped her pistol in place. Not wanting to take the time to twist her hair into its usual bun, she stuffed her flowing tresses into her hat. Pulling the stampede string tight, she left her room and headed for the stairs.

Annie urged her horse along the now-familiar cattle trail. Things looked different in daylight, less menacing, but even so, she stayed alert.

The cool morning air nipped at her cheeks like a playful puppy, but the blazing sun rising over the distant mountains promised another hot day. Prairie dogs popped in and out of holes and grazing cattle lifted broad faces to stare as she raced by.

She had just about given up looking for Taggert when she spotted his black steed hidden in the shadows of the towering rock formation.

After tying her horse to a bush next to his, she followed the same trail taken the night before. This time she noticed something she'd missed: a cave.

She cautiously ducked inside and stood perfectly still. The sound of dripping water echoed from the hollow depths but otherwise all was quiet.

Someone had built a campfire in the center of the main chamber but the ashes were cold. A rusty canteen and an old boot were scattered on the ground along with a book.

Annie picked up the dime novel and recognized the title: *Miss Hattie's Dilemma* by K. Mattson. Aunt Bessie's daughter-in-law and former "heiress" seemed to have quite a following. Judging by the dog-eared pages, the book had been well read.

She tossed it to the ground and moved to the back of the cave. The ground slanted downward and led to what appeared to be an underground tunnel. Fresh wood shavings dotted the entrance. Wishbone's? She couldn't be sure.

A moving light shone in the center of the otherwise dark passageway and she held her breath. Someone was coming this way. She turned, looking for a place to hide. It was probably Taggert but she couldn't be certain. She scraped the wood shavings away with the toe of her boot. Let Taggert find his own clues.

Her back against a rough rock wall, she slid her hand into her false pocket and wrapped her fingers around her gun.

Taggert stepped out of the passage and she exhaled. "Imagine meeting you here."

He swung around. If he was surprised to see her, he kept it to himself. Instead he gave her a crooked smile. "Does this mean you've decided we'd best pool our resources and work together?"

"Certainly not." She moved away from the wall. "Find anything?"

He shook his head. "Just some pickaxes and shovels. Looks like our mystery lights belong to a prospector."

"Would you tell me if you'd found anything else?" she asked.

He laughed and the warm, pleasant sound bounced off the rocky cave walls all around her like a dozen rubber balls. "Would you?"

"You know I wouldn't," she said, though oddly enough she felt guilty for hiding the wood chips.

He extinguished the light and hung the lantern on a hook jutting from the rocky wall. Half of his face was in shadow, and even now that she knew his true identity, much of him remained a mystery.

"What made you become a detective?" she asked. Everyone had a reason for doing what they did, and it was usually personal.

It took a moment for him to answer, as if he wasn't sure that he wanted to. "My father was shot and killed during a bank robbery," he said at last. "I was fifteen at the time."

"I'm so sorry." She knew what it was like to lose a father to a violent death and her heart went out to him.

His eyes clouded with visions of the past. "When the police failed to find his killers, I found them myself and brought them to justice. The day the three men sat on trial was the day a Wells Fargo representative offered me a job. I was nineteen."

"So young."

He shrugged. "Never thought of myself as young." He regarded her with a speculative gaze. "What made you become a detective?"

"Operative," she said. After the word *detective* became synonymous with bullying tactics, the Pinkerton founder had devised a new word.

"Nothing like a new name to erase negative public opinion." He stared deep into her eyes and for the first time in her life, she felt like someone could see the real Miranda Hunt.

She started to say something but he stopped her. "Don't tell me. Let me guess. You followed in a relative's footsteps. Probably your father's." He lifted an eyebrow. "How am I doing so far?"

"Not bad. My father was an operative until he died."

He grimaced. "I'm sorry. It seems like you and I have more in common than we knew."

"Except, unlike you, I have no military training."

He drew back, obviously surprised by her observation. "Does it show that much? The military part?"

"Sometimes," she said.

He considered this for a moment. "I was sent to military school at the age of twelve to learn discipline."

"Just as I thought. A delinquent."

His gaze made a slow sweep over her face as if to memorize every plane. "You were the only girl in the family and so you had to prove you were every bit as good as your brothers."

He was good, no question, and not to be outdone, she continued the game, keeping her tone light. "Let's see . . . the way you pronounce certain sounds tells me you're from the East. Not Boston. Closer to New York, but not the city."

Like a worthy challenger he didn't miss a beat. "And the way you speak tells me you're from Illinois, not Chicago. Closer to the southern border. Probably Peoria. Which means one of your parents, most likely your mother, was Kickapoo. Either your father or his parents were British." He slanted his head and studied her.

"My father's mother was born and raised in London," she said.

"There had to be a reason for all those afternoon teas," he teased.

"Spying again, no doubt." When he neither denied nor confirmed the accusation, she changed the subject. "Since you're so good at reading people, why didn't you know I was a Pinkerton operative?"

He shrugged. "Why didn't you know I worked for Wells Fargo?"

"Probably because you looked so utterly believable as a thief."

His mouth curved in a half smile. "Is it true that Pinkerton operatives never sleep?"

"Of course," she said. "And Wells Fargo agents never forget, right?"

"Absolutely. Since we're being honest with one another, how about at least telling me who GTF is?"

Reminded of how she found him going through her things, she lifted her chin. "Most certainly not!" It was a good thing she wrote even her most personal thoughts in cipher. She had been taught well.

"Is GTF the *big* man?" Taggert asked.

She almost burst out laughing. "Most definitely."

He frowned. "So you *do* know who the big man is."

"Let's just say I have an idea," she said. If only he knew . . .

He pondered this for a moment. "Tell me who hired you."

"I'm not at liberty to say." It wouldn't do to let a competitor know a Pinkerton's business.

"Ah, that must mean you're working for the governor."

"It means nothing of the sort," she snapped.

He laughed. "The lady doth protest too much, methinks."

"You can think all you want," she said, "and you would be wrong."

He moved a step closer, effectively blocking her escape. "And what else would I be wrong about?" he asked softly.

She sucked in her breath. "I don't know what you mean."

"If I said you want me to kiss you, would I be wrong?"

Her heart jolted and her cheeks flared. "Most definitely." Her voice hoarse, she swallowed hard and began again. "Why would you even think such a thing?"

She lifted her hands to his chest to push him away but he caught her by the wrists. He gazed at her for a moment before gently but firmly pulling her all the way into his arms. Her hat flew off and her hair tumbled to her shoulders and fell down her back.

Lights of approval flared in his eyes. "Call it my powers of deduction."

He angled his mouth onto hers and everything went blank except for the taste and feel of him. His lips were gentle at first, persuasive, like a musical note starting soft and increasing in volume. Warm sensations flooded through her, filling an aching need, while at the same time creating another. Rising on tiptoes, she thrilled to the way her body molded neatly to his. Throwing caution to the winds, she flung her arms around his neck to deepen the kiss.

He lifted his mouth from hers and gazed into her eyes. "Who knew kissing an operative could be so much fun?"

Had he slapped her he couldn't have hurt her more. Feeling like she'd suddenly been doused with ice water, she pulled out of his arms. "Oh no you don't!" she stormed.

The Pinkerton Agency frowned upon the use of romantic or sexual favors to gain information, but obviously Wells Fargo detectives had no such qualms. She bent to pick up her hat and rushed past him.

He chased after her. "Annie! What did I do?"

She whirled about to face him and they almost collided. "You're not using me to gain information."

He drew back. "Is that what you think I was doing?"

"That's what I *know* you were doing, but it's not going to work."

"Annie, listen to me —"

"No, you listen to me. We are *not* working together. Just the fact that you know I'm working undercover goes against Pinkerton policy. I could lose my job."

"And you don't think I can't? We're both in the same boat and we either row together or sink. It's your call. But what happened back there . . . that had nothing to do with us professionally."

"What happened back there . . . can't happen again." She turned and hurried to her horse and this time he didn't follow.

The sun beat mercilessly against her back as she raced her horse back to the ranch house. Tears blurred her vision and ran down her cheeks.

Memories overwhelmed her. Tired of childhood chants from her brothers that she was only a girl, she devoted her teens to proving she was as good as any man. She learned to ride better than her brothers, shoot better than they, and, should her job as a Pinkerton require it, could even play a mean game of poker and faro.

By the time she was twenty, men looked at her like one of their own. She was never asked out to dances or church socials like the other girls, but that never bothered her. Instead she was invited to target shooting and horse racing and other male endeavors. Until today, that had been enough.

She had her job and that was all she ever

wanted — that and her name posted along with Pinkerton's best. This sudden desire for a man to look at her like a woman surprised her. More than that, it frightened her.

Taggert made her aware of feelings never before acknowledged. She now knew how it felt to be kissed — really kissed — by a man. His kiss accomplished what no amount of sleuthing or following in her father's footsteps had done; it filled the hole in her heart, if only for a short while.

But the damage was done and things would never be the same. Now she wanted a man to admire her for who she was and not because she could outride or outshoot him. She wanted a man to love and cherish her and to keep her under his protective wing.

And she wanted that man to be Taggert.

Taggert watched her ride away and grimaced. Her accusations still stung. Did she really think he was so shallow as to kiss her to gain information? Nothing had been further from his mind. He kissed her good and he kissed her hard for all the right reasons.

Still, he shouldn't have done it. Big mistake. Not only professionally, but personally. He blew out his breath. Kissing her sure hadn't done much for him physically either, except make him want to kiss her again.

Now that he knew the sweetness of her lips and how neatly she fit in his arms, it would be that much harder to stay away from her. But stay away he must.

The lady wanted what he wanted: to capture the Phantom. Only his reason was more personal; he had to find out what happened to his friend. Only one of them would succeed, and he intended to make sure it was him. And if that meant depriving himself of the pleasure of her company, that's what he intended to do. God help him.

CHAPTER 21

Silence is golden except during an interrogation.

Annie tossed and turned that night. The burning torch of Taggert's kiss seemed to sear her very soul. She hated that he tried to use his considerable charm to obtain information. Hated even more that he made her long for things that, for her, didn't — couldn't — exist.

Hers was a world of make-believe, filled with pickpockets pretending to be upright citizens and private detectives acting like criminals. Nothing was as it seemed, not even love. No one was real and sometimes she even wondered if GTF was.

Realizing the futility of trying to sleep, she flopped on her back and stared at the ceiling.

Frowning, she lifted her head off the pillow. It was still dark, yet weird-shaped shadows danced across her bedroom wall. From the distance came the tinny, yet urgent, sound of the triangle calling bell.

She was halfway out of bed when she caught a whiff of smoke. She rushed across the room and flung open the balcony door and gazed in disbelief at the sight that greeted her. The stables and barn were ablaze.

Flames shot upward and battled the sky with fiery swords. A line of men worked a fire brigade and buckets quickly moved from hand to hand between the water tanks and burning buildings. Other cowhands led blindfolded horses out of the stables and away from danger.

Shocked wide-awake, Annie darted inside and grabbed her dressing gown. Shoving her arms in the sleeves as she ran, she raced out of her room. Miss Walker was in the hallway on crutches.

"Stay here," Annie said, rushing past her and down the stairs.

Miss Walker said something in reply but Annie kept going. She practically collided with Able in the entry hall as they reached the front door at the same time.

"It's bad, real bad," he said. He dashed outside ahead of her and stopped to stomp on the glowing embers in the courtyard before running to help the others.

Pillars of thick smoke burned her eyes and her throat closed in protest. The fire sizzled beneath the onslaught of water. Flames crackled and sparks flew in the still-dark sky like fireworks on Independence Day.

Taggert emerged from the stables with a blindfolded horse and she ran to his aid.

"I'll take him!" she croaked. It was Miss Walker's horse, Baxter.

Taggert thrust the rope in her hand and dashed into the next stall.

"Be careful," she called, but her voice was drowned out by the crackling fire, shouts of men, and whinnies of frightened horses.

"You're all right, boy." She rubbed her hands along Baxter's slick neck and then led him to the pasture. He seemed to sense safety inside the enclosed area and stopped trying to pull away. She removed the rope from his neck and pulled off his blindfold.

She let herself out of the gate just as several frantic horses thundered past her. The roof of the barn and stables collapsed amid shouts and men scrambling out of the way.

Hands to her bosom, she prayed, *God, don't let anyone be hurt. Taggert . . .*

Smoke burned her eyes and her watery gaze flitted from man to man. Stretch,

297

Wishbone, and Able were still tossing buckets of water onto the flames while Mexican Pete and Ruckus put out nearby fires with shovels. Brodie battled to hold on to a rope around the neck of a frenzied stallion.

The men frantically worked to keep the fire away from the ranch and bunkhouse.

Taggert was nowhere in sight and icy fear twisted her heart. Spotting Stretch by the windmill, she raced to his side. "Where's Branch?" she cried.

Stretch, face black with ashes, dipped his bucket into the water before answering. "Why, he's right there, Miz Annie."

She whirled about just as Taggert looked up from hauling bales of hay away from the flames. She noticed for the first time that he was dressed in long johns and was suddenly conscious of her own state of undress. But it was Taggert all right, blackened face and all. She would recognize that quick, arrogant smile anywhere.

She found Taggert digging in the still-hot ashes the next morning. Nothing of the barn remained except for pieces of charred metal and a scorched leather saddle. Fortunately, no one had been injured and every last horse was saved. The men had also managed to haul out most of the saddles and harnesses in time.

Taggert glanced up as she approached. For a brief moment, she imagined herself back in his arms. Judging by his grim face, no such pleasant memories drifted through his mind, only the stark reality of the ashes at his feet.

She picked her way through the smoldering rubble. Tendrils of smoke curled upward and the acrid smell of ashes scorched her throat and stung her eyes.

The sun had yet to rise but the silvery light of dawn slowly uncovered the extent of the damage. Except for a quick glance in her direction, Taggert kept his head lowered. He seemed focused and efficient — every bit the detective.

Following his lead, she picked up a stick of her own. If he could act like nothing had happened between them, so could she. At least she could try.

"Arson," she said in a crisp, no-nonsense voice. She could never understand the power that some people derived from setting fires. Never having worked an arson case, she nonetheless knew what to look for. Black smoke indicated a fuel accelerant, but her assumption was also based on how quickly the fire had spread.

He responded with a grunt and continued to poke around with his stick. After a while, he lifted a piece of blackened fabric out of the ashes. He pulled the cloth off the stick with thumb and forefinger, sniffed it, and tossed it aside.

"But why?" she asked. "What reason would anyone have for burning down the barn and stables?" It made no sense, but then, neither did poisoning cattle.

"There are only two reasons for arson." He paused for a moment before locking eyes with hers. "To hide something or gain something." He stood the stick on end. "Let's start with the gain."

"If you're thinking insurance fraud, you can forget it," she said. She'd seen the ledgers, and though the ranch barely made a profit during the last year, it was still in the black. "I don't think Miss Walker even carries insurance." Few people outside the city did. "And even if she had insurance, she'd have a hard time setting a fire while on crutches."

He lifted one shoulder in a half shrug. "Unless she paid someone to do it."

She shook her head. "She wouldn't do that. This ranch means everything to her." Her gaze traveled beyond the horse pasture to the little cemetery on the hill. It wasn't just the old lady's roots that went deep, it was her heartstrings.

"She won't even consider selling the property and has turned down two offers that I know of," she added.

Taggert poked at a tin can with his stick and pushed it aside. "Does she have any enemies?"

She knew what he was thinking. Arson was often a crime of revenge. "Most definitely," she said. "Miss Walker can be brusque and brutally frank. Such traits could make foes out of choir boys."

"That makes it easy, then. There's nothing more exasperating than a victim who claims to have no enemies."

She stepped over a charred beam. "Do you think there's a connection between the poisoned cattle and the fire?"

"I sincerely hope so," he said. "I'd hate to think we have two crazies running around intent on ruining the ranch."

Her thoughts exactly. She studied him. "Do you think it's the Phantom?"

Taggert poked at the pile of ashes at his feet. "What would be his motivation?"

Good question. If the Phantom was indeed hiding here, why would he want to draw attention to himself? It made no sense.

"I don't know." Once they knew the

301

motivation, finding the culprit should be easy. "We can't discount the possibility."

"I'm not discounting anything," he said. He stabbed at something with his stick.

Thinking he'd found something more in the ashes, she moved closer. "What is it?"

"Nothing . . . I was thinking." He looked straight at her. "You said Miss Walker turned down some recent offers. What if someone was trying to force Miss Walker to sell?"

It was something she hadn't considered. "Anyone who thinks poisoning cattle and burning down the barn will get Miss Walker to sell doesn't know her very well."

"Maybe not, but we don't know what the person will do next."

The thought made her shudder. "It's hard to imagine anyone destroying property they wish to purchase."

"There's got to be some sort of connection," he said. "The timing is too coincidental. Do you know who made the offers?"

"Someone back east. Your boss would know."

"Stackman?"

"He's the one handling the offers," she explained.

He took a moment to consider this. "I'll ride into town and talk to him."

"I'll go with you."

He stared at her for a moment, his expression inscrutable. Only the light in his eyes gave him away. "Do you realize we're actually working together?"

He caught her by surprise. They had fallen into such easy rapport she'd momentarily forgotten that he was a competitor and not a Pinkerton colleague with whom she might readily exchange theories.

"We're discussing a fire," she said with a toss of her head. She welcomed the reminder because as long as they remained competitors, there was little danger of repeating what happened in the cave. "Nothing more."

She tried her best to maintain a serious demeanor, but there was nothing — absolutely nothing — to be done about her flip-flopping heart.

Annie stood at the counter of the telegraph office and printed her message in code. She and Taggert had parted company the moment they reached town, agreeing to meet at the bank at two.

Since code could easily be misinterpreted, it was necessary to print so the operator did not send the wrong message. In cryptic she wrote: *Fire at the ranch; arson suspected.*

Taggert sidled up to the counter and she glanced at him in surprise. She hadn't expected to run into him so soon. He arched his neck and tried to read what she wrote.

Since her note was written in cipher, it wouldn't do him any good. Nevertheless, she moved away from him, sliding her note along the polished wood counter.

He reached for a sheet of paper of his own and began to write. Keeping her head lowered, she cast a sideways glance in his direction. The bold strokes of his hand were followed by the scratching sound of his pen, but she was too far away to see what he wrote. No doubt his message to his home office was similar to her own.

After finishing her report, she handed it to the telegraph operator at the same time Taggert handed over his.

"Ladies first," she said.

"That's true only for sinking ships," Taggert said. He slapped a gold coin on the counter and the youth's eyes widened.

Not to be outdone, Annie reached into her purse and pulled out two gold coins.

"I . . . I have some telegrams ready to send ahead of yours," the youth stammered.

A third gold coin did the trick. "Send it collect," she said. The youth snatched the paper out of her hands and sat down on his stool.

She turned to face Taggert. "You did it again," she said. She tapped her chest to indicate his pocket. "You stole the fountain pen."

He drew the writing implement out of his pocket and stuck it in the penholder. He then slapped two coins on the counter in front of her.

"What's that for?" she asked.

"It seems only fair that I share investigation expenses."

"We're *not* working together." She pushed his money toward him. "I agreed to join you to talk with Mr. Stackman, but that's as far as I'll go."

He stayed her hand with his own, sending waves of warmth up her arm. "You have no idea what you're missing. Two heads are better than one, and the same can be said for private eyes."

"Sorry, but this eye prefers to work alone."

He released her hand. "What a pity." For one brief moment it seemed as if they were no longer talking about the Phantom or the fire or even mystery buyers from the East, but rather something far more personal, and her mouth went dry.

CHAPTER 22

You can learn a lot from a stakeout, mainly what bad company you are.

Less than twenty minutes later, Mr. Stackman hustled Annie and Taggert into his paneled office. The mere mention of a problem with Miss Walker seemed to unsettle the otherwise businesslike banker.

"Have a seat."

Stackman sat behind a conservative oak desk, hands folded. The desk was equipped with fountain pen, inkwell, and rocking ink blotter but was otherwise bare.

"What is this about? Is Eleanor all right?" The banker's expression was suffused with concern.

Taggert pushed his hat back. "Miss Walker is fine. There was a fire at the ranch last night."

Stackman frowned. "The house?"

Taggert shook his head. "Just the barn and

306

stables."

Stackman started to say something and stopped. He glanced from Taggert to Annie.

"You can speak freely," Taggert assured him. "Miss Beckman is a Pinkerton operative."

Stackman sat back in his chair and blinked. "You can't be serious. A Pinkerton?"

Annie leaned forward. "It's essential that no one else knows my true identity," she said. "And that includes Miss Walker."

"Yes, of course, of course. I won't breathe a word, but . . . Eleanor . . . Miss Walker will kill me if she finds out I've been keeping something like this from her." He sighed. "So what can I do for you?"

"We want to know the name of the person who made an offer on the ranch," Annie said.

"Ah, don't we all? I tried to find out but the attorney refused to tell me. He cited client/attorney privilege or some such thing."

Annie thought about this for a moment. "Why would a prospective buyer not wish to have his identity known?"

"It's not as unusual as you might think," Stackman explained. "Some people wish to keep their assets hidden. Then, too, speculators are snapping up property left and right. They hope value will increase should Arizona become a state. If word got out, it could start a land rush and that's the last thing these land grabbers want."

Annie glanced at Taggert. "Perhaps you're right. Maybe someone is trying to force Miss Walker off her ranch."

Stackman frowned. "Why would you think such a thing?"

"For one thing, the fire was no accident," Taggert said. "And someone poisoned the water, causing the loss of more than a dozen cattle."

"Good heavens!" Stackman's gaze flitted back and forth between Annie and Taggert. "And you think the buyer has something to do with it?"

"Right now we don't know what to think," Taggert said. "But we have to consider every possibility."

Stackman rubbed his temples. "What does any of this have to do with the Phantom?"

"That we don't know," Annie said. "Maybe nothing."

"Or maybe everything," Taggert added.

Annie glanced at him. Did he know something she didn't? She wouldn't put it past him.

Stackman wagged his head. "I'm sorry I

can't be of more service." He hesitated. "My main concern is Eleanor's safety. Is there a chance that she might be in any sort of danger?"

"We'll keep an eye on her," Taggert promised, meeting Annie's gaze.

"Yes, *we* will," she said. But she sent a visual message that said, *That's all we'll do together.*

As if to read her thoughts, Taggert frowned before turning his gaze back to the banker. "We won't take up any more of your time." He slapped both hands on his thighs and stood.

Annie stood too, as did Mr. Stackman.

"I'll see if I can speed up the telephone work," Stackman said. "I'll feel a whole lot better when the telephone is installed at the ranch."

Taggert checked his watch. "That would be a great help."

Annie offered the banker her hand and he took it. "A Pinkerton, eh. I never would have guessed it."

If the astonishment on Marshal Morris's face was any indication, hc obviously hadn't guessed Annie's profession either.

"Well, I'll be a skunk's uncle." He lowered himself on the chair behind his desk, his eyes wide beneath his craggy brows. "I should have known something was up that day you came in here and started asking all those questions."

"She thought you and I were in cahoots," Taggert said and laughed.

"Which of course you were," Annie said, "but not how I imagined."

The marshal shook his head. "If we can't figure out the good guys, how in tarnation will we ever figure out the bad?" He stared at her like he still couldn't believe it. "What would make a woman decide to be a Pink?"

"My father was an operative."

"I guess that explains it, then."

"Nothing on this end, eh?" Taggert asked.

The marshal clasped his hands. "No clues as to who the Phantom might be, but I'm afraid I do have some bad news. I checked out the deserted cabins north of town and I found a corpse. We were able to identify the body as the missing Wells Fargo detective."

Taggert sat forward and the blood drained from his face. "How did he die?" His voice was ragged and sounded unlike him.

"Blow to the head."

Taggert sucked in his breath.

Annie frowned. "Do you think the Phantom had something to do with it?"

"I wouldn't be surprised if he did." The

marshal's gaze traveled between the two of them. "And if so, that means we're not just dealing with a thief, but a killer as well." His horseshoe mustache twitched. "If you know what's good for you, you'll watch your backs. Both of you."

Taggert shot out of the marshal's office like cannon fire. He'd suspected his friend was dead, but that hadn't made the news any easier to bear.

"Branch!" He stopped at the sound of Annie's voice but didn't turn around. He wanted — needed — to be alone.

She caught up to him and the concern in her eyes pierced the heaviness of his heart. "He was a friend, wasn't he? The Wells Fargo agent was your friend."

"Yeah." Forcing the word out was like pushing a boulder up a mountain. He swallowed and tried again. "He was a friend." Not only was Paul Lester his best friend, Taggert had talked him into becoming a Wells Fargo detective.

Her face darkened with emotion and her thick lashes lowered as if in prayer. "I'm so sorry," she whispered. After a moment she touched his arm. "We'll find who did this."

We. She said *we.* A short time ago he wanted to work with her, but not now. With one undercover agent dead, the stakes were now a whole lot higher.

He touched a hand to her cheek and nudged away a tiny strand of hair from the side of her face with his fingertip. "You must leave the ranch," he said, his voice hoarse. "It's too dangerous."

She pushed his hand away and he could almost see a determined streak race across her face. "I know it's dangerous."

"No, you don't know." He grabbed her roughly by the arms, his fingers digging into her flesh. "Go home, Annie. This is no job for a lady."

Anger flashed in her eyes and she pulled away. "I'm every bit as capable as a man."

"Which means you're also capable of getting yourself killed." The thought of anything happening to her nearly crushed him. "Annie, please . . ."

She lifted her chin. "I'm staying." She whirled about and stormed away.

"Have it your way," he yelled after her. He pounded a fist into the palm of his hand. Fool, stubborn woman!

That afternoon Annie walked into the parlor, tray in hand. Miss Walker looked up from her writing tablet and grimaced. She looked every bit the ranch owner in her divided skirt, masculine shirt, single booted foot, and wide-brim hat. Even her plastered leg didn't take away from her cool, efficient appearance.

"What poison do you have planned for me this afternoon?" she asked.

Annie set the tray on the low table in front of the sofa. "Jasmine. It has a lovely aroma that should help take away the awful smell." She'd kept the windows and doors tightly shut and candles lit but the smell of ashes permeated the house.

Miss Walker set her pencil and notebook next to the tea tray.

Annie reached for the pad. The page was filled with lines and boxes. It was a simple drawing, almost childish in nature. "What's this?"

"My new barn and stables," Miss Walker replied.

Annie stared at the sketch, her detective mind spinning like the works of a clock. The ashes weren't even cold and already Miss Walker had drawn up plans, but that didn't mean she had instigated the fire. The woman had somehow managed to turn every setback of the past into an advantage. Evidently she intended to do so now. It was one of the things Annie most admired about her.

"It looks enormous." There were at least

twice as many horse stalls.

"Of course it does," Miss Walker assured her. "What good is a fire if something bigger and better doesn't come out of it?"

Annie set the sketch down and picked up the teapot. "Branch . . . believes that it was arson," she said carefully.

Miss Walker didn't look the least bit surprised or even disturbed. "Hmm. An arsonist." She shrugged. "Then I owe him my most profound gratitude. I wanted to rebuild and now I shall."

Miss Walker's casual attitude would normally be cause for suspicion, but unless there was insurance money involved, there would be no need to resort to such tactics. Had she wanted to rebuild that badly, Miss Walker would have simply done so.

"Does the ranch have fire insurance?" Annie thought she knew the answer, but she had to make sure.

Just as she suspected, Miss Walker shook her head no. "Insurance for what? Stucco and sand? An old wooden barn that should have been replaced when I built the ranch house?"

Annie poured the tea and handed a cup of the steaming brew to Miss Walker. She tried to think how best to phrase the next question but then decided to come right

314

out with it. "Do you by chance have any enemies?"

Miss Walker's eyes shone with a wry but indulgent glint. "Of course I have enemies. Making enemies is so much easier than making friends, and they're far less trouble to maintain."

Her answer was just what Annie had come to expect from her. She filled her own cup and sat in the chair opposite. "Is there anyone in particular who might wish to see you harmed?"

"No, but I daresay many would gladly dance on my grave." She laughed at Annie's expression. "Some people say to forgive your enemies. My plan is to simply outlive them." Miss Walker took a sip of tea and grimaced. "That is, if you don't poison me first."

CHAPTER 23

Imitation might be the sincerest form of flattery, but to a forger it's also the quickest route to riches.

Annie had just finished serving Miss Walker her breakfast in the dining room when shouts sounded from outside.

Miss Walker's fork stilled. "Don't tell me my men are fighting again."

"I'll go and see." Annie hurried from the room and stepped onto the veranda. A group of men was gathered in front of the bunkhouse. Wishbone, already on his horse, flew by the ranch house, kicking up dirt in his wake.

She strained to get a better view and Miss Walker joined her on crutches.

"It looks like someone's hurt," Annie said.

"Well, don't just stand there," Miss Walker snapped. "Go and see who it is."

Moments later Annie broke through the

ring of men circling the injured man. It was Taggert. She covered her mouth and watched in mute wretchedness as the men struggled to lift him off the ground.

Stretch held Taggert under the arms and Feedbag held him by the feet. He was breathing but unconscious.

"What happened?" she managed.

"Thrown from his horse," Ruckus said. "Looks like he's got himself one of them there concussions. Wishbone's on his way to town to fetch the doctor."

She turned to the black steed tethered to the hitching post in front of the bunkhouse. Her detective skills dulled by the fog of worry, her instincts nonetheless remained sharp. Frowning, she ran her hand along the horse's slick neck.

"Wait," she called, stopping the two men. "Take Branch to the main house. He can stay in one of the guest rooms."

Stretch and Feedbag exchanged looks.

O.T. stepped forward, his craggy face all serious. "I don't know that the boss lady will like a cowhand staying in her house like he's a guest or somethin'."

"He's injured," Annie said in a tone that forbade further discussion. She didn't want to tell them that she feared for Taggert's safety.

O.T. shrugged and tossed a nod toward the ranch house. Stretch and Feedbag reversed directions and Annie led the way.

The two men carried Taggert up the stairs and placed him in the room next to Annie's. They didn't bother to undress him except for his boots and holster. The bed seemed too small for Taggert's large form and his feet hung off the edge of the mattress.

"Would you ask Able to bring me some ice?" she asked.

"Sure thing," Stretch said. The two men left the room, leaving the door ajar.

Moments later Able entered wearing a flour-covered apron and carrying a chunk of ice wrapped in a towel. It looked like he'd been working over a hot stove and his face was almost as red as his hair. "Is he going to be all right?"

She took the ice from him. "I think so. Would you let the doctor in when he arrives?"

Able nodded. "I'll make gumbo soup," he said, and she smiled. Gumbo soup was Able's cure-all for everything. "And I'll put on a kettle for tea." He glanced at Taggert. "For when he's conscious. Any special kind?"

"Gunpowder tea," she said. "And make it

strong." *That will wake him up.*

"Just let me know when you want it."

"Thank you, Able."

After the cook left, she leaned over the bed.

"Say something," she urged. Taggert's eyes fluttered open for an instant, but only enough to let her see the whites of his eyes.

She shook him gently but he didn't respond. Her eyes blurred and a tear trickled down her cheek. Already she missed his crooked smile. If anything happened to him . . .

The last words she said to him were spoken in anger and she regretted that more than she regretted anything.

She leaned over and pressed her lips on his forehead. "Say something. Speak to me. Please."

Taggert didn't move. She pulled back and wrung her hands. Where was the doctor? What was taking so long?

Needing something to do, she filled a basin from the pitcher on the dry sink and wet a washcloth. Ever so gently she cleansed the wound on his head and then arranged the pillows so the ice pack covered the worrisome lump.

And then she waited in silent prayer.

It was almost an hour later before the

rumbling of Dr. Fairbanks's horseless carriage drifted through the open window, followed by the sound of its horn. *Ah-ooh-ga.*

Moments later two taps on the bedroom door made her rise to her feet. Dr. Fairbanks entered the room. "Well now, what have we here? His name is Branch, right?"

She moved the chair away from the bed. "Yes."

The doctor set his black bag on the floor and leaned over Taggert's motionless body. He removed the ice pack and checked the wound. One by one he lifted Taggert's eyelids and peered at his retinas. He then pulled his stethoscope out of his black bag.

"It's a concussion, all right," he said. "Some people call it a bruised brain."

The doctor started to expound on the marvels of the organ and she quickly stopped him. "Is it serious?"

"Any trauma to the head is serious," Fairbanks said. He lifted Taggert's shirt and planted the chest piece of his stethoscope on the upper torso. He then pulled away, letting the medical instrument dangle down the front of him. "Got a good strong heart."

Annie pressed her hands together. She knew about the good part. Maybe she always did, even when she suspected him of being a criminal.

After Fairbanks had affixed gauze to the wound at the back of the head, Taggert opened his eyes. Annie clasped her hands together. *Thank You, God, thank You!*

"Ah, there you are," Dr. Fairbanks exclaimed. "From what I understand, you and your horse parted company."

Taggert blinked as if trying to clear his vision. He looked pale and his gaze batted around the room, as if he didn't know where he was.

Fairbanks tossed his scissors and gauze into his black case and straightened. "Suppose you tell me your name?"

Taggert frowned as if trying to pull something out of the recesses of his mind. "Taggert," he slurred. "Jeremy . . ."

Annie froze. Oh no! He really was out of his head. Under no other circumstances would an undercover detective reveal his true identity unless absolutely necessary.

Fairbanks drew back. "I thought your name was Branch."

"He doesn't know what he's saying," Annie said quickly. "Taggert's the name of his friend." She hated lying to the doctor, but she really had no other choice.

Taggert thrashed from side to side as if trying to sit up.

Fairbanks held him down by the shoulders. Taggert was strong but so was the young doctor. "Whoa, there! You aren't going anywhere. At least not for a while."

Taggert sank back on the pillows and shook his head as if to clear it.

"Hello, *Branch,*" she said with emphasis. "You certainly gave us a scare, *Branch.*"

He gazed up at her but she couldn't tell by his blank expression if anything she said made sense to him.

Dr. Fairbanks gave her a strange look and bent over his patient. "Now that we've established who you are, perhaps you can tell me the name of the president of the United States?"

Taggert pinched his forehead and groaned. "Lin . . . coln."

Fairbanks straightened. "We'd better not let our southern friends know he's still president or we may have another war on our hands."

Annie chewed on a nail. "Is . . . is he going to be all right?"

"We'll have to wait and see. Let him rest for a while but watch him. Don't let him sleep for long periods of time. Wake him every hour or so. If the swelling in his brain doesn't go down, I'll have to drill a hole to relieve the pressure."

Annie shuddered and swallowed hard.

"Don't look so worried. Did you know that trepanning is the oldest known surgery to man?" The doctor chuckled. "Can you imagine cavemen drilling holes in each other's skulls? That must have been something."

Knowing that the surgery had been around for thousands of years did nothing to relieve her anxiety.

The door flew open and Miss Walker hobbled into the room. "So how is he?" she demanded.

Dr. Fairbanks gave a quick but no less thorough rundown on Branch's condition. He picked up his black bag. "If he gets worse, have someone come and get me." He turned to Miss Walker. "I may as well check you out while I'm here."

"I don't need you checking me out. I need to get rid of this cast."

The two left the room arguing and Annie drew a chair next to Branch's bed. His eyes were closed, but his breathing sounded normal. The doctor said to wake him every hour but she didn't want to wait that long.

She leaned forward and took his hand in hers. It was a large hand, his fingers nicely shaped. She squeezed it tight. If anything happened to him . . . She couldn't bear to finish the thought and tears burned the backs of her eyes.

"Who . . . who did this to you?"

"How do you know anyone did?"

She dropped his hand with a gasp. He peered at her through one eye before opening the other.

"You . . . you were faking!" She jumped to her feet and glared down at him, hands on her waist. She couldn't make up her mind whether to hug or shake him. "You nearly scared the life out of me."

He looked like he was trying to smile but grimaced instead. He pressed his hand against his forehead and groaned. "I didn't know what else to do."

"What is that supposed to mean?"

"When I first woke I *was* confused. After I realized I had given the doctor my real name, I decided I'd better not let on that I was of sound mind. So I continued to act confused. For your information, McKinley is the president. See? Perfectly normal."

"You're lucky the doctor didn't drill a hole in your head," she said.

This time he did manage a wan smile. His boyish grin melted away the last of her annoyance and she smiled back. She couldn't help it.

He grew serious. "Okay, it's your turn." He spoke slowly as if he had to search for each word. "How do you know someone did this to me?"

"You're a good horseman. The best."

"No horseman's so good he can't be thrown," he said.

"True. But it takes real talent to be thrown before mounting."

He narrowed his eyes. "What are you talking about?"

"Your horse wasn't even saddled." During the confusion of finding Branch on the ground, no one seemed to have paid any attention to his black steed.

He rubbed his forehead as if trying to recall the order of events, but he didn't fool her.

"Come on, Taggert. 'Fess up. What really happened?"

He let out his breath. "I couldn't sleep. I kept going over everything trying to figure out what I might have missed. The fire, the cattle . . ." He paused for a moment as if trying to remember. "I decided to check out the cave again, but as I was getting dressed I heard something. I let myself outside, but everything was quiet. I decided to check the horses to see if any had been ridden. Stretch's horse was still warm."

A shadow flitted across his face and he grimaced. "That's all I remember."

She lowered herself onto the edge of the bed. "Do you think Stretch hit you?"

"I don't know."

"Was he in the bunkhouse when you left?"

"It was dark and it never occurred to me to do a bed check."

Dark? That meant he'd been unconscious for a while before anyone discovered him. The thought sickened her and her mind raced.

He narrowed his eyes. "I can see the wagon wheels turning."

"That's how the other Wells Fargo agent died — a blow to the head."

"Thank you for reminding me."

"Do you think your assailant knows you work for Wells Fargo?"

"I doubt it." He reached for her hand. "It could have been you that was attacked, and if anyone hurt you, I —"

He held her gaze and the concern in his eyes reached deep inside to a previously untouched part. No one had ever made her feel the way he did. Never had she felt so feminine, and in her mind this translated to vulnerability, perhaps even weakness. As a Pinkerton operative, she couldn't afford such feelings. She had a job to do and nothing could be allowed to interfere.

She pulled her hand from his and straightened the bedcovers, but all too soon she ran out of diversions. "While you're resting, I'll look around the crime scene." She doubted she would find anything but she had to make certain.

"I wish you weren't working the case," he said.

"It's my job."

"It's dangerous. I don't think Pinkerton would have sent you had he known just how dangerous it was."

"But he would have sent a man, right?" she snapped.

"That's not what I meant. One man is already dead and we still don't know who or what we're up against."

Something tiptoed on the back of her mind, but it slipped away before she could grasp it. "I have the feeling we have all the pieces of the puzzle. They just haven't fallen into place."

He stared at her for a long moment, but his expression offered no clue to his thoughts. "Annie . . ."

His low voice forced her to lean closer. "What is it?"

"Be careful. I —"

She quickly covered his mouth with her fingertips. "Don't talk," she whispered and a silent plea exploded inside. *Don't say*

327

anything we will both come to regret. Don't say the words that my heart longs to hear.

"Y-you need to get some rest." She pulled her hand away and stood, her cool, efficient manner belying the knot of emotions nearly tearing her apart. "I'll go and look around."

He started to laugh but ended up grimacing in pain.

Hands on her waist, she gazed down at him. "What?"

"Do you realize we're working together?"

She relaxed. His teasing banter she could handle. As long as they remembered their roles as private detectives, they were on safe ground.

"What a pity," she said. "You're still confused. Looks like the doctor is going to have to drill a hole in your head after all."

Since the fire, the ranch hands kept their horses tied to the hitching post in front of the bunkhouse.

Sitting on her haunches, Annie checked the ground. The sandy loam was covered in footprints and U-shaped hoofprints.

By the looks of Taggert's wound, she suspected he'd been hit with the butt end of a gun. She nonetheless checked for rocks and other possible weapons, but found none.

She did find an impressive pile of hand-rolled cigarette butts by the side of the building.

Someone had obviously been standing in that spot for quite some time. The question was why. She mentally counted off the ranch hands who smoked. Most did, including Michael. Stretch chewed tobacco. Only Ruckus was without a tobacco habit.

She picked up a butt and examined it. The cowhands sat in the shade almost every afternoon and smoked. It would be a simple matter to find a cigarette that matched. She slipped the butt into her pocket.

"You looking for something, Miz Annie?"

The voice made her jump and she swung around to find Feedbag standing at the door of the bunkhouse. She still couldn't get over how odd he looked without his black square-cut beard.

Her training came into play. "Branch asked me to make sure his horse was taken care of."

Feedbag's gaze drifted to the steed and back again. No doubt he was wondering why she was by the side of the bunkhouse and not by Branch's horse. "Me and the boys will take care of him."

She nodded. "Thank you."

One cheek bulged with a wad of tobacco.

"Is Branch gonna be okay?"

He looked and sounded genuinely concerned. "Yes, Feedbag, I believe he is." She hesitated. "Do you know who found him?"

"That would be me. I walked outside to saddle my horse and there he was. I would have bet a month's salary he was ready to be laid out all respectful-like in a cigar box."

The thought nearly tore away her tightly held emotions. "Branch wasn't thrown from his horse. Someone hit him over the head."

Feedbag's eyes widened. "You don't say."

She studied him. "Who do you think would do such a thing?"

He shrugged. "Maybe Branch caught someone trying to steal our horses. Could have been a drifter. Wouldn't be the first time someone tried to take off with our stock."

It was a plausible theory, and had it not been for all the strange happenings, she might have given more credence to the idea.

He spit out a stream of tobacco juice and it hit the ground with a plop. "You weren't thinking it was one of us?"

"I don't know what to think." She turned and walked back to the ranch house. Pausing by Dr. Fairbanks's horseless carriage, she glanced back. Feedbag hadn't moved. She was too far away to see his face beneath

the brim of his hat, but she nonetheless felt
his gaze.

CHAPTER 24

A man who keeps looking o'er his shoulder is probably only two jumps ahead of the sheriff.

The telephone wires reached the ranch the following week and by Thursday afternoon the instrument had been installed on the wall in the entry next to the staircase.

The ranch hands crowded by the front door to admire the wondrous new contraption. Not everyone was so enamored. Miss Walker sat in a chair Annie had arranged for her and glared at the phone box as if she expected it to attack.

Taggert had fully recovered from his injury. Annie envied his ability to appear relaxed even as his sharp, assessing gaze traveled around the room.

Each time his gaze met hers it lingered for a moment before moving on. He stared at the cigarette dangling from Wishbone's mouth and sent her a message with a raised eyebrow. It wasn't a match for the cigarette butts found outside the bunkhouse.

They read each other's expressions like lawyers reading briefs. It didn't take much — a quirk of his brow, twist of the mouth, or narrowing of the eye and she immediately knew what he was thinking.

Not good, not good at all. Not only did working with a Wells Fargo detective go against Pinkerton company policy, she never thought to work with the competition, not after what happened to her father. But, God forgive her, never had she enjoyed herself more.

Wishbone moved halfway up the stairs and leaned over the stair rail. "Ladies and gentlemen, it's now official. We have entered the nineteenth century."

"And it's not a moment too soon," Taggert whispered in her ear. His warm breath on the back of her neck sent goose bumps rippling down her spine. "Since the twentieth century is right around the corner."

Miss Walker glared at the bill Ruckus handed her. "There goes free speech."

O.T. stroked the walnut box like one would stroke a prize horse. "Never thought I'd see the day we'd have a telephone all the way out here."

"How does it work?" Able asked. He wiped his hands on his apron, releasing a cloud of flour. Today he smelled like cinnamon and Annie's mouth watered just thinking of the dessert he was no doubt concocting for dinner.

"It's simple," Ruckus said, "but it seems only right that Miz Walker try it out first." He lifted the horn-shaped receiver and held it out to her.

Miss Walker pushed it away. "The telephone has only just been installed and already it's turning out to be a nuisance." She rose on her crutches and hobbled into the large room.

Shrugging, Ruckus lifted the receiver to his ear and turned the hand crank. He grinned when a voice came over the line. He spoke into the mouthpiece. "I don't want a number, Bessie, I'm just testing the phone."

He hung up.

"Let me," Wishbone said. He did what Ruckus showed them to do. "Hello, hello, hello, hello." He kept yelling into the mouthpiece and turning the crank.

"You only have to say hello once," Feedbag said, snatching the receiver away.

One by one, the other ranch hands tried it

out. "Your turn, Branch," Ruckus said after a while.

"I'll pass," Branch said. "But we should let Miss Annie try it."

Annie was quite familiar with the telephone. The Pinkerton Agency led the way in utilizing the telegraph, railroads, photography, and telephones in the fight against crime. Nonetheless, she decided it was best to play along.

The voice on the other end of the line sounded impatient. "What num-BER?"

"Mrs. Adams — Aunt Bessie — it's Annie Beckman. We're just testing the phone." She cast her gaze among the expectant faces. "Would you like to speak to your nephew?"

"That would be mighty nice," Aunt Bessie responded in her ear.

Annie handed the receiver to Michael.

"Not bad," Branch said under his breath. "For a *beginner*."

"Who said I was a beginner?" she whispered back.

"My mistake," he said quietly, and something in his voice made her pulse race.

By the seventh or eighth test, Bessie's voice shot out of the earpiece like the blast of a horn.

Stretch dropped the receiver and pounded

the side of his head with the palm of his hand.

"Ours must be the only telephone with *two* cranks."

Ruckus caught the swinging receiver and placed it on the hook.

Feedbag raised his hand. "Hey, this is the first thing we've ever done that Ruckus hasn't gone and quoted the Bible."

Stretch rolled his eyes. "You ninny! That's 'cause they ain't nothing in the Bible about telephones."

"Sure there is," Ruckus said. "The Lord called his people all the time. And if I'm not mistaken, He's calling us back to work right now."

"But I didn't get a chance to talk," Brodie complained. It was the first complete sentence Annie had ever heard the horse trainer say.

Ruckus held the door open. "Tomorrow the phone will be hooked up to the bunkhouse and you'll get your chance then. Now git, all of you!"

Taggert waited for Annie to return from taking the nightly tray of sweets to the bunkhouse before stepping out of the shadows. "Psst."

She spun around and he moved in front

336

of a lit window so she could see him.

She glanced around to check for eaves-droppers. "What are you doing here?" she whispered.

"I know who the cigarette butts belong to." He kept his voice low.

Flashing him a smile, she set the empty tray on the veranda steps. "You sure do know how to get a girl's attention."

He stepped closer and caught a pleasant whiff of lavender. "Don't I, though?"

She gazed up at him. "Well? Are you going to tell me or not?"

The way she looked all smiling and warm, he would have told her anything she wanted to know. "They belong to Feedbag. They're from Egypt. Some of the boys don't like the strong odor so they make him smoke out-side. What I don't understand is how he can afford Egyptian cigarettes on a ranch hand's salary."

"They were a gift from his brother," she said.

Ah, so she was testing him. "He doesn't have a brother. Since obviously you've checked up on the man, you must know that his real name is Willard Day."

"Willard *R*. Day from Indiana," she said without missing a bcat. "His father was a flatboats man."

"And his mother a teacher," he added.

"He left home at sixteen," she continued. "Went to Mexico and eventually wound up in Texas."

"Where he worked for a time on the King Ranch." He couldn't remember enjoying himself more. He didn't touch her, at least not physically, but it wasn't hard to imagine her in his arms. Imagine kissing her. He shook the thought away.

She gave her head a slight toss. "He left the ranch under suspicious circumstances."

"Nothing suspicious about them. He was having an affair with one of the owners' daughters."

Her eyes turned the light from the ranch house window into stars. "And was later tried and almost hung for horse theft."

He shrugged. "But obviously got away."

"So do you think he's the Phantom?" she asked.

"Do you?"

Her lips curved into a smile. "Let's just say I'm keeping an open mind."

"An open mind is good." He lifted his hand to her face and ran a knuckle down her silky soft skin. "So where does this leave us, partner?" He lowered his head but stopped short of capturing her mouth with his own.

338

She pressed her hands against his chest and her touch seemed to burn right through him. "We're not —"

"Don't worry," he breathed. "I'm not going to kiss you. I don't want to be accused of using you to gain information." It took every bit of effort he could muster to pull away. "The next time I kiss you — and there will be a next time — there must be no question as to my real motive."

He turned and walked away. Hearing her quick intake of breath, he smiled. Unless he missed his guess, she craved his kiss every bit as much as he craved hers.

"You're wrong," she called after him. Her voice was loud enough for him to hear, but too low to carry much beyond the courtyard walls. "Feedbag does have a brother. A *half* brother."

He kept walking. He might have been wrong about Feedbag, but he wasn't wrong about the lady.

CHAPTER 25

You can't take it with you — but an embez-
zler will try.

On the day of the church bazaar the tem-
perature soared into the high eighties.
Despite the heat, Annie enjoyed the festivities.

Held outside on church property, the
bazaar's main purpose was to raise funds
for the Children's Aid Society. It also afforded townsfolk the opportunity to catch
up on the latest gossip.

As head of the decorating committee,
Aunt Bessie had left no stone, cactus, or
telephone pole unadorned. Planks of wood
strung across whiskey barrels served as
booths and were decorated with ribbons
and colorful fabric. Even the church steeple
was wrapped in red, white, and blue
bunting.

Annie felt bad that she hadn't been able

to talk Miss Walker into coming, but the ranch owner refused to even consider it.

According to Ruckus, it was because some church ladies protested her divorce by refusing to buy her beef. "After that she even stopped going to church," he'd explained.

What a pity. It would do the ranch owner a world of good to get out of the house and socialize. Since nothing could be done about Miss Walker, Annie concentrated on her own reasons for coming.

Social affairs often proved valuable to operatives. The best way to glean information was when people's guards were down, and that was usually when they were having a good time. However, it wasn't the chatter around her that commanded attention — it was Taggert. No matter how many times she pulled her drifting thoughts together, she couldn't seem to stop looking at him.

A small group of musicians struck up the band and music filled the air, adding to the festivities. She recognized some but not all of the musicians. Stretch played the fiddle, Able the harmonica, and Wishbone a drum.

Annie held her parasol at an angle so she could watch Taggert unseen. He had his disguise down to perfection. Everything from his well-worn boots to his work-stained hat pegged him as one of the many migrant cowpokes who drifted from ranch to ranch taking whatever work was available.

Men ate up his joking banter, women blushed and giggled at his smile, and Annie's heart ached with envy. God forgive her, but she wanted Taggert all to herself.

He moved from group to group like a friendly puppy looking for a treat. His sharp glances and attentive ear told Annie he was on full investigative alert, though no one would ever guess it by his easy smile.

"The next time I kiss you . . ." The memory of those words filled her with such longing she could hardly breathe.

With a shake of her head she strolled from booth to booth.

She avoided the crowd lined up in front of the baked goods. Able's cinnamon rolls and macaroons were selling fast. When he wasn't playing in the band, the affable cook seemed to enjoy swapping recipes with some of the older women.

Spotting Michael, she hurried over to join him. She had to do something to take her mind off Taggert.

The smithy greeted her with a polite tip of his hat. "Miss Beckman."

"Michael."

"Do the locks work to your satisfaction?"

he asked.

"Yes, thank you. They work just fine." She followed his gaze to a small group. "Your young lady . . . is she here? You must point her out to me."

Michael's face turned tomato red. "Yes, ma'am, she's here." He cast a worried glance at his aunt before pointing her out. "That's her over there."

The object of his affection was a pretty blonde dressed in a blue gingham dress. The perfectly coiffed hair beneath a flower-trimmed hat seemed almost too staid for such lively features.

"I'm going to ask Charity to marry me."

Judging by the attention the girl was drawing from a bevy of other young men, Michael had better do it soon. "She's very pretty," Annie said, bringing a grin to Michael's face. "You really ought to tell your aunt. She's going to find out sooner or later."

"She thinks she knows better who I should marry." He made a face. "You won't believe the women she's picked out for me."

"Your aunt means well."

Charity's high-pitched laughter drew Michael's loving gaze.

Annie gave him a little shove in the girl's direction. "I have a feeling she needs to be rescued from that annoying man." The man in question was clinging to Charity's every word. "You'd better go and save her."

After Michael left, she made a valiant but fruitless attempt to ignore Taggert. Accepting defeat, she scanned the crowd and spotted him in deep conversation with the banker. Both men looked serious and she wished she could hear what they were talking about.

Aunt Bessie sidled up to her side. "I'm so glad you could make it, dearie."

"So am I." Annie drew her gaze away from the two men and checked out the display of aprons, embroidered linens, and bonnets for sale at one of the booths. "How are you?"

"Busy." Aunt Bessie ran her hand over a quilt. "Now that the telephone has reached the ranch, I hardly have a moment to myself."

Annie frowned. "But Miss Walker refuses to use the phone."

Aunt Bessie rolled her eyes. "The ranch hands more than make up for it."

"Really? I wouldn't think they'd have that many calls to make."

"You'd be surprised. That new man, Branch, is always calling the bank. Doesn't it seem strange that a cowhand would have so much financial business to discuss? And what they discuss never makes sense. It's like they're talking in a foreign language. Not that I listen in, of course."

"Of course not," Annie said politely.

"Then of course there's Stretch. He calls twice a day to ask if Miss Winston has a phone yet. Then O.T. is always calling Green's to see if some order has arrived."

"Sounds like the town's going to have to hire a second hello girl," Annie said.

"They've already talked about hiring Charity." Not even Aunt Bessie's heavy-handed face paint could hide her disapproval. "What an annoying girl." She pointed to the object of Michael's affection. Every last suitor seemed to be mesmerized by the girl, Michael most of all.

"She looks like a very nice person," Annie said.

"Maybe so," Aunt Bessie muttered, "but she hasn't got a brain in that head of hers. I'd sooner spend my days with a dumb mule."

It appeared that Michael had good reason to worry about his aunt's opinion. Annie picked up a dime novel, which earned Aunt Bessie's approving nod. The title of the book was *Cactus Joe: Master of Disguise*.

"That was written by my nephew's wife."

"Oh yes, I met her at church. Is she here?"

"Yes, but she doesn't plan to stay long because of the heat." Aunt Bessie pantomimed a rounded belly with her hand. "I'm sure she'll be happy to sign it for you." She chose a book from the stack. "This one is better," she said in a hushed tone. She shoved it into Annie's hand. The title read *Miss Hattie's Dilemma.*

"That's the one I told you was banned in Boston." Aunt Bessie fanned her face with her hand and Annie laughed.

Annie reached into her purse for her money. "I guess that explains why it's so popular. I've seen it in the most unexpected places." The memory of the cave and Taggert's kiss brought a flush to her already heated face.

"Oh dear, I made you blush, but don't worry. It's not *that* bad. It's just very romantic."

"I look forward to reading it," Annie said, paying the woman behind the counter.

"Oh, there's that nice-looking man again." She pointed to Taggert. "The one who's always calling the bank. Do you think I could interest him in Miss Chase?"

"The one who hasn't got a brain in her head?" Annie asked.

Aunt Bessie didn't look the least bit chagrined. Instead she turned her gaze on her nephew in the distance and frowned. "I've got to do something to get her away from Michael."

"I don't think Branch plans on staying in Cactus Patch for very long," Annie said, surprised by the sudden surge of emotion that rushed through her upon thinking of Taggert with another woman. Not jealousy. It couldn't be jealousy. *God, please don't let it be jealousy, because that would mean . . .*

Michael had managed to pull the young woman away from the others and the expression on Aunt Bessie's face looked like a storm cloud. "What on earth does Michael see in the girl?"

"Michael said she reads the stories he writes," Annie said. "That seems to mean a lot to him."

"*Harrumph.* I didn't even know she could read."

"It would seem like the two of you have a lot in common. You didn't know she could read and she doesn't know what a kind, charitable woman you are."

Aunt Bessie scoffed. "Like I said, hasn't got a brain in her head."

Annie sighed. Michael had his work cut out for him. She tucked her newly purchased book in her purse, excused herself, and made a beeline to the lemonade stand where Taggert had just purchased a drink.

She armored herself with an air of professionalism, but he immediately disarmed her with his smile. "Having a good time?"

She fought for composure. "Not as good as you're having."

He turned to the youth in the booth and tossed a coin on the counter. "Pour one for the lady."

The youth filled a glass with lemonade and handed it to Annie.

"Thank you." She took a sip of the cool, sweet beverage. They moved from the booth and away from the music where they could talk.

She sensed his disquiet. "Find out anything?"

Troubled eyes met hers. "There was another bank robbery."

She stiffened. "When?"

"Day before yesterday. Stackman and I decided to keep it quiet for now."

Thursday. "What do you know? Lightning does strike twice," she said. "Any ideas?"

"A couple." He took a sip of his beverage. "Ladies first."

"Always a gentleman." She purposely kept him waiting while she took a long drink. "Sorry, I can't help you. I left the ranch early that morning." Now that Miss Walker was on crutches, Annie was expected to learn ranching. "Ruckus and I repaired fences and checked the water on the north boundary."

"See anyone else while you were out there?" he asked.

She shook her head. "No one." She waited and when he failed to volunteer any information, she inclined her head. "Your turn."

"I saw you talking to Michael."

Knowing he'd been watching her made her feel all tingly inside.

"I think it's him," he continued. "Do you?"

Okay, so he hadn't been watching her; Michael was his object of interest.

"No!"

Her emphatic response made him draw back. "Me either." When she didn't respond, he added, "Still, we can't discount him completely. He wasn't at morning prayer that day, nor did he show up for work until noon."

Michael was definitely not an early bird, but for good reason. According to Ruckus, if Michael wasn't with Charity, he stayed up late writing. She started to explain Michael's absence but a nearby group of youths playing mumblety-peg yelled out, drowning her voice. Another boy stepped forward to take his turn throwing the knife and the group fell silent.

"Michael has taken a fancy to that young woman over there in blue." Annie pointed to one of the game booths where Michael and Charity were taking turns tossing rings onto milk bottles. "I can assure you that robbing banks has never crossed his mind."

"Is that the opinion of a private eye or simply women's intuition?" he asked, and the intensity in his eyes made her blush.

"Both."

He cleared his voice and looked away as if the shared moment had been as powerful for him as it was for her. "And I don't remember seeing Stretch."

"Stretch drove into town that day for supplies." She remembered distinctly because he mailed a letter for her. "He likes to get an early start."

He seemed to weigh her words. "Stretch just happened to be in town during both bank robberies. He's in town almost as much as Michael. And don't forget, the day I was attacked, Stretch's horse appeared to have been ridden."

Her gaze drifted over to where Stretch danced with a short redheaded woman. Miss Winston, no doubt. The tall ranch hand was practically doubled over to accommodate their differences in height. Was he the one? She fervently hoped not, but she couldn't allow personal feelings to interfere with an investigation.

"Do you think it's Stretch?" she asked.

"He did admit to robbing a bank."

"*Accidentally* robbing a bank." She still couldn't shake the nagging feeling that she'd missed something. "The time element bothers me. The robberies are getting closer together."

"I've been thinking the same thing." Taggert thought for a moment. "He now seems more interested in robbing banks than trains and stages, which means he's probably working alone."

"It seems like our guy is under some sort of pressure and he's starting to take risks." She took a sip of lemonade. "Do you think all that talk about a Wells Fargo detective being in town has him running scared?"

"If that's true, he has a funny way of showing it. If I was scared I wouldn't be robbing banks. I'd lay low."

What Taggert said made sense.

He finished his lemonade and set his empty glass on a tray. "Stackman is meeting me tomorrow at the bank so I can have a look around."

"I'll be there too," she said, though she

doubted they'd find anything.

His brows drew together. "That won't be necessary. I'll . . . let you know if I uncover any clues."

"How very thoughtful of you." She had no intention of being shut out. "But if you don't mind, I prefer to do my own investigating."

She set her glass down on the counter and turned to leave. He stopped her with a hand to her arm.

His eyes caught hers and held. "Annie —"

A high-pitched scream pierced the air and a woman's voice yelled, "Help! We need a doctor."

The music stopped and a hushed silence followed as all eyes turned to stare at the home goods booth where a matronly woman frantically waved her arms.

Dr. Fairbanks rushed to the woman's side and dropped to his knees. That's when Annie saw the banker, Mr. Stackman, lying facedown on the ground.

CHAPTER 26

Running a shady business is no way to
live a sunny life.

"Poison!" Miss Walker's face turned almost
as gray as her hair. "You can't be serious. Is
Robert all right?"

Annie sat on the sofa. "He's at the dispensary, but he's going to be fine. Fortunately
he received excellent medical care." Thank
God the doctor was nearby, saving precious
time.

She took hold of Miss Walker's hands. The
palms were calloused, the nails square cut,
and the skin brown as old leather and
almost as tough.

"Was it something he ate? I told him not
to eat any beef but mine." Miss Walker's
voice held its usual sharp edge and only the
tremor and coldness of her hands gave her
away.

"It wasn't beef." Annie hesitated. "Dr.

Fairbanks believes it was arsenic."

"Arsenic!" Miss Walker pulled her hands away. "That means it was no accident."

Annie nodded. "I'm afraid that's exactly what it means."

Miss Walker made a funny choking sound. "But who in heaven's name would want to poison Robert?"

It was a good question and Annie had no answer. Never had she felt so inadequate. "We don't know, but the marshal is doing everything possible to find out."

Miss Walker sniffed. "That old tin badge couldn't catch a wolf in a chicken coop." She would never admit it but she was obviously shaken. Still, Annie had a job to do and there was no time to waste.

"Does Mr. Stackman have any enemies?"

"Of course he has enemies," Miss Walker snapped with an impatient wave. "He's a banker."

Annie debated on how little or how much to say. "I wonder if there's a connection between what happened to Mr. Stackman and what's been happening on the ranch."

Miss Walker's thin brows rose. "Certainly you don't mean the fire and poisoned water?"

"I do. And don't forget someone attacked Mr. Branch." She made no mention of the dead Wells Fargo detective. "Everything that's happened recently, including Mr. Stackman's poisoning, could be the work of a single person."

"But that makes no sense," Miss Walker sputtered. "Robert has no connection to the ranch."

"Except through you," Annie said. "Someone may be trying to get to you through him."

The older woman seemed to shrink before Annie's eyes, as if someone had taken the stuffing out of her. "Why would anyone want to do such a thing?"

"I don't know." That very question had been burning in Annie's mind since Robert collapsed. She and Taggert had discussed it at great length while waiting for the doctor to finish examining the banker. "I have a feeling that once we figure it out we'll have the answer to all our questions."

"Take me to him." Miss Walker reached for her crutches but Annie stayed her.

"There's nothing you can do for him. He's in good hands and he's resting." She searched for something to say, for something to do that would put Miss Walker's mind at ease.

"Would you . . . like to pray with me?"

Miss Walker didn't say anything, but she

didn't resist when Annie took her hands a second time. "God the Father, please comfort and heal Mr. Stackman . . ."

"And tell Him to put an end to all the nonsense that's been going on at the ranch," Miss Walker interjected.

Annie peered at Miss Walker through lowered lashes. "Would you like to tell God that yourself?"

"Why would I want to do that? You're doing just fine." She clamped her mouth shut. After a moment she added, "What are you waiting for? Go on, tell Him."

Annie resumed her prayer. "And please, God, help" — she almost said *me* — "the marshal catch the . . . culprit who's been causing all the trouble at the ranch."

"And tell Him to get on the stick."

Annie opened her mouth to say something but changed her mind. Talking to God through a third person was better than not talking to Him at all. She finished her prayer and released the older woman's hands.

Miss Walker sank back, eyes closed. She claimed that nothing meant as much to her as the ranch, but Annie had seen beyond the rigid exterior. The poisoned cattle and fire hardly fazed her, but she still grieved the loss of her daughter and was clearly shaken by her banker friend's near brush with death.

"If anything happens to Robert . . ." Miss Walker didn't finish; it wasn't necessary.

"I'll have Able make us some tea," Annie said, standing.

The old lady's eyes flew open and the piercing gaze seemed to bore a hole through Annie. "Before you go, answer me one question. Who are you, really?"

Taggert wrapped the reins of his horse around the hitching post in front of the bank. Stackman's medical emergency had postponed their meeting, which meant having to conduct his investigation during bank hours.

Annie was nowhere to be seen. Professionally, he was relieved. Personally? That was another matter. He missed her when she wasn't around and worried about her safety, but nothing he said convinced her to leave the ranch. She was determined to see the job through to the end. *Stubborn woman.*

Stackman greeted him the moment he entered the bank. He still looked a bit peaked around the eyes, but otherwise appeared to have recovered from his ordeal.

Taggert shook the banker's offered hand. "It appears that Miss Beckman won't be joining us."

"Nonsense. She's been here for ages." Stackman turned and led the way through the bank. "Checked out all our customers' shoes."

Taggert winced inwardly. He should have known she would want to get a head start on the investigation. Were his personal feelings making him careless?

"Did you say shoes?"

"Yes. Miss Beckman explained that bank robbers often wear low-heeled shoes so as not to get caught on the metal bar leading to the vault. Did you know that?"

"Can't say that I did." Taggert didn't like having another detective show him up, even one as competent as Annie.

"I'm happy to tell you that all today's customers are well-heeled." Stackman laughed at his own joke and a couple of bank employees looked up to stare from behind the bars of the teller cages.

Stackman ushered Taggert into his office where Annie sat waiting. She quickly closed her notepad and dropped it into her handbag along with her pencil.

Taggert would give anything to see what she'd written. He abandoned his cowboy swagger and donned his efficient detective persona, matching Annie's. It was easier to concentrate that way. He sat in the chair next to hers, careful not to get too close.

"I didn't see your rig," he said.

She afforded him a slanted glance that hid more than it revealed. "I didn't think it wise to let anyone know we were at the bank together."

It never failed to amaze him how her mind worked, but that didn't make him any less concerned for her safety. If only she would listen to him.

Stackman sat on the corner of his desk and folded his arms. "As I was telling Miss Beckman before you arrived, we didn't even know we'd been robbed until we counted the money after closing."

"Even so, I don't believe it's an inside job," Annie added.

"We can't rule it out," Taggert said, though he suspected Annie was right; most dishonest bank clerks targeted customers, not the bank. It was a simple matter to shortchange a distracted client either at the teller booth or counting table. "Show us where the robbery occurred."

"This way." Stackman slid off the desk and opened a second door.

They followed him down a hall to the bank vault behind the cashier cages. It was an older vault with concrete walls, typical of the kind prevalent in most western towns.

Eastern banks had newer vaults with combination locks and cast-iron doors that, unlike the cheaper metal doors, were torch-proof.

Without such modern amenities, this particular strong room offered better protection against fires than thievery.

"This is the day door," Stackman explained. "After hours we set the night door."

Taggert examined the lock. "Who has access?"

"Each teller has a key." He pulled out his own key and opened the door. "As you can see, the door has a spring lock. It locks by itself." He swung the door shut to demonstrate.

Taggert put his hand out to Annie. "Quick, give me your hair clasp," he said beneath his breath.

Without question or argument, Annie reached for the wooden barrette holding her bun and handed it to him. Her fingers brushed his and their gazes caught. Her hair stayed in place, but the memory of lush dark tresses falling to her shoulders flashed through his mind, along with the kiss that had followed.

Forcing the memory away, Taggert turned to Stackman. "Pretend you're a teller. Go to the vault. Show us how it's done."

Stackman inserted the key into the keyhole

and unlocked the door. The tall heel of his shoe caught on the iron bar as he stepped inside. Taggert glanced at Annie but said nothing.

The door swung shut and locked. After a moment, Stackman opened the door and emerged. Before it locked, Taggert quickly inserted Annie's hair clasp in the casing. This he did with such finesse that Stackman didn't seem to notice — but Annie did.

Taggert would have missed the quick upturn of her mouth had he not been looking straight at her.

"So what do you think?" Stackman asked.

Before Taggert could reply, a bespectacled young man dressed in dark trousers, vest, and bow tie called to Stackman. "Sir, I need your signature."

"Excuse me," Stackman said and walked away.

Taggert pushed the vault door open. Annie's hair clip fell to the floor and he scooped it up with one quick move and slid it into his vest pocket. He then took Annie's hand and pulled her inside the concrete vault. He closed the door but didn't shut it all the way. A stream of light filtered through the crack.

In such close quarters, he could smell her sweet lavender fragrance.

"Very clever of you," she said softly.

"An old trick," he said without the least bit of modesty.

"Do you think this was the work of the Phantom?" Only half of her face was visible in the vault's dim light, but it was enough to know that she had not dropped her professional air.

He narrowed his eyes. He ached to reach beyond her studied expression. Longed for those dark eyes of hers to gaze at the man and not the detective.

"Maybe," he said, his voice hoarse. "Maybe not."

She gazed up at him through a fringe of dark lashes. "How can you be so sure?" she teased.

His grin was rewarded with a smile that practically turned his heart inside out. He felt himself sink into the velvet softness of her eyes and everything went out of his head but her nearness.

"If I kiss you, will you still accuse me of having ulterior motives?" he asked.

"Probably," she whispered and in a stronger voice added, "Yes."

Then she did something totally unexpected. She threw her arms around his neck and kissed him fully on the mouth.

He crushed her in his embrace and her

hat went flying. Hands pressed against her back, he smothered her lips with an urgency that left them both breathless.

He pulled his mouth away but only to brush kisses across her silky smooth forehead. "Who are you?" he whispered, burying his face in her sweet-scented hair.

"What kind of question is that?" With her arms still around his neck, her expression seemed to beckon for more. "You know who I am."

He kissed her again before answering. "You know my real name, but I don't know yours." It suddenly seemed imperative that he know everything about her.

She hesitated and he knew why. An undercover agent could never be too careful.

"Miranda," she whispered.

At that moment he knew that she trusted him, not only with her name but with her life. No one had ever given him a greater gift. "Miranda," he lipped silently to show he would never betray that trust by saying her name aloud. He pulled her closer still and could feel her heart beat next to his.

She nestled her head against his chest. "Hunt. Miranda Hunt."

No sooner were the words out of her mouth than he felt like the ground had caved beneath his feet. Had she suddenly stabbed him with a knife the pain wouldn't have been more intense.

He pulled back and stared at her. "Hunt?"

She nodded. "It's a good name for an operative, don't you think?"

It can't be. God, don't do this to me. "Your father . . . ?"

"My father's name was Charles Hunt." She tilted her head and her smile died. She said something more, but his mind was a blank. "Is . . . something wrong?"

He worked a finger along his collar but he still couldn't breathe. Feeling as if the walls of the safe were closing in, he tore open the door and staggered out of the vault.

Stackman's mouth dropped open. "How did you get in there?"

Taggert moved as far away as possible from Annie. He needed air. He needed to think. "An old t-trick," he stammered.

"It would seem Mr. Taggert is full of tricks," Annie said, her face suffused with confusion and hurt.

Stackman's gaze swung from Annie back to Branch as if he sensed the strain between them. "I'll instruct my tellers to make certain that the door is closed and locked before they leave."

"The Phantom seldom uses the same M.O. twice," Annie said. The banker didn't seem to notice the tremor in her voice but Taggert did. "That's what makes him so difficult to catch."

"M.O.?"

"Sorry." She took in a deep breath as if trying to brace herself. "*Modus operandi.* It's a method of operation. Like a calling card. We're all creatures of habit, and that includes criminals. But in this case, no one *modus operandi* has been established. Salt, fire, and arsenic hardly sound like the workings of one man."

"Which means what, exactly?"

"It means that if this is the work of a single man, he's extremely clever," she explained. "Or there's a pattern we've yet to identify."

While Annie and Stackman talked, Taggert's thoughts shot back in time three years to that fateful day that made him question himself and God's purpose for him. He had been dispatched to the Wells Fargo bank in Chicago. He worked the case for two weeks before finally catching one of the bank clerks stealing notes from an unsuspecting customer. His name was Sam Vander.

Taggert had stepped in front of Vander, badge in hand. The man panicked and ran. Taggert chased after him. Vander dashed outside the bank just as a band of union picketers walked by.

"Don't let him get away," Taggert yelled.

Vander pulled out a gun, and in the scuffle that followed, a shot was fired and what turned out to be a Pinkerton undercover operative fell to the ground. Taggert now knew that man was Annie's father.

The death of an innocent man took a toll on him and reminded him in the worst possible way of his own father's death. He'd joined the agency to protect people like his father, who was shot down for no reason; instead he caused an innocent man's death. For two years he refused to accept an assignment, choosing instead to work at a desk.

"Branch?"

Startled, Taggert looked up to find Annie and Stackman staring at him. "I'm sorry —"

"I was just asking what we should do to increase security," Stackman said.

"Uh . . ." Taggert cleared his throat. "Just stay alert. It might be a good idea to post someone by the door to keep watch."

Two lines of worry filled the space between Stackman's eyebrows. "I'll be sure to keep my guard up. You too. Both of you. I don't want to lose another detective."

Annie drove the wagon back to the ranch.

Her heart still raced with the memory of Taggert's kiss. So what happened?

After their meeting with Stackman, he refused to look her in the eyes. Even more puzzling, he took off without so much as a good-bye.

She went over every word exchanged in the bank vault, every look, every nuance. Something had triggered a strong reaction in him, but what? Certainly not their kiss.

"If I kiss you, would you still accuse me of having ulterior motives?" Her pulse skittered.

A sudden thought made her yank on the reins to slow the horse. Had he figured out who the Phantom was? That would certainly explain his haste in leaving the bank and why he refused to look at her. The thought nearly crushed her. Was all that business of working together just a ruse?

He wanted to catch the Phantom and evidently would do anything to reach that goal — even if it meant using her. To think otherwise was just plain foolish.

Taggert wasn't a drinker. No detective could afford to take a liking to alcohol, but today he was tempted. Something had to dull the pain that seared through him like a piercing bullet.

Miranda *Hunt.* He couldn't believe it.

367

The saloon was crowded, a lively game of faro in progress. He bellied up to the bar and the bartender placed a shot of whiskey in front of him. Taggert picked up the glass but memories of Annie were reflected in the amber liquid.

She would never forgive him. How could she? Her father was cut down in the prime of life, because of him.

The image of Charlie Hunt lying on the ground in a pool of blood would forever be engraved on his mind. At the time, he thought the dead man was another rioting union worker. He didn't find out he was an undercover Pinkerton operative until much later.

He had wanted to quit then and there, but his boss talked him out of it. "You're a good detective. We need you."

"Good detectives don't get innocent people killed," he'd argued, but in the end he stayed. Instead of field work he settled for an office job. He handled stagecoach holdup reports and dispatched detectives as needed. He also sent out wanted posters and issued reward checks.

He'd asked for God's forgiveness and through God's grace had learned to live with his guilt . . . more or less. Nothing he did could justify an innocent man's death, but upon learning of his friend's disappearance he pledged himself anew to physically fighting crime. His days of hiding behind a desk were over.

It was a decision he now regretted. Learning the dead man's identity was horrific enough, but nothing compared to finding out that Annie was the man's daughter. Had Hunt reached from the grave to seek revenge, he couldn't have exerted worse torture.

Taggert shook the glass and the amber liquid whirled around. *Annie . . .*

Every moment spent with her left him wanting more. He admired her intensity when she puzzled over something. Loved the rare occasions she dropped her professional persona and allowed him to see the passionate, beautiful woman beneath the cool exterior. At such times her eyes lit up whenever they met his.

They did light up, didn't they? Or was it his imagination playing tricks on him? Crimes must be solved, a friend's killer brought to justice, and here he was thinking of Annie yet again — the last woman in the world he should be thinking about.

If only he hadn't kissed her; if only he hadn't held her in his arms. Perhaps then he would be better able to put her out of his mind.

With a groan, he slammed the shot glass down, spilling the untouched whiskey. He then tossed a bill on the counter and stomped outside.

CHAPTER 27

"Elementary, my dear Watson."

Annie couldn't sleep. Instead she stood on the balcony staring out at the thick darkness of night. She wanted to talk to Taggert in the worst possible way, but it seemed as if he had purposely avoided her.

Shivering, she walked inside, closed the glass door, and lit the kerosene lamp. She reached for her GTF file and flipped through the pages until she found her favorite scriptures.

She traced her finger over the sentence written in cryptic. *"I was blind, now I see."* It seemed like the perfect biblical verse for a private eye. She closed her eyes and forced herself to concentrate on the words. *But, God, what don't I see?* Something . . .

So many questions; so many unsolved puzzles, but none had anything to do with her low spirits. What depressed her —

scared her — was the gnawing suspicion that no amount of problem solving or detective work could fill the empty hole that festered inside.

For as long as she could remember it seemed as if part of her was missing. At first she blamed it on her mother's early death. During her teens she was convinced her father's aloofness created the void inside. Later she blamed it on a lack of meaningful work assignments. The petty thief cases assigned to her weren't challenging enough. What she needed and wanted was to sink her teeth into a "real" case. Then the hollow in her heart would go away — or so she thought.

Her current assignment had turned out to be more challenging than she ever could have imagined and it had truly fulfilled her, at least for a while. But then Taggert entered the picture and the feeling of emptiness became want . . . and want became need.

"I was blind . . ."

When she was a child she heard the minister of their church talk about God's plan and she asked him what that meant.

"How do you know what God's plan is?" She still remembered her pastor's answer.

"Follow the joy. You know God's plan by doing the things that give you great joy."

The day she told her father she intended to follow in his footsteps would forever be ingrained. "You're a girl," he said as coldly as a tormentor might point out a cripple's useless legs.

"I wouldn't be the first woman in the agency," she'd argued. That honor went to Kate Warne, who joined the firm in '55 and was instrumental in helping the agency's founder foil a plot to assassinate Lincoln.

Her line of reasoning held no water with him and he continued to ignore her. It was her brother Travis who taught her to use a gun, ride a horse, and defend herself.

"Are you sure you want to do this, sis?" he asked one day after sneaking up behind and grabbing her by the waist.

She reached for his hand and bent back his finger.

"Ow!" he cried, letting her go.

She whirled to face him. Her brother had taught her well and she was ready to tackle the world. "Yes, I want to do this." She would prove to her father she was every bit as capable of being an operative as a man. Maybe then he would see her, not as a child to ignore, but as the woman she had become.

William Pinkerton hired her on the spot, but only because she was Charlie Hunt's daughter.

By the time her father learned that she had joined the firm, she had already completed the extensive training program, which included dramatizations of crime scenes and lessons on disguises. He stormed into the principal's office and their raised voices could be heard throughout the building, but William Pinkerton's decision prevailed and Miranda was allowed to stay.

From that moment on, she never questioned God's will for her. She was certain that God had removed the blinders from her eyes so she could follow the path He had set for her.

If only she hadn't met Taggert. If only she hadn't experienced such joy when they were together. Like a thief in the night, he stole her heart and all that remained now was an empty space. She didn't know exactly when or how it happened, but there it was, plain as day.

Years of training had taught her to control her feelings. She learned to control body language, words, and facial expressions so as to conceal her true identity. But the womanly part — the part that craved Taggert's touch and kisses — that part she didn't know how to control.

But she had to find a way. Otherwise her

goal of restoring the Hunt name to its former glory as Pinkerton's best and finest would be in jeopardy.

She stared at the open Bible in her hands, but no answers materialized. It was as if God had snatched the road map of her life away and purposely left her in the wilderness to fend for herself.

She set the Good Book on the desk with a sigh and reached for the dime novel purchased at the church bazaar. Perhaps a little light reading would put her mind to rest and help her sleep. There was nothing to do until she could talk to Taggert.

For the next hour she was thoroughly engaged with the lively story.

Miss Hattie's Dilemma was a romantic tale of a woman torn between two men, but it was also a story of the lust for gold. Mrs. Kate Adams, who wrote under the pseudonym K. Mattson, was a good writer. Descriptions of the cave where gold was found seemed so real it felt like Annie was there on the spot. She could almost hear the drip of water, see the indentations on the cave wall, the light in the dark tunnel.

Feel the kiss . . .

Startled, Annie dropped the book on her lap. Maybe the cave seemed familiar for a reason.

The cave in Kate's novel was almost identical to the cave on Miss Walker's ranch. She shook her head — that was crazy. This was fiction, pure and simple, written before its author even set foot in Arizona Territory.

Shaking the thought away, Annie turned the page and tried to concentrate, but the words kept blurring together. Flashes of memory bombarded her. Was it just coincidence that a copy of the book had lain in plain sight on the cave floor?

Work the clues. How often had she heard William Pinkerton utter those very words?

Go back to the beginning.

She considered everything that had happened during the past several weeks. The mysterious lights, the poisoned cattle, the fire, Mr. Stackman, even the train and bank robberies. Slowly, the crazy, mixed-up puzzle pieces fell into place and a disturbing picture began to emerge.

She jumped out of bed and threw on her clothes. Fingers trembling, she had trouble fastening the hooks and eyes at her waist, and it took every bit of effort to buckle the holster around her thigh.

In her hurry, she accidentally knocked her GTF file on the floor. She stooped to pick it up and her gaze fell on the verse *"I was blind, now I see . . ."*

She dropped the folder on the desk. Indeed she did see, and what she saw, she didn't like.

William Pinkerton accused her of taking unnecessary risks, but she had no intention of doing so tonight. There was too much at stake. She needed Taggert's help. More than that, she *wanted* his help.

She crept along the hallway in the dark. She stopped to listen but could hear nothing over the sound of her pounding heart. She treaded ever so carefully down the stairs and avoided the middle where they were most likely to creak.

Reaching the bottom, she felt her way through the darkness to the telephone. She lifted the receiver to her ear and turned the crank. She hated waking Aunt Bessie in the wee morning hours, but she didn't dare leave the house. Through the horn-shaped receiver plastered to her ear came a ringing sound that seemed to go on forever.

"Come on, come on," she muttered beneath her breath. "Answer."

The incessant ringing of the switchboard woke Bessie out of a deep slumber. Ignoring it, she buried her head beneath her pillow. It was probably some lovesick goon calling and wanting to be connected to his lady friend.

It was shameful, that's what it was, the goings-on in this town. Men calling women, women calling men, and it didn't seem to matter what time it was. When she first agreed to be the hello girl, she was told the phone would be used primarily for emergencies. *Ha! Emergencies, my foot!*

She turned over and gave her pillow a good thump, but it did no good; the switchboard kept ringing and her husband kept snoring and her overactive mind began to imagine the most awful things. What if it really was an emergency?

Finally she slipped out of bed, but more out of curiosity than a sense of responsibility. Walking barefooted from the bedroom to the dining room, she paused to light a lamp.

"All right, all right. Hold your horses." She sat on the stool and donned her earphones. Much to her surprise, it was the Last Chance calling. The main house, no less.

"What num-BER?"

"Please connect me to the bunkhouse."

Bessie Adams recognized the hushed voice immediately. She glanced at the long clock in the corner of the room. It was a little after 2:00 a.m. "At this time of night? What is it with women today? Why, in my day —"

"It's Annie. Please hurry. It's urgent!"

The line suddenly went dead. Bessie played with the switch, checked the jack, and tried ringing the ranch number back with no luck.

She slammed her headset down. For this she was awakened from a sound sleep! She knew something was going on between Annie and that new man, Branch, and now her suspicions were confirmed. A body would have had to be blind not to notice the way the two gazed at each other at the church bazaar, or how they snuck off together afterward. No wonder Annie's nose was out of joint when Bessie suggested she introduce Branch to Charity.

"*Harrumph!* If Mr. Bell knew how his instrument would be put to use, he might have thought twice about inventing it."

She turned off the lamp and shuffled back to bed. Tomorrow she'd ask her nephew to check the new lines going out to the ranch for problems. Then she intended to give Annie a motherly talk.

Her husband, Sam, snorted twice and rolled over. "Who was calling at this hour?"

"Don't worry about it. Go back to sleep."

The line dead in her ear, Annie dropped

the receiver. A man's form stood no less than ten feet away. Though it was dark, she knew immediately who it was. She reached into her false pocket for her gun.

"Hello, Able."

He stepped forward into the circle of moonlight streaming through a narrow window.

"How did you know?"

Something in her voice must have told him it would do no good to act innocent. She pulled her derringer slowly out of her pocket, careful to keep it hidden behind the folds of her skirt. "That you're the Phantom?"

"How did you know?" he repeated.

In retrospect, there had been so many clues, but she had failed to put them together.

"The night of the fire. Something always bothered me about that night, but I couldn't put my finger on it. You and I reached the front door at the same time, but you went out first. I always turn the lock before retiring, but the door wasn't locked when you went out. That meant that someone had left the house prior to the fire, and that someone could only have been you."

"Foiled by a lock," he said.

"That wasn't the only thing. You always

go to town on Tuesday for supplies," she said.

"So? What does that have to do with anything?"

"I arrived at the ranch on a Thursday and you were nowhere to be found. I rang the bell and called, but the house was empty. It turns out that was the same day the bank was robbed."

"Go on."

"Then there was the night Branch and I were at the cave. We heard someone leave, but when I checked the horses, none appeared to have been ridden. That bothered me, but I think I solved the puzzle. The day in the garden when you were digging for carrots, I noticed an old barn. That's where I'll find your horse. Am I right?"

"No one uses that barn anymore. Miz Walker said I could keep my horse there."

"Then there was the dime novel. I first saw it in the kitchen but it never occurred to me that the one in the cave was the same copy."

"How careless of me."

"Yes, wasn't it?" Her mouth dry, she forced herself to continue. "What I don't understand is the significance of the book. It's fiction."

"That's what I thought. But then one day

I happened to come across the cave and what do you know? It was almost identical to the one in the book. So I started digging."

Another piece of the puzzle fell into place and she nodded. "And you found something."

"I found gold, just like it said in the book."

"Then why bother with robberies?" she asked. "If you found gold, you're already rich."

"Not me. Miss Walker. The gold belongs to the boss lady."

Ah, more pieces of the puzzle. "So you decided to buy the ranch," she said. "And you needed money. But why rob? Why not just mine the gold?"

"To mine that much gold I'd need proper equipment, and that would have drawn attention to the cave."

"You had to have known Miss Walker would never sell."

"Everyone's got a price, and I figured Miz Walker couldn't hold out forever. Once the ranch was mine, I could start mining."

"But you couldn't do it on your current salary," she said. "So you hired others to do the dirty work."

"Yeah, but it took too long. That's 'cause they were cheating me out of money. So I got rid of them."

"By getting rid of them, you mean you called the marshal." How the marshal knew to greet the train always puzzled her. "That's why he was waiting for them when the train pulled into the station."

"They got what was coming to them." He shrugged. "Besides, it was quicker and more lucrative to rob the bank. Didn't need anyone for that. What I needed was the ranch."

"But Miss Walker refused to sell, so you decided to scare her off by poisoning her cattle and burning down the barn and stables." When he didn't deny it, she continued, "What about the Wells Fargo agent? Why did you kill him?"

"I didn't know who he was. All's I know, he was following me."

His matter-of-fact tone filled her with contempt. Sometimes criminals were found in the most unlikely places. In the last year alone, the agency had uncovered a pickpocket priest, a counterfeiting doctor, and an arsonist fireman. Still, it was hard to believe that the same hands that created such delectably light pastry could kill a man in cold blood.

"What about Branch? Why did you knock him out?"

"He's been nosing around and I figured he wasn't who he said he was. I don't know where he was heading, but I sure didn't want him going back to the cave."

"And Mr. Stackman? How does he fit into the picture?"

"Everyone knows he wants the old lady to sell the ranch and marry him. I figured if she thought she was gonna lose him, it might scare her into taking him up on his offer."

"You thought of everything, didn't you?" she asked. "Except for this." She raised her arm and pointed her gun straight at him.

At that moment, the light came on in the big room, revealing the gun in Able's hand.

Undaunted, she said, "Drop it!"

He gave her gun a cursory glance. "My barking iron's bigger than yours."

Just then Miss Walker hobbled into the entry on crutches, her gaze darting from gun to gun. It was obvious she'd been sleeping on the sofa in the big room. Less obvious was how much she'd heard.

"What in the name of Betsy —"

In one quick movement Able wrapped his arm around the old lady's neck and pressed the muzzle of his gun against her temple. Miss Walker's crutches fell to the floor with a clatter.

He glared at Annie. "Now will you drop that can opener you call a gun?"

Annie lowered her weapon to the floor.

Miss Walker's face grew red from the pressure of his arm and her eyes bulged. "What is wrong with you, Able? What's going on? Answer me!"

His laughter held no mirth. "I have the gun, so that means for once I give the orders, not you. Once again I'm the king of the range. Me!"

His manic voice made Annie's flesh prickle with cold shivers but she willed herself to remain calm. The freckles she once thought gave him a boyish look now stood out like angry ink blots. How had she previously missed the cruel, tight mouth and cold, fish-stare eyes?

He backed into the living room, dragging Miss Walker with him, and motioned Annie to follow with a toss of his head. He glanced around, face grim, a wild look in his eyes. He made no effort at deception now, although he'd certainly managed to dupe everyone in the past with his easygoing manner and fine cookery.

"Pull the cords off the draperies," he ordered, and Annie did as she was told. She could hardly do anything else, not with a gun pointed at Miss Walker's head.

He forced the ranch owner down onto a ladder-back chair. "Now tie her hands and feet," he ordered.

Miss Walker glared at him. "You can't do this. You're the cook."

His eyes glittered. "And you're the goose."

Annie kneeled in front of Miss Walker. "Sorry," she mouthed.

Able kept his gun pointed at her while she wound the cord around Miss Walker's one good leg and cast. Just as Annie tied the last knot, someone pounded on the door.

"Annie!"

It was Taggert. Relief escaped in one long breath. Never did she think to hear a more welcome sound.

Able momentarily froze. With a shake of his head he motioned her with his gun. "Make him go away."

Wiping damp hands on her skirt, Annie rose and walked out of the big room, through the entryway, and to the door. The lock designed to keep intruders out now seemed like a coffin nail keeping them in.

She leaned her forehead against the wood. "It's late . . . What . . ." She glanced over her shoulder and Able motioned her to continue with a wave of his gun.

She faced the door. "What do you want?"

"Annie, are you all right?" Taggert called,

his husky voice failing to mute his concern. "Mrs. Adams asked me to check. She said you tried to reach the bunkhouse and it sounded urgent."

When she didn't respond, Able moved so close she could feel his breath in her hair.

"Get rid of him." He slammed the muzzle of his gun into her back. Startled, she gasped and squeezed her eyes shut.

Swallowing hard to clear her voice, she called, "Everything's all right. I thought I heard something, but it was just . . . nothing." *Keep talking, got to keep talking.* "I couldn't sleep and —"

"Annie, we need to talk about what happened earlier —"

"Make him go away," Able growled. "Now!"

Her heart pounded and she was shaking so hard her knees threatened to buckle. She placed her hand on the door for support. For some reason the action reminded her of the day Taggert held her palm to her desk.

"GTF? Give to Phantom?" he'd asked.

"You really ought to work on your spelling," she'd said.

The memory gave her an idea. "You've . . . Got . . . To . . . Forget." She emphasized each word, spacing them out evenly. Such an unnatural speech rhythm would alert a

Pinkerton operative, but would a Wells Fargo agent detect her plea for help?

She held her breath and waited. The silence that followed seemed to stretch on forever, sapping her of all but the slightest hope.

Apparently satisfied that the immediate threat had been resolved, Able gestured her back to the big room. Reluctantly she pulled away from the door.

CHAPTER 28

Every cattle rustler, horse thief, and crooked politician deserves a fair trial, followed by a respectful hanging.

Taggert pressed his hand hard against the door. It was as if some magnetic force held his palm in place. Even with a thick wood plank between them, he could feel her presence, and when he closed his eyes he could visualize her. *You've got to forget.*

Forget? What exactly did she want him to forget? That he was responsible for her father's death? But how would she know that? No, it couldn't be that. It had to be something else. His friend's death? Work related, perhaps?

Maybe it was their kisses she wanted him to forget. Or the way she felt in his arms. No matter; he could no sooner forget the few precious moments he'd held her than he could forget his own name.

The truth was, he had fallen head over heels in love with her and nothing would make him forget that.

He pulled away from the door and headed back to the bunkhouse. *God, why did You do this to me? All the women in the world I could have loved — why did it have to be the one woman who would never forgive me enough to love me back?*

The drapery cords cut into Annie's flesh. Able had tied her to a chair, the rope so tight around her chest she couldn't breathe. It took every bit of strength she possessed to wiggle her body; the chair moved but the cords remained intact.

Hands damp from gripping the palm nippers, she continued working. Confiscated from the New Orleans Society Thief, the tool was designed to cut through delicate chains. The tiny wire clippers were a boon to pickpockets, but they weren't much help in cutting through thick cord. She finally resorted to moving the blade back and forth in a sawing motion.

"He's crazier than a sheepherder," Miss Walker hissed. Able was in her office, and by the sound of the slamming drawers, he was searching for something. This seemed to annoy her more than being bound hand

and foot. "What is he looking for?"

"I don't know." Annie held the palm nippers still. The cord cut into her flesh with each sawing motion. The pain shot up her arms and brought tears to her eyes. She gripped the clippers tighter and again attacked the cord. The woven cloth cable was thin, yet strong enough to swing a locomotive.

"I was good to that man," Miss Walker muttered. "I hired him and gave him a home. I never thought —"

Annie grimaced. She couldn't blame Miss Walker. If two trained detectives couldn't see past the ruse, how could anyone else?

"Gold" — gritting her teeth, she worked the palm nippers harder — "does strange things to a person's mind."

Miss Walker's head spun in her direction. "What are you talking about? Gold?"

Annie quickly filled her in the best she could without going into details. She kept her voice low and spoke quickly. "That's why he's been trying to buy your ranch." She stopped sawing to catch her breath.

Miss Walker's eyes widened. "There's gold on my property? But this is a cattle ranch."

"Shh." Annie glanced at the office door. "I don't think the cattle care one way or another."

"But I don't understand. How could Able afford to buy my ranch? None of this makes sense." Miss Walker's voice was low but didn't waver. Did she not understand the dire predicament they were in?

Annie pressed the tiny clippers harder. "Mostly by robbing banks and hiring others to rob trains and stages."

"Are you saying that *he's* the Phantom?"

"That's exactly what I'm saying."

"Well, he sure fooled me." Miss Walker snapped her mouth shut.

"He fooled all of us." Annie pressed harder still and the clippers cut into her hand. Thank God Papa couldn't see her now. The thought gave her pause; she was no longer a little girl needing her father's approval. Come to think of it, she hadn't been for a very long time.

She continued hacking at the cord behind her back. *Please, please help us!* She glanced at the ranch owner. *And, God, please get on the stick.*

Miss Walker studied her. "Are you all right?"

Annie clenched her mouth tight. "I. Will. Be."

"I still can't believe that Able —" She narrowed her eyes. "How do you know all this?"

"I'm a Pinkerton operative. I was sent

here to work undercover."

Miss Walker stared speechless while Annie explained how Kate Adams's dime novel helped solve the mystery. The cord gave way and in her haste to work her hands free, she dropped the clippers and they fell on the rug by her chair.

"I don't know what surprises me more," Miss Walker lamented. "To find out that my cook is the Phantom or my heiress is a detective." She shook her head. "What I don't understand is how Kate knew about the gold."

With one eye on the office and the other on the clippers in plain sight, Annie unraveled the rest of the cord. "I don't believe she did. She wrote the book before coming to Arizona. The cave she described in her novel just happened to match one on your ranch. After reading the book, Able decided to do some digging. He got lucky."

The cord fell away, but before she could reach for the clippers, Able walked into the room. Annie froze and Miss Walker clamped her mouth shut.

The palm-sized clippers on the floor seemed to stand out like a blaze of light. How could he not see them?

Behind her back she rubbed the rope burns on her wrists and tried to think. Her hands were free but her feet were still tied. Pinkerton operatives were taught how to avoid such situations, not how to escape them.

Able barely glanced her way before turning his attention to Miss Walker. "I don't know what it is about this place, but someone keeps walking off with the pens. Do you ladies know where I can find something to write with?"

Miss Walker threw back her head and let go a string of curses that could fry bacon. "What do you want a pen for?"

He thrust a paper in the ranch owner's face. "So you can sign this bill of sale giving me full ownership of the ranch."

Miss Walker clenched her jaw. "Over my dead body."

Able straightened. "First things first. You sign." He pointed his gun at her. "Then we'll discuss the rest."

Considering her dire situation, Miss Walker continued to keep her calm demeanor. "You'll never get away with this."

"Oh, I think I will. After Mr. Stackman was taken ill, you decided there were other things in life besides cattle. So you finally agreed to sell your ranch, and then when you realized what you'd done, you decided to end it all." He looked straight at Annie.

"You tried to take the gun away from Miss Walker but — oops! — it went off and you both ended up knockin' on the pearly gates." An evil smile followed his words. "What do you think?"

"I think you've been reading too many dime novels," Annie said. *Got to keep him talking.* "No one would believe such a story." Certainly Taggert wouldn't.

"Of course they'll believe it. Everyone knows how much this ranch means to the boss lady."

"That's why no one will believe she sold it," Annie said.

Able faked a sad face. "And she never would have, had Mr. Stackman not visited death's doorstep."

Annie blew out her breath. The man's brain fairly dripped with dime novel phrases, but the plan was clearly his own.

"You forgot one thing," she said. "People might wonder how you could afford to purchase the ranch on a cook's salary."

"Oh dear. That *is* a problem." He thought for a moment. "How about this? My uncle recently died. The war affected his mind . . . yes, that works. Everyone thought him dirt-poor but he left piles of money hidden under the mattress. Old war wounds make people do the strangest things."

Annie's spirits plummeted. He just might get away with his crazy plan.

"All right, ladies, let's start again. Where can I find a pen?"

Annie's mind raced. "There's one upstairs. On the desk in my room." If she could get him to leave the room for even a few moments, she might be able to free her legs. Taggert's habit of stealing pens might be a lifesaver.

Able's gaze shifted back and forth between them. "Don't go anywhere, you hear?"

He shoved his gun in his waistband and left the room.

"You've got to forget . . ."

Taggert turned over in bed. Annie's voice kept repeating in his head. Something . . .

"You've got to forget . . ."

It seemed like a strange thing to say to a Wells Fargo agent, whose very motto is *never* to forget. He flopped over again, the cot squeaking beneath his weight. Even if he hadn't been indoctrinated with company policy, he could never forget Annie. Didn't want to forget her.

He frowned. *Got to forget . . . got to forget . . . got —*

He sat up. *Got . . . To . . . Forget: GTF!*

"Is he the big man?" he'd asked Annie,

referring to the manila folder he found on her desk.

"Most definitely," she'd replied.

He jumped up off his cot and stubbed his toe. Hopping around on one foot, he reached for his trousers. "Stretch. Wishbone, Feedbag, Michael, wake up!"

Annie retrieved the clippers and frantically hacked at the cords around her ankles.

"He's coming," Miss Walker said, keeping her voice low.

Annie quickly straightened and flung her hands behind the back of her chair. Her heart pounded and beads of sweat rolled down the sides of her face.

Able walked into the room waving a pen. His face looked flushed and his reddish hair stood up on end. "Success!" he announced. "Now we can get down to business." He pulled out a knife and worked on the cords at Miss Walker's wrists.

A pounding on the door was followed by Taggert's voice. "Annie!" He pounded again.

Able dropped his knife and reached for his firearm.

Fearing that Taggert was about to break down the door, Annie screamed, "Watch out! He's got a gun!"

Swinging his body around, the cook glanced about the room, eyes darting.

The banging increased. "Open up!"

Able slammed his back flat against the wall. He held his gun with both hands, the barrel pointing upward.

"You'd best give yourself up," Annie said. "You'll never get away now."

"Shut up!" He stuck his gun in his waistband and pulled a second knife from his boot. He started toward her and she drew in her breath.

Taggert's hammering fists now caused the windows to rattle and a wall hanging crashed to the floor. Eyes filled with panic, Able hesitated for a moment, knife posed, then spun around and dashed from the room.

While Stretch and the others covered the front of the house, Taggert raced around the side to the back. A door opened and someone stepped out.

"Put your hands up!" Taggert yelled.

The man fired a shot before disappearing inside. Bent at the waist, Taggert raced to the door and grabbed the knob; it held tight. He hadn't been able to identify the gunman in the dark, but it had to be either the cook or Ruckus. All the other men had been in the bunkhouse with him.

He kicked an imaginary rock and a silent cry rose from his depths. *Not again, God, not again.* He'd caused Charlie Hunt's death, but he had no intention of letting anything happen to the man's daughter.

"Psst. Is that you, Branch?" The hushed voice belonged to Michael.

"It's me."

"You okay?"

"Yeah," Taggert said. *As okay as possible under the circumstances.* "Stay here and keep watch. I'm going in."

He holstered his gun and patted his shirt pockets, hoping to find a pen. Instead he found Annie's barrette — the one he could never bring himself to return. It was just what he needed. He straightened the clip and, working blindly in the dark, finally managed to fit the pin into the lock. It took some jiggling but the tumblers clicked and the door sprang open. He shoved the barrette back into his pocket and pulled out his gun.

Walking on the balls of his feet, he stalked quietly through the dark kitchen and down the hall. The big room was lit and light spilled into the entry. He paused, his body alert. Only the sound of his pounding heart broke the silence. Where was she? *God, let her be all right.*

Sweat trickled on his forehead. He crept past the stairs.

The telephone receiver dangled from its cord. He stopped to pick up Annie's gun and stuffed it in his waistband. He stepped over Miss Walker's crutches.

His back against the wall separating the big room from the entry, he held his Peacemaker in both hands. He waited a beat, then whirled his body into the doorway. Both women were tied to chairs but he only had eyes for one.

"Annie!"

She greeted him with a smile. "It's about time you got here, partner."

Never could he think to see a more welcome sight. He glanced around. "Where?" he mouthed.

She lifted her gaze to the ceiling. "Upstairs."

He stuffed his firearm in his holster and set to work. Dropping on one knee in front of her, he drew a knife from his boot and cut the cord away from her ankles.

She practically threw herself in his arms. "I was so afraid you wouldn't understand my cryptic message." Her voice was hoarse and he could feel her tremble.

Holding her tight, he buried his nose into

400

the sweet fragrance of her hair and cursed himself for not understanding sooner. "Thank God you're all right. But . . . who . . . ?"

"Able."

He drew back. "But how — ?"

Speaking in a whisper, she quickly filled in the details.

He shook his head. Hard to believe. To think that his friend's killer had been under his very nose all these weeks. Still, it made some sort of crazy sense. "But why did he poison Stackman?" he asked, his voice low.

"Everyone knows that Miss Walker refuses to marry him because of the ranch."

His mind raced. "But if she thought she'd almost lost him for good —"

"Exactly. She would sell the ranch and marry him. At least that's what Able hoped." Her gaze softened. "I thought I'd never see you again . . ."

He grimaced. "If he had hurt one hair on your head . . ."

Miss Walker's strident voice cut through their hushed whispers. "Now that we've established that you two are glad to see each other, would you mind giving an old lady a hand?"

Annie inhaled and pulled out of his arms.

"Here." He put Annie's gun in her hands.

"You might need this." As an afterthought he added, "Partner."

He hurried over to Miss Walker and cut through the cords on her hands and feet. She rubbed her good ankle. "Don't tell me you're a Pinkerton detective too."

"Wells Fargo," he said.

Miss Walker groaned. "Next you'll be telling me that my cattle are really sheep."

He slipped his knife in his boot and pulled out his gun. He checked the entry before walking out to fetch her crutches.

A moment later he was by Annie's side.

"You okay?" he asked.

Nodding, Annie flexed her foot in an effort to get the blood flowing. She glanced at the ceiling but all was quiet. "Do you think he's still in the house?"

"The house is surrounded. He can't get away." His gaze flew to the open office door. "Take Miss Walker in there and lock the door. Don't leave until I tell you it's safe."

Her eyes flashed. "And miss all the action? I certainly will not!"

He frowned. It was no time to argue. "Annie —"

"Don't you 'Annie' me." Her hushed voice failed to dampen the angry sparks. "I have a job to do and I intend to do it."

402

"Wells Fargo takes priority over a Pinkerton."

"Since when?"

"Since I said so."

She tossed her head and the look on her face made him wish she wasn't carrying a gun. "I'm the one who figured out it was Able."

"Exactly. So I should take it from here. It's only fair."

"Fair my —"

"He killed my friend!" he said in a hoarse whisper.

The determined look on her face softened, but only slightly. "I know."

"Then you must also know why I have to do this."

She shook her head. "You're too personally involved. One of us has to keep a straight head and that someone is —"

A thump followed by a groan made them both spin around. Able was sprawled on the floor facedown. Miss Walker stood over him, crutch held high, ready to clobber him again if necessary.

"Now you can both take credit," she said.

CHAPTER 29

If the wages of sin is demise, an outlaw
would be wise to quit before payday.

The eastern sky was edged with the silver
thread of dawn. It was cold but Annie
hardly noticed. So much had happened in
such a short time.

Able was handcuffed and tied to the
saddle. He still looked dazed when the
marshal hauled him outside, but whether
from the bump on his head or knowing that
his outlaw days were over, it was hard to
tell.

Michael and the rest of the ranch hands
had returned to the bunkhouse. Only Taggert remained. He stood beside her in the
courtyard and together they watched Marshal Morris ride away with his prisoner in
tow.

"You all right?" he asked.

"Yes." She didn't want to worry him, but

she was anything but all right.

Her assignment was complete, but instead of elation, her heart churned in sadness. She liked Able and even considered him a friend. It took a long time to see through his guise, but *his* failure was greater. He was a talented cook and valued employee, but he measured success by worldly goods and allowed himself to be blinded by gold.

The marshal and his prisoner were mere dots in the distance and she pulled her gaze away to study Taggert's profile. She could hardly see his features in the dim light of dawn, but she felt his strength and her heart ached. Now that the Phantom was caught, she and Taggert would go their separate ways. It was a job requirement.

Like tumbleweeds in the wind, private detectives traveled from town to town, state to territory, and sometimes even country to country. Love didn't last long when separated by time and distance, as many of her colleagues had learned the hard way.

Marriage, home, and family were luxuries she couldn't afford. Not now. Not when everything had gone her way. She had proven she could do a man's job. No longer would she be dispatched to track down petty thieves. Pickpockets and the ilk would be left to inexperienced detectives yet to prove their worth.

At long last, she felt like she had earned the right to be called a Pinkerton, and that was all she'd ever wanted. The job required sacrifices, but she always knew that, had willingly made them in the past and would do so again.

If only it didn't hurt so much.

Marshal Morris and his charge vanished in the folds of darkness and she shivered. "I'd better go in. I want to make sure Miss Walker is all right." She hated the thought of leaving the ranch, but her job was done and she had no reason to stay. "Then I'll write my report."

"I have to write mine too," Taggert said. His voice sounded oddly distant.

A lump rose in her throat and she battled back tears. It wouldn't do to get sentimental. "Are you taking all the credit for capturing the Phantom?"

"Of course," he said. "And you?"

"Naturally."

"I might give you some credit," he said. "A little bit, just to be fair."

"That's mighty considerate," she replied.

"Don't forget, I did figure out your cryptic message. GTF. The big man." He turned to face her, his head outlined with fading stars. "So how did you get GTF out of Able? Do the initials stand for his real name?"

She laughed. She couldn't help it. His expression remained hidden, but she sensed the intensity of his eyes.

"What's so funny?" he asked.

"GTF stands for God the Father."

"But you said —" Suddenly it dawned on him and he laughed too. "The *Big* Man." He pointed upward.

"The Big Man," she agreed.

"And it had nothing to do with the Phantom?" he asked.

"Not a thing," she said.

"Hmm." He was silent for a moment. "You keep a dossier on God?"

She was grateful for the darkness that hid the rush of heat to her cheeks. "It's more of a study guide," she explained.

"Do you have a *study* guide on me too?"

"Of course." She tilted her head. "Do you have one on me?"

"Naturally. But God . . . never thought to keep one on Him. You got me there."

After a moment he stepped closer. "Annie." There was something heart-wrenching in the way he said her name, as if he, too, knew they had come to the end of the road.

She cleared her voice. "I . . . I guess this is good-bye —"

He didn't wait for her to finish. He pulled

her into his arms and once in the warmth of his embrace, she had no desire to leave. His lips brushed her forehead ever so gently and her pulse quickened.

"If anything had happened to you . . ."

Something in his voice made her pull away. The sky was gray now, almost silver, but his eyes were dark as night. He didn't sound like a man who had just seen a criminal hauled off to jail; he sounded like he was about to face a firing squad.

"There's something you don't know." His voice was ragged. "Something you need to know."

Her heart thudded and apprehension coursed through her. "What . . . do I need to know? You're scaring me. Is it about Able?"

He shook his head. "It's about . . . your father."

"My fa—" She stared at him. What could he possibly know that she didn't?

He rubbed his chin. "I was there the day he died. The Wells Fargo agent that —"

She gasped. "Don't say it!"

He grabbed her by the arms. "You have to hear this and you have to hear it from me."

She shook her head. "No!"

He told her anyway. He described how he spotted Vander in the bank and chased him outside just as a parade of union workers passed by. "I'm the one who caused your father's death."

She pulled away. "And you're just now telling me this?"

His shoulders sagged and his chest caved in like a deflated pillow. His military training was no match for the weight that seemed to crash down on him. "I just found out myself, the day in the bank vault. I didn't even know your real name until then and —" He reached for her.

She moved away. "Don't touch me."

"Annie, please, I can't tell you how sorry I am. Please forgive me."

"Don't." She put her hands on her head. This wasn't happening. *God, please let this be a nightmare.* She turned and ran up the veranda steps and into the house, her way blurred by tears.

Annie couldn't stop shaking. It was all she could do to keep her hand steady while offering Miss Walker a cup of tea. "It's chamomile and it's very calming."

The ranch owner scoffed. "I just found out that my cook is a madman. I don't want to be calm."

Holding on to the teapot with both hands to keep it steady, Annie poured herself a cup, spilling tea all over the tray. Miss Walker didn't seem to notice. For a woman her age, she seemed to be holding up remarkably well, but Annie was nonetheless worried about her.

She placed her teacup on the low table and sat. It wasn't quite six o'clock in the morning. Only four hours had passed since encountering Able in the entryway, but it seemed a lifetime ago. So much had happened; so much had changed.

"I'm sorry I had to lie to you about my real reason for coming here."

Miss Walker took a sip of tea, grimaced, and put the cup down. "I guess this means you're leaving."

"Just as soon as I receive my next assignment." Annie leaned forward. "I'll help you find a new cook and housekeeper, if you like. I don't want you to be alone."

"I'm not alone. I have two thousand cattle to keep me company."

"Yes, but can any of them make a pot of tea?" Annie asked.

"I sincerely hope not." Miss Walker quirked a thin eyebrow. "What about your Wells Fargo friend?"

"He's leaving too." Just thinking about Taggert made her nearly double over in pain. She reached for her cup. "We'll go our separate ways."

"Because of your father?"

Annie spilled her tea. She set her cup on the saucer and reached for a linen napkin. "You heard?"

Miss Walker shrugged and offered no apology. "So how did it happen?"

Annie dabbed at the damp spot on her skirt and explained. "He asked me to forgive him."

"In the name of Sam Hill, what is there to forgive? He was only doing his job."

Annie blinked. "He put lives in danger. My father's —"

"The thief put lives in danger. Branch or whatever his name is was simply trying to stop him." In the early morning light, Miss Walker's eyes looked more gray than blue. "Are you saying you wouldn't have done the same thing?"

"I wasn't there. I don't know what I would have done."

"Hmm. I think you do." Miss Walker swiped a strand of hair away from her face. "I always thought forgiveness overrated, but then, so is Shakespeare. So, for that matter, is tea. But these last few weeks I've had a generous dose of all three and I have to say that forgiveness is perhaps the least painful. You might want to try it."

"I thought you said there was nothing to forgive. He was doing his job."

Miss Walker gave a wry smile. "He's a man. There'll always be something to forgive."

Annie studied her. "Does that mean you'll forgive Able?"

Miss Walker thought for a moment. "That remains to be seen. He did a lot of damage to the ranch and county, but you wouldn't have come here otherwise. For that I am grateful."

"Even though I caused you to break your leg?" Annie asked.

"I could have done without the broken leg, but then I wouldn't have found out how stubborn you are."

Annie fought to keep her tears at bay. If she hadn't seen the suspicious gleam in Miss Walker's eyes, she might have succeeded.

Annie finished packing her carpetbag and glanced around the room one last time. She would miss the ranch, miss the wide-open spaces, and miss the easy banter of the ranch hands. Mostly she would miss the old lady.

A private eye's existence was a lonely one. The secretive nature of the job prevented getting too close to any one person. She had no friends and didn't even have a home. In between assignments, she bounced from one brother's house to the next, like a ball in a game of catch.

She had accepted her lot in life as a necessary part of the job she loved so much. Yet in a matter of a few weeks, the ranch had come to feel like home and Miss Walker like family. How careless of her to grow so attached to any one place or person. She was a professional and there was no room for sentimentality.

As for Taggert . . .

"I'm the one who caused your father's death."

Grief ripped through her like a metal blade and her knees nearly buckled. She thought she was over her father's death, but now she wasn't so sure. So much had been left unsaid between them. They should have talked about the elephant of her mother's death but now it was too late.

She grabbed hold of the desk chair to keep from falling. After a while, the sharp, excruciating pain abated, but the dull throb in her heart remained.

She picked up the GTF folder from her desk and flipped through the pages.

"I was blind . . ."

The words jumped out at her and she realized the world looked a whole lot different since coming to Cactus Patch. She once saw only the bad in people; now she saw the good. She'd learned to look past Miss Walker's bullheaded ways to see the caring, lonely woman inside. She had come to admire and respect Ruckus's faith, Stretch's love of story, and Feedbag's loyalty. She even saw that Aunt Bessie's bossy way was how she expressed love.

The eye: We never sleep. Maybe not, but the Pinkerton eye saw only the worst of human nature, and now she knew it was a very narrow focus. She might never fully understand God's ways or find the answers to all her questions, but she'd much rather see the world through His eyes than Pinkerton's.

CHAPTER 30

Thou shalt not steal — unless, of course, it's another's heart.

Four days later Annie walked into the bank to cash her check. Signed by Robert Pinkerton, the check covered her salary, plus expense money for her next assignment.

It was noontime and only two teller cages were open. The pale-faced clerk pushed his spectacles up his nose. "Good day, ma'am."

"Good day." She slid her check through the pigeonhole beneath the iron window grill.

Already she was about to be dispatched to her next job. As soon as the dossier on James Flanagan, aka the most cunning counterfeiter the country had ever known, arrived, she would head to Denver, Colorado, to track him down.

Flanagan. She couldn't believe her luck in landing such a plum assignment. So why did she feel so downright miserable? So utterly distraught?

Chasing down the Irish counterfeiter would surely cure her melancholy — or at least, she hoped so.

He was every bit as big as that "king of counterfeiters," William Brockway, and had proven to be as difficult to catch. Already three Pinkertons had pursued him to no avail; the Irishman could smell an operative a mile away, no matter how good the disguise. Would he be as good at detecting a female operative? That question kept running through her mind.

The clerk finished counting out her money. "There you are, ma'am."

"Thank you." She slid the stack of bills into her handbag and turned away from the teller cage. Taggert stood at the next cage and it was all she could do to breathe. He'd left the ranch the day of Able's arrest and she had hoped he'd also left town. As painful as his absence was, it hurt even more to see him.

But there he was, bigger than life. He looked much more rested than when she saw him last, and every bit as handsome.

He met her gaze and tossed a nod in the direction of the counting desk where an elderly man stood verifying the count of a bank teller. A much younger man, probably in his thirties, hovered a short distance behind him, presumably waiting to check his own money.

At first glance, he looked like a salesman. He wore a white flannel suit and a derby hat. His black mustache and hair offered a startling contrast to his pale skin. On the floor next to him stood a brown leather sample case.

Taggert lifted his foot to draw attention to the young man's shoes.

Annie glanced downward and could barely contain a smile. The drummer wore shoes with no heels.

Taggert completed his business and walked toward her. "Good to see you, Miss Beckman," he said with a tip of the hat and in a voice clearly meant to be heard by one and all.

Like an actor on stage, she spoke her lines as if they had been rehearsed. "Good to see you too, Mr. Branch." The prospect of catching a thief in action paled in comparison to the joy of seeing Taggert again, but she nonetheless played her part to the hilt. Sarah Bernhardt couldn't have done better.

"I thought you'd left town," she said.

"I had to arrange for a burial."

She drew in her breath. "Your friend."

A shadow flitted across his face. "Reverend Bland performed a simple ceremony."

"I . . . wish I could have been there," she said.

He studied her. "I shipped his belongings to his widow."

"I'm sure she'll be most grateful."

"Annie . . ." For a moment it seemed as if he'd forgotten their purpose for standing there.

She reminded him with a slight toss of her head and he quickly changed the subject and increased the volume of his voice. "So what brings you to town today?"

Keeping the drummer in sight, they stood talking like two old friends. Their chatter took a light turn, but the glances they exchanged were filled with meaning. After they had run through a litany of polite amenities and exhausted the subject of the weather, the conversation turned to the ranch.

Annie, I'm sorry, his eyes seemed to say. Out loud he said, "I hope Miss Walker has recovered."

"Yes, she's doing quite well." *Don't make this any harder than it already is.* "Dr. Fairbanks plans to take the cast off next week."

"Ah, next week, you say?" His gaze settled on her lips. *Do you remember the times I*

418

kissed you?

How could I possibly forget? Feeling her cheeks grow warm, she lowered her lashes and that's when she noticed the pen. "That wouldn't happen to belong to the bank, would it? In your pocket?"

He slapped his hand to his chest. "I believe you're right." He pulled the pen out of his pocket and tossed it onto a nearby desk. "Some habits are hard to break."

While his voice still held its neutral tone, the tenderness in his gaze told a different story, and she felt a tingling in the pit of her stomach.

Catching a subtle movement from the corner of her eye, she slid a sideways glance at the two men on the opposite side of the bank.

The drummer casually dropped a bill and it fell three feet from the old man's left foot. It was a good thing the suspect had made his move — a very good thing, for she didn't know how much longer she could continue acting her part.

After dropping the bill, the younger man stepped forward and politely tapped the older man's stooped shoulder. "I believe that's yours, sir," he said.

"Thank you. You're very kind." The unsuspecting victim did what anyone would do;

he reached down to pick up the bill. While he was occupied, the thief quickly snatched a handful of money from the pile on the desk and headed for the door. He was too smart to take all of it. By the time the older man discovered his funds missing and recounted to make sure there was no mistake, the thief expected to be long gone.

And he would have been, too, had he not had the misfortune of meeting up with Annie and Taggert. Standing side by side, they blocked the door.

"Excuse me," the thief said roughly, his face hidden by the brim of his hat.

"What you did is beyond excuse." Taggert grabbed the thief by his collar. The man raised his sample case like a weapon but his slight frame was no match for Taggert.

With one easy move, Taggert grabbed the man's raised arm before he could do any damage and knocked the case to the ground. He then pushed the man against the wall and held him there while Annie snapped the handcuffs he handed her around the thief's wrists.

"Do you want to turn him over to the marshal or shall I?" Taggert asked.

Annie pulled a wad of bills from the man's vest pocket. "I think we should both turn him in. That way we can both claim credit."

■ ■ ■ ■

The thief's name was Walt Mason and he turned out to be a known bank robber. After he was locked in a cell, Annie and Taggert left the marshal's office together.

Once outside, Taggert dropped his professional air. "Annie, about your father. I can't tell you how sorry —"

She shook her head. She had done a lot of praying in recent days, and a lot of thinking. "Don't say any more, Taggert. I don't blame you."

His eyebrows shot up. "You don't?"

"What you did . . . I would have done the same thing."

"You would have chased a criminal into a group of innocent people?"

"I would have chased him to the ends of the earth. So would my father."

Taggert looked dumbfounded. "I don't know what to say."

"There's nothing to be said. My father died doing what he loved best."

Taggert sucked in his breath and rubbed his chin. "Have . . . you received your next assignment?"

"Y-yes," she squeaked out. The heaviness in her chest made it difficult to breathe. She

421

cleared her throat. "And you?"

"I'm due in Denver at the end of the week."

Her jaw dropped. "Did . . . did you say Denver?"

Taggert leaned against a telephone pole, arms folded. "You sound surprised."

"It's just . . . it wouldn't have anything to do with James Flanagan, would it?"

"What makes you think — ?" He straightened and dropped his arms to his sides. "As a matter of fact, it does. Don't tell me. You're —"

She nodded.

He burst out laughing. "What do you know? If that doesn't take the cake. It looks like we're going to be working together again."

She stared at him, speechless.

He grew serious. "He won't be an easy catch. He's a clever one."

"Extremely so." Personally she was a mess, but professionally she could still hold her own. "He's passed more than a million dollars of bogus money in the last two years alone."

"A large portion of which he used to bribe police," Taggert added.

"Few men have succeeded in copying the scrollwork on treasury notes so precisely," she said. His ability to bleed the color from small-value notes to make larger-value notes was nothing short of genius.

"Like I said, it's not going to be easy."

"Agreed." She gazed up at him through a fringe of dark lashes. "So may the best man — or woman — win." She started down the boardwalk and he fell in step by her side.

He glanced both ways to check for eavesdroppers before pulling her to the side of an adobe building. His hand on her arm felt warm and strong.

"We need to talk." He released her. "I'm not kidding, Annie. Flanagan's a tough bird. The Secret Service hasn't had any more luck capturing him than Wells Fargo or Pinkerton."

What he said was true. Created following Lincoln's death to suppress counterfeit currency, the Secret Service had, for the most part, done a good job. But if Secret Service agents couldn't capture Flanagan, what chance did she have?

She afforded him a guarded look. "So what are you saying? That I'm not up for the task? Because I'm a woman?"

"I'm not sure that either one of us is up to the task." He rubbed his forehead. "First, I have to know. Did you mean it when you said you didn't blame me for your father's death?"

"I blamed you at first," she said honestly. "But then I realized I was doing the same thing to you that my father did to me."

He narrowed his eyes. "I don't understand. What did your father do?"

"He blamed me for my mother's death. She never fully recovered from my birth and died when I was two." She sighed. "Some things just happen, you know."

"Did it ever occur to you that it wasn't you he blamed, but himself?"

Her brother had said something similar, but coming from Taggert it sounded more plausible. "That doesn't explain why he was so against me being a Pinkerton operative. Had it been one of my brothers . . ."

Taggert shook his head. "Annie, he loved you and was worried about you. Just like I —"

Her heart thudded. "Just like you . . . what?"

He took in a deep breath. "If I could go back and change what happened . . ."

"I know." She laid her hand on his arm. "You're a good man and a good detective." She couldn't resist adding, "For a Wells Fargo agent."

"You're not bad yourself . . . for a Pink."

He grew serious again. "Of course, if we combine our talents . . ."

She pulled her hand away. "Don't say it. Don't even think it. We're not working together." Not only would that make life more difficult for her personally, but William Pinkerton would never allow an operative to join forces with its competition.

"We just did."

"That wasn't planned," she said.

"If we can work so well together by chance, think what we could do if we actually sat down and made a plan."

"It's not going to happen."

"At least hear me out." He hesitated and his galvanizing look made her senses spin. "What if we go as a newlywed couple? Denver's a great place to honeymoon. So what do you say?"

"I say you're . . . you're out of your mind." She would do almost anything to catch Flanagan, but compromising her morals was where she drew the line. "We'd have to share the same hotel room and . . ."

"That's what honeymooners usually do." He lowered his voice to a silky whisper. "They share a lot of things. Think about it. Flanagan will be looking for a single agent, not two. And you know yourself that those Secret Service men don't know how to work

425

undercover."

"I know no such thing."

"It's true," he said. "A child could pick one out a mile away."

"It won't work. Flanagan will see right through our disguise and —"

"Disguise?" He drew back. "Who's talking disguise? I'm talking the real thing." Hands at her waist, he drew her near. "Marry me, Annie. Marry me, Miranda."

Anger flared inside her and she pulled away from him. "Do you think this is some sort of game . . . ?"

"I love you."

"Marriage is sacred. It's not something that you can fake or —"

"I love you."

"And another thing — a Pinkerton operative does not work with Wells Fargo —"

"The reason I never guessed you were a Pink is because I was too busy falling in love with you."

"And another thing —" She stopped midsentence as the full force of his words hit her. Was the same true for her? Had she been too busy falling in love with him to notice what was now as plain as the nose on his face? Was that why she failed to pick out a fellow detective?

"I love you." He pulled her a tad closer.

"What's more, I'm willing to bet the feeling is mutual. Why else would you so readily forgive me?"

She closed her eyes. She was shaking so hard she could hardly think. *Love.* Why did he have to say *love*? She fought for composure. It was no time to waver. She chanced a look at him — big mistake.

"I . . . I never said I loved you," she stammered. She knew she had feelings for him but she never admitted to love. Didn't dare.

"You don't have to. I'm a detective." His hands moved up her arms. "I can read smiles." His hands moved to her shoulders. "I can read eyes." He cupped his fingers around her face. "I can read lips."

What few defenses she had left deserted her, along with all pretenses. Through the years, she had worn so many disguises she'd almost forgotten who the real Miranda Hunt was. All she knew was that the woman standing in her place right then was real and she didn't have to prove anything to anyone.

"It's true," she said softly. "I do have certain feelings for you."

His eyebrows rose. "Feelings?"

"All right, I admit it. I love you too." If she didn't know it before, she knew it now. "Are you happy that you made me say it?"

She clenched her fists. This was so hard —
so very hard, and he wasn't making it any
easier.

"Annie . . . Miranda . . ."

"Don't . . . please . . . don't." She backed
away. "Private detectives can't be married.
You know that. It never works. We'll both
be in Denver this time. But what about the
next time and the time after that? We may
not see each other for months. Years."

"There's one simple solution," he said.

"Forget it." She shook her head. "I'm not
giving up my job."

"I'm not asking you to. I say we get married, go to Denver, and track down Flanagan. After that, we resign from our respec-
tive jobs and start our own detective
agency."

Her mouth dropped open. "Are you out
of your mind?"

He moved his hand through the air as if
reading an invisible sign. "Taggert and Wife:
Detective Agency. In memory of your father,
Charlie Hunt, our slogan will be 'We Hunt
the Bad Guys.' "

She couldn't help but laugh. "That's
dreadful."

He shrugged and lines crinkled at the
corners of his eyes. "Okay, we'll work on
the slogan, but I think even GTF would ap-

prove the rest."

The mention of God brought another thought to mind. Never before had she been able to see a future without the Pinkerton National Detective Agency, but maybe, just maybe, God had opened another door.

She tilted her head sideways. "Are . . . are you serious?"

"Never been so serious in my life. I may be out of a job soon. The newer safes are harder to break into and stagecoach robberies are becoming few and far between. And what about your job? The Pinkerton Agency is heading into the security business. Your future there will be preventing crime, not tracking down criminals. Somehow I don't think Charlie Hunt's daughter would relish spending time as a security guard."

Taggert spoke the truth. It was something she hadn't wanted to think about. Oddly enough, being the best and brightest Pinkerton operative held less appeal than it once did.

But owning her own agency? It never occurred to her that she could have it all; she could still pursue outlaws without having to give up the man of her dreams.

The very thought would have made her heart pound had Taggert's declaration of love not already done so.

"Well, what do you say?" he asked, his voice husky. "Will you marry me, partner?"

She gazed up at him. *"How do you know what God's plan is?"*

"That's simple, my child. Follow the joy. That's how you know God's plan for you."

Just the thought of being Mrs. Jeremy Taggert filled her with unspeakable joy. She loved this man and wanted to spend the rest of her life proving it to him. As for his plan — it could work. It *would* work. She would make certain of that.

It took every bit of willpower not to run into his arms. "Taggert and Taggert Detective Agency. And the first Taggert's me."

He blew out his breath. "You drive a hard bargain."

She put out her hand. "Do we have a deal?"

He took her hand in his own, then weightlessly pulled her into his arms and locked her in his embrace. "Deal." He then sealed it with a heart-pounding, breathtaking kiss.

CHAPTER 31

The way some people carry on about weddings should be a crime.

"It's beautiful," Annie cried. She stared at herself in the mirror and fingered the delicate lace that hugged her figure. The wedding dress had been loaned to her by Aunt Bessie's nephew's wife, Kate, and it only took a few stitches to make it fit perfectly.

"Do you think it's too fancy? We're just having a simple wedding."

Aunt Bessie stood back. "Simple wedding or not, you have to look like a bride. This dress is perfect for you with your dark hair and honey skin. It's like it was made for you." She sighed. "Too bad your family can't be here."

Annie thought about her father. Getting married was perhaps the first conventional thing she'd ever done. Somehow she knew he would approve. The thought brought a smile to her face and a satisfied nod from Aunt Bessie.

"I wish you weren't in such a hurry to get married." Bessie glanced at Annie's waist. "You're not in a family way, are you?"

Annie blushed. "Oh no, of course not." The real reason the marriage had to be rushed had to be kept secret. Only a few people, including Miss Walker, the marshal, and Mr. Stackman, knew her and Branch's true identities, and that was how it had to stay. To make it all legal, they would sign the paperwork with their real names in private.

"It wouldn't be the first time a bride was accompanied down the aisle." Aunt Bessie reached for the wreath of white flowers on Annie's head and straightened the flowing ribbons. "Mary Hopkins practically burst out of her seams when she walked down the aisle, and she didn't tell anyone she had the baby until months later."

"As I explained, Branch has business . . . out of town." Miss Walker was given full credit for Able's capture, and no outsiders knew what really happened.

"Well, it's a crying shame. You haven't seen anything until you see the weddings I put on. Of course, after Molly's wedding to

Dr. Fairbanks, that no-good marshal put a moratorium on weddings for a year, but that's about to end."

Annie turned away from the mirror. "Why would he do such a thing?"

Bessie stooped to straighten Annie's train. "He doesn't like me insisting that the saloons close the night before a wedding. It's the only way to keep everyone sober so that there're no mix-ups at the altar. Why, Harry Laine was so drunk at his own wedding he nearly married the bride's sister by mistake."

Annie reached for her bridal bouquet and sniffed the sweet scent of roses. "I can see why closing saloons might cause ill feelings."

"Maybe, but the marshal also disapproves of the way I decorate the town."

"You decorate the town?" Annie laughed. "Now I really am sorry we don't have time to experience one of your productions." She pecked the old woman on her rouged cheek. "You're very kind. I really appreciate all you've done for me."

Not even the heavy paint on Bessie's face could hide her pleasure. "I just want you to be happy. And you'd better come back and visit us."

"I will, I promise."

"Come along now. Let's not keep your handsome groom waiting."

Just then Lula-Belle rushed through the door, the feathers on her hat doing a wild dance. "The wedding's off," she announced.

Fists on her hips, Bessie whirled about to face her sister. "What crazy talk is that?"

Lula-Belle looked down her nose at her sibling. "I'm just telling you what the marshal said."

Bessie glared back. "And why is that, pray tell?"

"He said that Annie and Branch can't get married. It's against the law!"

Eleanor Walker felt every one of her sixty-seven years. Her housekeepers had left, her cook was in jail, and Annie was gone.

She missed Annie the most. Even more than she missed Kate Tenney and Molly Hatfield after both had upped and married. But a Pinkerton operative — Eleanor still couldn't believe it.

A ringing sound made her turn her attention to the telephone. Apparently someone was using the one in the bunkhouse. What in the world did her ranch hands have to jabber about in the middle of a workday?

Earlier her telephone rang but she refused to answer it. If anyone wanted to speak to

434

her, they could jolly well do so to her face.

She sighed. The world was changing so fast she could hardly keep up. Telephones, automobiles . . . even raising cattle had changed from open to closed range. What would be next?

Not one to feel sorry for herself, she reached for her crutches and hobbled out to the veranda. Fresh air would do her a world of good. Dr. Fairbanks said the cast could come off as early as next week and she couldn't wait. She longed to be back in the saddle again. Now that all the excitement was over, perhaps they could get some work done.

She sat in the rocker and reached for a stick she kept for the purpose of scratching her leg. The worst part of wearing a cast was the itching.

The chugging sound of Dr. Fairbanks's automobile caught her attention.

"Now what?" Far as she knew, the doctor wasn't scheduled for a visit.

The car sputtered to a stop and backfired. A chicken squawked and flew away. Dogs barked. The doctor and his newfangled auto had once started a stampede. If he started another, she'd have his head.

Much to her surprise, it was Robert and not the doctor who jumped out of the auto and dashed toward the house. Fairbanks remained seated behind the steering column.

Alarmed, she reached for her crutches, but before she was able to stand, Robert bounded up the steps. "What are you doing here? And why are you running? A man your age!"

"If you'd answer the blasted telephone I wouldn't have to run," he said. "There's a problem in town. Annie needs your help."

"What does she need my help for? Isn't she supposed to be getting married or some such thing?"

"That's just it. Morris won't let her wed."

"Why not? What business is it of the marshal's what Annie does or does not do?"

"He said he has no choice but to uphold the miscegenation law. Annie is part Indian, and as you know, it's against the law for an Indian and a white to wed."

"That's ridiculous." She was wrong: some things never changed. "Annie is just like you and me. She was like a daugh—" She stopped but not soon enough.

Robert arched a silver brow. "Why, Eleanor, I never thought I'd hear you say such a thing."

Nor did she ever think to say it. Her gaze drifted to the distant hill where her one and only child was buried. She'd always wanted a family, and when she lost her little girl and her marriage fell apart, she thought that was the end of it. It wasn't until years later that she got the idea to advertise for an heiress. She hoped to find one young woman to take the place of her daughter. Some came close, but Annie came the closest.

Aware that Robert was staring at her, she pulled her gaze away from the hill. "So what do you want me to do about it?"

"Some of our public officials are coming up for reelection. I thought perhaps you might wish to make a friendly donation to the cause. Providing, of course, they waive certain unfavorable laws."

"You want me to bribe officials? Why, Robert, I'm shocked."

He grinned. "No, you're not."

"Well, I should be."

"So what do you think?" he asked.

"It would take too long — Annie and Taggert have to leave soon." She thought for a moment. She recalled reading something recently in the Tombstone newspaper about a similar situation. "I have a better idea."

She inched herself to the edge of the chair and pushed up on one foot. She then tucked the tops of her crutches beneath her arms. "Quick, call the marshal and tell him to

437

meet me at the church. Tell him to make sure that Annie, Taggert, the preacher, and the justice of the peace are present when I get there."

"You want me to use the telephone?" he asked.

"Unless your voice can carry five miles, I don't see what choice you have."

Robert's mustache twitched. "What do you plan to do?"

"You'll see. Now make the call . . ." She stopped at the top of the steps and stared at the horseless carriage. Mercy! Was she really going to ride in that thing?

CHAPTER 32

Stealing another man's wife is a serious
crime, second only to horse rustlin'.

Annie couldn't stop crying. Clutching her
bridal bouquet, she sat on a church pew
while Taggert and the marshal argued.

Taggert's angry voice seemed to rattle the
stained glass windows. Reverend Bland
wrung his hands and tried to keep the peace.

"I don't make the laws," Marshal Morris
said, sounding peevish. "I just uphold
them."

She'd been so eager to marry Taggert she
hadn't even thought to ask about miscegenation laws in Arizona Territory. She didn't
even remember her Kickapoo mother and
identified with her father's side of the family, who raised and educated her. She never
thought of herself as Indian or even white.

Taggert moved to her side. "It's all right,
partner. We'll get married elsewhere. Fortu-

nately, not every state or territory has such ridiculously *dumb laws.*" He shouted the last part for Morris's benefit.

"I know, but these are my friends." She waved her hand to indicate the ranch hands gathered in back of the church, casting sympathetic glances her way. "Getting married in a strange place won't be the same."

Aunt Bessie came bustling down the aisle and plopped herself next to Annie. "I tried to call Miss Walker and she didn't answer, but Mr. Stackman kindly agreed to drive out to the ranch. He just called and said to stay here at the church. Miss Walker is on her way."

Annie dabbed at her eyes with her handkerchief. Knowing how Miss Walker felt about the town, it was hard to believe she was coming. "Thank you, but there's nothing she can do." There was nothing anyone could do.

Taggert dropped down on one knee in front of her. "Don't cry. We can marry elsewhere."

"What good will that do?" Annie wiped away a fresh tear. "Our marriage will be legal in some states but not others. We won't be able to travel the country as husband and wife."

"Blast it!" As if recalling they were in

church, Taggert lowered his voice. "I don't care about that. I just care about us."

"Being married in some states is better than not being married at all," Aunt Bessie said, her expression less convincing than her voice.

Ruckus had just joined them. "And if you marry before God, that's the only authority that counts."

Annie smiled at the ranch hand. "That's very kind of you to say."

"It's the truth, Miz Annie. Just as soon as I become an official preacher, I'll marry you."

Annie dabbed at the corner of her eye. "You're going to become a preacher?"

Ruckus got all red in the face. "This town needs a full-time preacher, and since my son's got his heart set on Africa, I reckon it's up to me. Ugly feet and all!"

She left her seat and threw her arms around him. "Oh, Ruckus. That's wonderful news."

A rumbling, growling sound, followed by a loud bang, announced the arrival of Dr. Fairbanks and his automobile.

A short while later the church door flew open and Miss Walker hobbled through it on her crutches, followed by Mr. Stackman and Dr. Fairbanks.

Annie didn't think it possible to march on crutches, but somehow Miss Walker managed to do just that. She looked like a soldier marching to war. Even the ranch hands stood at attention like military men waiting to pass inspection.

Miss Walker positioned herself directly in front of the marshal and looked him straight in the eye. "What's this nonsense about not marrying these two?"

Morris threw up his hands. "As I explained" — he glanced around the church — "and explained, Miss Beckman has Indian blood. According to Arizona law, that means she cannot marry a white man."

"Horsefeathers!" Miss Walker exclaimed. "Where's the justice of the peace?"

A short, skinny man stepped forward. "Here, ma'am. Harvey Wilson at your service."

Marshal Morris shook his head. "I don't make the law and neither does Wilson."

"It doesn't matter because the law doesn't apply here. Annie is my daughter and that makes her white no matter what color her blood."

A stunned silence followed Miss Walker's declaration and no one moved. Even Wishbone stopped whittling.

Once the shock of her words passed, Annie leaned toward Taggert and whispered in his ear, "Did she say what I think she said?"

"I think so," he whispered back.

The marshal was the first to recover. "Your daughter?"

"My *adopted* daughter, and I'll sign an affidavit to that effect."

The marshal turned to Wilson. "Is that legal? Does an adoption make a person white?"

The skinny man nodded. "Well . . . there have been a couple of cases in the territory where a judge ruled an Indian white by way of adoption."

The marshal scratched his head. "Well, I'll be a son of a gun. As soon as we get the paperwork out of the way, it looks like we're going to have ourselves a wedding."

Ruckus led a cheer and Stretch pulled out his harmonica. Annie flung her arms around Miss Walker. "Thank you, thank you . . . *Mother*!"

Miss Walker looked positively stunned, but then her face softened into a broad smile. "Well now. It looks like at long last I have my heiress."

Taggert stepped up and slid his arm around Annie's waist. "And it looks like I am about to have a wife."

Michael, who had been watching from the

sidelines, joined the group, pulling Charity along with him. "Me too," he said. "Charity and I plan to get married too."

"Why, that's wonderful," Annie exclaimed. Seeing the frozen look on Aunt Bessie's face, she slipped her arm around the older woman's waist. "Now you can put on another wedding of the century."

Much to her relief Aunt Bessie rose to the occasion. A bright smile broke through her face paint. She pulled free from Annie and took Charity under her wing. "What do you think about a July wedding? And you know those awful telephone lines. I was thinking we could drape satin ribbons over them and . . ." Her voice faded as the two walked away. Charity looked overwhelmed by the plans Aunt Bessie had for her wedding but managed a respectful nod or two.

"It looks like things are going to work out just fine," Annie said.

Michael scratched his head. "I can't believe that Aunt Bessie accepted my choice of a bride, just like that."

"Maybe she simply opened her eyes and saw the same traits in Charity as you do." If she hadn't yet, she soon would — Annie was convinced of it.

Michael grinned. "Well now . . ."

Taggert stepped forward and held out his

hand. "Shall we?"

It took nearly an hour to complete the paperwork. After everyone, including all the ranch hands, signed as witnesses, Taggert took her hand in his. Together they walked up to the altar and everyone formed a circle behind them.

While they waited for Reverend Bland to locate the missing Book of Common Prayer, Taggert leaned over to whisper in her ear. "Flanagan was born in Edinburgh."

"One of seven children," she whispered back, not wanting to be found remiss.

"His father was a businessman."

She took the bouquet of flowers from Aunt Bessie and held them in front like a proper bride. "But not a very good one. His mother was an art forger who supported the family by selling 'original' copies of the *Mona Lisa*."

"He started his life of crime at the tender age of ten," he continued.

"No surprise there," she said, as Aunt Bessie straightened the gown's train. "Pinkerton did a study that showed most evildoers started their life of crime between the ages of ten and sixteen." She often wondered what could be done to better protect children.

"What a shame." He shook his head

before continuing. "Flanagan got his start manufacturing bogus coins and quickly advanced from there." His voice sounded like velvet in her ear.

"He was married three times and fathered, in all, twenty-three children," she whispered back. Astonishment crossed his face and she laughed. "Got you!"

"What are you two yammering about?" Miss Walker demanded.

"Probably making plans for their honeymoon," Stretch called out.

Taggert grinned down at Annie and her heart fairly danced with excitement. "Do you think our newlywed status will work?" he asked.

"I do," she said, forgetting to keep her voice low.

"I do too," he replied.

Neither had noticed Reverend Bland in front of them until he spoke. "I'm the preacher and you can't say 'I do' until I say you can say 'I do.'"

Taggert winked and tucked her hand in his. "Are you ready to marry me, partner?" he asked.

She smiled and her heart felt about to burst with happiness. "More than ready."

EPILOGUE

"That's done," Eleanor said. She and Robert were the only two remaining at the church. It had been a long time since she'd stepped foot inside a house of worship and she wasn't in any hurry to leave.

"Yes, it is," Robert said. "I have to say, Annie or Miranda or whatever her name is made a beautiful bride." He shifted in the pew to look directly at her. "You did a fine and noble thing by adopting her, Eleanor."

"Fiddlesticks! You make it sound like I raised the dead or something."

He chuckled and ran a finger over his mustache before growing serious. "Since you're in the wedding mood, I wonder if you would reconsider and marry me." He cleared his voice. "I love you. Always have. Always will."

She stared at him. It wasn't the first time he'd proposed. Heavens, no. He'd proposed every year on her birthday for the last fifteen or more years. But never once in all that time had the word *love* escaped his lips.

"Aren't you getting sentimental all of a sudden?"

"Blame it on the poison," he said. "When you're lying at death's door, you tend to think about all the things you never got around to doing, all the words left unsaid. The one thing I regretted was not telling you how much I love you. I guess I was afraid you'd scoff."

"Oh, Robert, I wouldn't scoff. If you must know, I . . . well, you know, feel the same way." They were words she never hoped to say or hear, because now it was so much harder to keep her resolve.

"And what way is that?" he asked.

She gave him a sideways glance. "You know." And because it seemed only fair, she added, "I have feelings for you too."

He drew back. "I can't believe my ears."

"Blame it on this confounded leg. Nothing makes you face mortality quicker than weeks of confinement." She lifted her chin. "But I'm still not selling the ranch." Now that she had a *daughter,* she couldn't sell even if she wanted to. Though there was little hope of her new heiress ever running the ranch.

"I don't want you to sell."

"You don't what?" She stared at him, stunned. They'd fought over this very thing for years. It was the main reason she never accepted his marriage proposals.

"I just want you to sell the cattle. The ranch, we keep."

"What are you talking about? If I sell the cattle we won't be able to maintain the ranch."

"Ah, but that's where you're wrong. I had someone check out the cave that Able was so determined to mine. Eleanor, you are about to become the richest person in the territory."

Eleanor gaped at him. "You can't be serious."

He shrugged. "You know me. Where money's concerned, I don't joke."

"I can't believe it. There's actually gold on the ranch? I thought that was a figment of Able's imagination."

"Believe it, my dear. And if it wasn't for Kate's dime novel, we might never have discovered it." He grinned. "What do you think about this — the Last Chance Mining Company?"

"Hmm. It has a nice ring, but I insist upon keeping a few cattle for old times' sake."

"Very well. The Last Chance Mining and Cattle Company. How's that?"

"The Last Chance *Ranch* and Mining Company," she said. "And that's not negotiable."

He grinned. "Very well. Do we have a deal? Will you agree to be my wife?"

"Oh, why not?" she said. "But first, I think you should know I always wanted a large family."

Robert's eyes nearly popped out of his head. "At our age?"

"I'm thinking of adopting Kate and Molly. Donny as well." Donny was Molly's brother. When the wheelchair-bound boy lived at the ranch with his sister, Eleanor had grown quite fond of him. Maybe Donny would agree to oversee the ranch should, heaven forbid, something happen to her. The more she thought about it, the more she liked the idea.

"What do you think? That way the future of the Last Chance Ranch —"

"And Mining Company," he interjected.

"— will always be in good hands."

Robert frowned. "They aren't going to move in with us, are they? All these *children* of ours?"

"Not if I can help it." She reached for her crutches. "Now that we've settled our future together, let's go home. It's time for my afternoon tea."

ACCIDENTAL DETECTIVE

Dear Reader,

Born in Glasgow, Scotland, in 1819, Allan Pinkerton might never have followed in his policeman father's footsteps had it not been for a chance encounter.

A barrel maker by trade, Allan's political affiliations got him into hot water, forcing him and his wife to flee Scotland. After arriving in America, the couple settled in Illinois and fighting crime was the last thing on Allan's mind. He was too busy running a successful cooperage company.

Then an odd thing happened: While cutting down poles for his barrels, he came across a counterfeiting ring. He reported his discovery to the sheriff, who immediately deputized him to help find the leader. In no time at all, Allan set up a sting and trapped the forger. Impressed, the Cook County sheriff offered Allan a job.

In 1850, he started his own detective

agency, the only one of its kind, and the Pinkerton National Detective Agency was born. The agency's "seeing eye" logo inspired the term *private eye.*

It wasn't until he uncovered an assassination plot on President Lincoln that the Pinkerton name became a household word. Lincoln then hired Allan to organize the Secret Service in an effort to stop rampant counterfeiting.

Allan was many things to many people. He was accused of being a traitor, a tyrant, and a patriot, but the one thing that can't be argued is that he and his sons changed the law-enforcement business forever. By 1870, the agency had the world's largest collection of mug shots in its criminal database and more agents than the standing army of the United States.

Pinkerton operatives tracked outlaws throughout the Wild West, but their heavy-handed and sometimes ruthless pursuit of outlaws like Jesse James (which resulted in the death of a child) soon earned the agency a bad reputation and tarnished the agency's name.

Following Allan's death in 1884, his two sons took over, but the Pinkerton National Detective Agency never recovered its former glory. The agency still exists today as a security consulting firm.

I hope you enjoyed Annie's and Taggert's story and wish them well as they start their own detective agency. This book wraps up the Brides of Last Chance Ranch series, but you can track my future projects on my website: MargaretBrownley.com.

"Excellent," says he.

"Elementary," says she.

Until next time,
Margaret

GUNPOWDER TEA

Gunpowder tea is from the Zhejiang province of China. Originally the leaves were hand-rolled and looked like little gunpowder pellets. Today the rolling is mostly done by machines. It's fun to listen to the little popping sounds as the leaves unfurl during brewing.

Brought to this country during the California gold rush, the tea was especially popular during the Civil War, and any soldier fortunate enough to secure some for his knapsack considered himself lucky indeed.

Gunpowder tea is good for what ails you and its health benefits range from preventing tooth decay to lowering blood pressure. It can even slow aging.

You won't find this in health books, but as Annie so aptly demonstrated, gunpowder tea can also issue a strong warning to an

annoying (though nonetheless handsome)
hero.

GUNPOWDER TEA BREAD

BY CHEF DANIEL

This is a recipe my son-in-law cooked up special for this book.

Ingredients
1 pound mixed dried fruit
12 tablespoons well-steeped gunpowder tea
6 ounces soft brown sugar
1 egg
1 ounce melted butter
9 ounces white flour
1/2 teaspoon baking soda
1/4 cup sugar in the raw

Directions
Cut up fruit to raisin size. Mix tea, fruit, and brown sugar in bowl. Cover and leave overnight. In the morning, preheat oven to 360 degrees. Coat loaf pan with butter and flour. Stir in egg and melted butter. Sift flour and soda and blend into wet mixture. Pour into prepared pan. Bake for 1 1/2

hours. When partially cool, top with sugar in the raw.

DISCUSSION QUESTIONS

1. Annie included John 9:25 in her "God the Father" file: "I was blind, now I see." In what ways does this verse describe your spiritual journey?
2. Annie's job as a Pinkerton detective made her see things through worldly eyes instead of God's eyes, which meant she was more likely to see bad than good. In what ways did living at the ranch change her vision?
3. It's been said that we see in others what we need or expect to see. Is this a hindrance, a blessing, or both?
4. Annie first met Taggert during a train robbery and this colored her judgment. Have you ever had a first impression turn out to be false?
5. Annie felt she had to work harder to prove herself because she was a woman. Do you think the same is true for women today?
6. Annie's relationship with Miss Walker got

off to a rocky start, but they ultimately grew close. Can you think of a similar relationship in your own life?

7. How did Annie's faith mature during the course of the story?

8. Annie's father said that a person had only one important decision to make in life and that was whether or not to follow the Lord; everything else was secondary. Do you agree or disagree?

9. As a Pinkerton detective, Annie/Miranda played so many roles through the years that she lost track of who she was. We all play many roles in life. In what ways can we fulfill these roles and still stay true to self?

10. Name a favorite scene in the book. Why did this particular scene stand out?

11. The telephone connects people verbally while at the same time disconnecting them physically. How do you think the telephone strengthens or weakens relationships?

12. What character did you most identify with? Why?

13. Annie strived to earn her father's approval but felt she never got it. How did this affect her? Have you ever done anything for the sole purpose of gaining approval?

14. The 1890s were a time of great change and upheaval. Banks failed, unemployment was high, and technology (telegram, electricity, telephone, and horseless carriages) changed the way people traveled, communicated, and lived. Miss Walker wanted to hold on to the old way of doing things. What changes have you resisted in recent years? Were they changes for the better or worse?

ACKNOWLEDGMENTS

Some of my most pleasant memories involve tea parties. As a child I spent hours wobbling around in high heels and pouring tea down my doll's throat. Those days are long gone, of course, but I still love a good tea party with friends — without the high heels. I also enjoy tea for two. This is what I call spending time with the Lord. He isn't much for tea, but He sure is good company.

Speaking of company, a tip of the teakettle goes to the many people who helped make *Gunpowder Tea* possible. First and foremost is my dear friend, champion, and agent, Natasha Kern, whose wisdom, knowledge, and encouragement deserve the highest praise.

I can't say enough good things about the talented Thomas Nelson team that turns each book into a labor of love. Special thanks to Natalie Hanemann, whose input helped strengthen my story and who has, through the years, made me a better writer.

A big thank-you also goes to Amanda Bostic, Rachelle Gardner, Katie Bond, Ruthie Dean, Ami McConnell, Daisy Hutton, and the terrific art department and sales team.

I don't know what I'd do without my dear friend, mentor, adopted sister, and first reader, Lee Duran. I'm also grateful for Diantha Ain's friendship and the many laughs we've shared over a cuppa.

Heartfelt gratitude goes to my family, who so graciously and lovingly put up with this writer's idiosyncrasies. Finally, I raise my cup in an Irish toast of appreciation to all my readers. Thank you for your continued support. May all your wishes come true but one, so that you always have something to strive for. Cheers!

ABOUT THE AUTHOR

New York Times best-selling author **Margaret Brownley** has penned more than twenty-five historical and contemporary novels. Her books have won numerous awards, including Reader's Choice. *A Lady Like Sarah* was a Romance Writers of America RITA finalist. Happily married to her real-life hero, Margaret and her husband have three grown children and live in Southern California.

Visit MargaretBrownley.com for more information.